Tales From the House Band

Volume 1

A Plus One Press Anthology

Contributions by:

Sam Cutler
Patricia V. Davis
Keith R.A. DeCandido
Barbara A. Denz
Susanne Dunlap
Kathi Kamen Goldmark
Deborah Grabien
Rain Graves
Erika Jahneke
Roz Kaveney
Brett Milano
Charles Shaar Murray
Madeleine Robins
Jeannette Sears
Clea Simon
Karen Williams

Tales From the
House Band

Volume 1

A Plus One Press Anthology

edited by
Deborah Grabien

Plus One Press
San Francisco

This is a collection of works of fiction. All of the characters, organizations and events portrayed in this anthology are either the products of the authors' imagination or are used fictitiously.

Plus One Press
www.plusonepress.com

TALES FROM THE HOUSE BAND, VOLUME 1: A PLUS ONE PRESS ANTHOLOGY. Copyright © 2011 by Plus One Press. All rights reserved. Printed in the United States of America. For information, address Plus One Press, 2885 Golden Gate Avenue, San Francisco, California, 94118.

Publisher's Cataloging-in-Publication Data

Tales from the house band, volume 1: a plus one press anthology / edited by Deborah Grabien—1st. Plus One Press ed.
        p. cm.
    ISBN: 978-0-9844362-4-8
    1. Fiction anthologies: multiple authors. 2. Short stories. 3. Music—Fiction.
4. Literary collections—General I. Title. II. Grabien, Deborah
    PS3568.O2774 T35 2011
    813'.54—dc22

2011936512

First Edition: December, 2011

10 9 8 7 6 5 4 3 2 1

For all the writers, the players and the listeners out there

Tales From the House Band

Volume 1

Contents

Introduction
– Deborah Grabien (ed.)

"Writing about music is like dancing about architecture."
– Martin Mull

If the above-cited, very famous quote is true, I've been dancing about architecture for the better part of half a century. Out of
(so far) sixteen published novels, ten are purely about music, and
music features prominently in most of the others. I've written
articles about music. I've reviewed music, and books about music. I've interviewed musicians. There's nothing in this world I
love more than writing about music, unless it's actually writing
and playing music.

So, when I decided to put together an anthology of short fiction that dealt entirely with music and musicians, I looked
around my fortunately broad acquaintance, and made a really
cool discovery: I know a lot of writers who also live and breathe
music, one way or another. And all of them jumped at the idea of
doing an anthology. Again, how lucky can a girl get?

The sixteen stories that make up *Tales From the House Band*
cover pretty much the entire spectrum. We have killer work from

world-class music journalists, brilliant fiction writers, superb essayists and memoirists who are generous with their history. We've got ghost stories, both traditional and twisted, from Patricia V. Davis, Barbara Denz and myself. From Karen Williams and Charles Shaar Murray, we've got breathtaking science fiction: the music of the stars and music made between the stars. Rain Graves gives us classic horror. Lyricist Jeannette Sears and former Rolling Stones and Grateful Dead tour manager Sam Cutler provide haunting vignettes, moments in time; with a slightly more bittersweet taste, so too do Brett Milano, Erika Jahneke and Clea Simon. There's speculative fiction that will knock you back on your heels, in stellar work from Madeleine Robins and Kathi Kamen Goldmark. From the classical music covered by Susanne Dunlap's wistful piece and Roz Kaveney's knockout *fin de siècle* fantasy thriller to the smackdown boogie offered up by Keith R.A. DeCandido's closer, it's all in here.

I really did get lucky, that so many of my writer friends are as much about the music as they are about the words. So whether it's architecture calling you, or a distance melody somewhere out there, grab your shoes and let's dance.

The Boy Who Played Air Guitar
– Madeleine E. Robins

Author's Note: This story perked along in the back of my head for years, as stories sometimes will. When I see kids playing air guitar the first thing I think, always, is "somewhere, someone is hearing that music."

The Boy Who Played Air Guitar

Mom was on her knees, arms wrapped around me, crying on my chest, apologizing, promising. Never hit you again. Used to be when she knelt she was as tall as I was standing, and she'd bow her head to cry on my shoulder.

Now I looked down and petted her the way you pet a cat. Mom didn't mean it—sometimes she just didn't know what else to do, and hitting was the thing that came easiest. And she hit like a girl, not the way Pop had; she didn't have the strength to slam a kid into the wall. Or the meanness.

"It's okay, Mama," I told her, and patted her head again. What else was I going to say? At least she never once hit Jerry. Pop had. It was one of the reasons why Mom had gathered us up and left him five years ago, when I was seven and Jer was ten. With Jer Mom was always patient and good. Mostly with me, too. Just sometimes the tired and the scared swept over her and she got that look and I said the wrong thing and—there it was. A smack, usually, open handed. Pop meant to hurt; Mom just got over-whelmed.

"I gotta go, baby. I can't be late. You look after Jerry." She got back on her feet, bent to kiss me. Her cheeks were still wet, and as she put her coat on over her uniform she was rubbing tears away. She stopped by the chair where Jer was sitting, looking at a book from the library, and dropped a kiss on his head. Jer didn't look up. "Bye, baby," Mom said from the door.

Without Mom the apartment was quiet, like Jerry sucked the sound out of it. Even the pages of his book didn't make noise when he turned them. The quiet made me want to yell, but Jer got upset by loud sounds, and I couldn't—didn't want to—upset him. Hurting Jer was like kicking a puppy. I sometimes had to defend him from the kids at school who called him "retard" or "spazz" or "spook," but he was all right as long as you kept things quiet and he didn't get scared.

Someone was at the door: a loud knock first, then a quieter one like the person had remembered Jer didn't like loud sounds. It was Rodey Kent from upstairs, his stupid cowboy hat pulled down over his eyes.

"Sammy, I got my cousin's X-Box. Come up n'play."

"I can't, man. I gotta watch Jer."

Rodey shrugged. "Bring 'im, dude. Mom's out 'til midnight." He said it as if his mother had left the key to Eisengard under the doormat. "I got food and stuff. Come on."

"We'd have to keep it quiet," I reminded him.

Again Rodey shrugged. "Headphones, dude. Bring the—bring him. Maybe he'll want to kill a couple of mercs or something."

I really wanted to. For a minute I stood there adding up the pluses and minuses. "Okay. We'll be up in ten."

Getting Jerry up and out of the apartment wasn't so hard. I had tricks to get my brother moving; a handful of M&Ms in my pocket, a new X-Men I'd been holding on to. Jerry was almost a head taller than me, skinny and long-armed and stronger than he looked; if he'd been hard to manage I wouldn't have had a prayer.

The M&Ms helped. I made Jer put on a fresh T-shirt—Jerry

could stink up a shirt just sitting still—and a flannel shirt over that; it was cold in the hallway, and Rodey's mother liked to leave all the windows open in their apartment. I checked to make sure I had my house key, then steered Jer up the stairs to Rodey's apartment.

Rodey's front door gaped open and he was playing Halo with the sound booted way up. It was like walking into a wall of noise: Jerry's face crunched up like wadded paper and his hands began to flap. "Wait," I said, low. I made a be-calm gesture with my hands, like I was pushing Jer's panic down, then went in and hit the TV's off button with a slap. Rodey gawked at me, outraged.

"Headphones, dude?" I brought Jerry into the room and closed the door. Rodey's apartment was like an icebox.

"Jeez, yeah, headphones. Sorry." Rodey ducked his head. "They're here somewhere." While Rodey rooted through an old milk crate filled with X-Box gear—controllers, a couple of Guitar Hero guitars, the plastic drum set, cables and guns and a skateboard—I settled Jer in an armchair, gave him a handful of M&Ms, and put his book and the X-Men on the table next to him.

"You be okay, bro?" Jer didn't look at me but he nodded and started sorting the M&Ms in the palm of his hand by color.

Rodey and I began to play Halo. I tried to keep an eye on Jer, make sure he was okay, but I kept getting sucked into the game. Once I looked around and Jer was reading X-Men; another time he was reading his book again. I figured I had a while before Jer got restless. I killed off some more of the forces of the Covenant.

The next time I looked up, Rodey's apartment was dark and even colder; the sun had gone down. Time to get Jer downstairs for dinner. When I pulled off the headphones and shook my head to get the headphone feel off my ears, I heard something, a rhythmic thapping behind me. I turned and saw: Jer had pulled one of the Guitar Hero controllers from the box and stood facing the window in a rockstar pose. The little flying-V-guitar-shaped controller was tight against his hips, his left hand flicking the colored buttons on the neck, his right hand scrabbling all over the strum bar as if he were plucking at strings. The controller wasn't hooked up, no sound came out, but Jer was rocking it anyway.

"Jerry? Dude, what?" We didn't play music at home, noise made Jerry freak, but here he was thumping away on that plastic guitar like Jimmy Hendrix. Where'd he get that from? I nudged Rodey, jerked my head in Jer's direction.

"Jerry, man, you're a natural!" Rodey said, too loud.

Jer stopped playing the controller, startled, his eyes wide.

"It's okay, dude." Rodey spoke softer. "I just meant you're, uh, doing a good job. You want to play for real?" Rodey switched the disk in the X-Box to Guitar Hero. I wasn't sure this was a good idea—so much sound could set Jerry off on one of his freak-outs.

"Turn the volume way down. Way down," I told him. "Jer? You want to try?"

Jerry clutched the guitar controller tight to his chest.

Rodey set up the level of play. "Want me to start it up?" He zipped through the logo screens and selected a tune. "Ready?" I nodded. Rodey hit play and unmuted the TV and the room was filled with backup music. Jer's eyes opened wide and the guitar controller shook in his hand; I grabbed the TV remote and turned the sound way down.

The panic ran out of Jerry like water; he held the controller to his hips and began to hit the buttons on the neck. Was he playing along with the song on the screen? Did he understand that was what he was supposed to do? He wasn't playing the way you're supposed to, pressing buttons that match the ones on the screen; it was like, if it were a real guitar he'd be playing real strings. Jer wasn't looking at the screen, he was just playing. And he was blissed out.

When the song was up Jer kept going, his body moving to music only he was hearing. It looked weird, but he seemed happy,

7

really in the zone. After a while, though, Rodey began to make little hmmphing noises and turned on a table lamp, impatient. It was full dark now, dinner time. Time to go home.

Making Jerry leave the guitar controller behind was tricky. He curled his body around the thing and wailed when I tried to take it away. M&Ms and the promise of another comic book didn't do it; threatening to tell Mom, which sometimes worked, didn't now. I flashed a look at Rodey, hoping he would say "Hey, take the controller down with you, bring it back later." But Rodey was doing a good imitation of clueless. Finally I told Jer I'd find him more music downstairs, and that—plus M&Ms doled out one at a time—got Jerry to give the controller to Rodey. Even so, I felt like I was peeling Jer's fingers from the slick black plastic.

When we got downstairs I made mac and cheese from the box and put a bowl on the table in front of Jer. Jerry ignored the food, even when I criss-crossed the top with ketchup the way he liked it. He just slumped in his chair looking like someone had taken away his toy, the best toy in the world, and he wasn't sure anything would ever be good again.

"Jer?" I kept my voice soft. "You want more music, bro?"

We didn't have a radio, not even an MP3 player. The music video stations were out: Mom didn't pay for cable. I looked through the old tapes in the TV cabinet; most of them we got cheap when Blockbuster was ditching inventory. There: a Metallica concert tape. I put the boxy old VHS into the player and adjusted the TV volume to just above a whisper.

"You want some music, Jer?"

Jerry said nothing, but he waited, his head not quite cocked in a listening tilt. I pushed play.

Jerry came to life. He stood up, took that rockstar pose again, his hip cocked, his left hand stretched out to fret an imaginary guitar, his right hand picking at strings that weren't there. He smiled, his eyes closed, his head moving fluidly in time with the music. It was amazing: Jer looked normal. Absorbed in his own world the way musicians sometimes are, but—like any kid.

I let the Metallica tape run and sat down to eat my own mac and cheese with a little hot sauce to hide the chemical taste. Jerry kept playing, fingers flying, body pulsing. Even when the tape jammed and the only sound was a low gray hiss, Jerry kept on. He wasn't playing Metallica. Something slower, less driving, from the way his fingers seemed to hover over some notes. I wondered what my brother was imagining.

It was almost eleven when Jerry dropped his hands to his sides. I'd finished some homework and read the X-Men Jerry had already looked at, and was watching TV with sound off and the captioning on, when I realized Jer wasn't playing air guitar anymore. He stood, his shoulders slumped, all the light gone out his face, sweat making his sallow skin shine.

"All done, Jer? You hungry?" I pointed to the mac and cheese. Jer sat down at the table and would have started in on the cold food, but I took it away to microwave it. "Warm it up for you, bro. It's almost bed time."

Jerry ate his dinner and came along when I led him to the bathroom. He was really ripe; I made him take a shower before he got into pajamas. Then I pointed Jerry to his bed. Usually he flopped around for a while like he was getting used to the feel of sheets against his skin, but tonight Jer was asleep almost at once. I lay there, awake, listening to his deep, rhythmic breathing.

I was on a beach, the sort of beach you see in movies: broad swath of sand, distant green of grass and trees, gray-blue ocean reaching out to forever. The sky was overcast but the air was warm. There was no one around, no footprints in the sand, but from over the rise in the distance I heard the sharp, bright tone of an electric guitar. I headed toward the sound, feeling coarse warm sand between my toes. The air smelled like sea and fruit

9

and broken grass; when I licked my lips I tasted salt and something sweet.

It took a long time to get to the crest of the rise. Looking out I saw dunes, beach grass, a couple of trees so twisted by the wind that they bent like dancers, and down the way to the left, someone standing on a rock, playing guitar. I started to trot along the side of the dune, sliding now and then when the beach grass under my feet gave way. The guitarist had his back to me but I knew him: his back, knobby under the black t-shirt; the bristly brown hair Mom cut herself.

It was Jerry, playing guitar.

Jer was wrenching sounds out of the guitar, moving his head and body as if each note ran through him into the instrument like an electric circuit. He was playing a big electric guitar, rosy-faced with black edges; the shoulders flared inward like devil's horns. What he was playing was pure rock, climbing up and down the scale, screaming over the gray landscape.

"Jer? Jerry!"

He stopped playing and turned. The last note hung in the air like mist. "Hey, Sammy." His voice was low and calm, with a smile in it. The voice I knew was higher, almost always frantic, whiny and wordless. This Jerry sounded older than fifteen. And he sounded pleased to see me.

"You're talking," I said. Way to state the obvious.

Jerry nodded. "Yup. Here, I can."

"What is this place?"

"I dunno. I just follow the music." Jerry looked down at the guitar and picked out notes like each one needed his attention. His mouth pursed.

"This is a dream," I said.

Jerry looked up at me. "No, it's not. Listen." He began to play again.

Mom was always up first. She had breakfast on the table and was drinking a glass of milk; when Jer and I left for school she'd go back to bed.

"Morning, Sammy." She squeezed my shoulder as I went past. "What did you guys do last night?"

I poured milk on my cereal. Jerry was already at the table, dressed and poking at his bowl with his spoon as if something might be buried there. "Went up to Rodey's for a while. Came back down and had dinner. Jerry—" how could I explain what Jerry had been doing? Jerry played guitar all night? "Jerry watched an old tape. I did my homework. Nothing much."

She nodded. "Sounds like a good evening. Everything okay?" Her eyes flicked to Jerry. Everything okay? was code for Jerry didn't have a meltdown? No screaming, nothing broken?

"Yeah, cool," I told her. Mom drank some more milk.

The bus came to pick Jerry up—he and I went to the same school, but Jerry got bussed there. As Jerry went down the steps with Aasif, the driver, I thought I saw Jerry's fingers twitch, playing ghost chords.

Mom went to work at four. After dinner, I started my homework; I left a book and some comics out for Jerry, but he didn't look at them. Instead he took a stance in front of the curtained window, arms dangling, head down. After a little while, like a signal had just come through, he began to play air guitar. He played with his whole body, eyes closed, that tight, focused smile on his lips. I watched for a few minutes; where had this whole music thing come from? From one time playing Guitar Hero at Rodey's?

I finished my homework and watched Jerry play some more. If I closed my eyes I could imagine the music he was making, an easy, rolling tune, plucked high notes against the drone of the lower strings, with a whiff of breeze to it. When I opened my eyes Jer was playing but the only thing I heard were his grunts, tiny

11

puffs of sound as he ran his fingers up and down the neck of the invisible guitar.

I closed my eyes again.

This time the sky that arched over the beach was clear china blue; I looked over his shoulder at an ocean that reflected the sky that reflected the wind-dimpled water. Jerry was sitting on the rock, playing the same tune I had imagined a moment before. Different guitar this time, a long-bodied acoustic with a light wood face, rosy-red sides, a black pickguard. I felt the music wicking through the beach grass, making it dance.

"What is that?" I asked.

"The song?" Jerry shrugged and the shrug went down his arm and into the music. "I dunno. Making it up as I go along. You like it?"

This time, with music sailing on the breeze, I wasn't surprised to hear Jer talk.

"Yeah, I like it. It's kind of—" I reached for the right word.

"Folky, maybe." Jerry smiled lopsidedly. "Think they like it?"

At first I thought Jerry was pointing to the black birds that wheeled overhead, chasing along the dunes like a line of music, scattering at the treeline. Then I saw something moving in the distance, tiny black dots moving, coming toward us. Shadows, or people.

The skin on the back of my neck prickled. "Who're they?"

Jerry shrugged again. "Guess they belong here. Coming to hear the music. What're you doing here?"

"What do you mean?"

"You don't belong here." Jerry said it like it was something I must have forgotten.

"What do you mean? How can I not belong in my own dream?"

"Not a dream, bro."

I opened my eyes. I was still at the table; Jerry was sitting on the arm of the sofa, head down, watching as his fingers plucked imaginary strings. I looked at the clock; it wasn't so late that I should have fallen asleep where I sat.

"Come on, Jerry. Bed time." I grabbed Jer's shoulder and pulled him up from the couch. He came, but he looked sulky. I pushed Jerry along in front of me to the bathroom, watched him brush his teeth. Looking at Jer's shuttered face in the yellow bathroom light it seemed impossible I had even dreamed my brother could speak.

Next morning, "What is he doing?" Mom had called us to breakfast, but Jer stayed by the window playing air guitar. This time I tried to explain.

"Rock and roll? But he can't handle music."

"He seemed okay if I kept it really soft," I told her. "It was like, when he saw the guy on X-Box he just knew what to do." I thought again of Jerry on the beach, real guitar in his hands, wringing notes into the salty air.

"Come on, sweetie. Even musicians need breakfast." Mom put her hand on Jerry's shoulder to bring him to the table. Jerry shook her off. His head bent, he watched his fingers. "Jerry, the bus will be here soon. Jerry, come on, baby." This time he came with her, let her sit him at the table, picked up his spoon and began to poke at the puffed rice and banana and milk in his bowl.

He was still eating when Aasif knocked. Mom pulled Jerry to his feet and slung his backpack over his shoulder and kissed his cheek and pushed him gently out the door into Aasif's care. Then she turned back to me. "Has he been doing that a lot? Pretending to play guitar?"

I was washing my bowl and glass. "Since Sunday, all the time."

Mom shook her head, thoughtful. "I never even tried playing music for him. I wonder if they do at school? I should call Mrs. Gonsalves and ask." She turned her attention to me. "Your turn, bud." She reached out to pat my shoulder; it used to be she'd ruffle my hair, then she realized that I didn't like it. "You don't want to be late."

That night, while Jer sat by the window playing the guitar that wasn't there, I did my homework with headphones on, listening to the TV. I needed to, to drown out Jerry's music. That wasn't there. It was stupid, I felt like I should be laughing at myself, but still I kept the bulky old headphones on and the sound booted up.

When my homework was done I packed our backpacks and made a snack—cut up apple and Ritz crackers—and put the plate where Jerry could reach it. I went back to the TV to finish the serial killer movie I'd been watching. When the movie was over I put the headphones away and turned off the TV. Jerry hadn't eaten his half of the snack, which annoyed me. The apples were turning brown under his nose.

"Wanna snack, Jer?" I held a slice of apple near Jerry's mouth; sometimes he needed the smell to remind him he was hungry. This time Jerry just dropped his head down further, away. "Fine. Time for bed."

Next day Aasif brought Jerry home with a note from Mrs. Gonsalves. I didn't get to read it, but Mom's face got the pinched look that meant *too much*, so I asked.

"Your brother's been acting out at school." Her voice was tight. "Had a screaming fit when they tried to stop him—" she wiggled her fingers in a parody of guitar picking. "They want me to come in tomorrow."

That meant she'd go in to school with Jerry, and miss sleep and be exhausted when she went to work. It seemed like she was tired already, thinking of it.

"Do you have to go?" I asked.

She didn't hear I was worried about her. She heard criticism, I could see that in her face. "What do you think, Sam? I should blow them off? Tell 'em to handle it themselves?"

"I just meant—"

"You're not helping," she said shortly. "Just be the kid and let me be the grownup. I'll take care of your brother." She moved around the kitchenette stiffly, already in her waitress uniform but barefoot; she never put on her working shoes until just before she left.

Jerry sat at the table eating Ritz crackers, drinking milk, reading. Mom slapped a plate of apple slices on the table. The sharp crack made Jerry recoil, his eyes wide and scared; his hands made tight warding gestures in front of his face. At once Mom put her hands on Jerry's shoulders; the pressure and her soft murmurs soothed him. Slowly Jer's hands lowered and he stopped the keening noise in the back of his throat. Over his head Mom looked at me as if somehow this was all my fault.

Jerry reached past his milk glass for the apple slices and the glass teetered at the edge of the table before it dropped and smashed. Jerry started moaning again, his hands flapping. I grabbed the paper towels to mop up the mess at the same time Mom went for the shards of broken glass; our heads bumped, Mom cut herself on the glass and reared back and smacked me in the face. Her hand dripped blood into the puddle of milk.

"Oh, God, Sammy. I'm sorry, baby. I'm so—Jesus God, baby, I'm sorry." The pinched look was gone, replaced by misery.

I tore off a piece of paper towel and handed it to her. "Here, Mama. It's okay. Wrap that up." I went back to sopping up the milk, careful to avoid the glass.

"Baby, let me do that. You might cut yourself." Mom's eyes met mine, and my mouth twitched and hers did, too. Suddenly the two of us were smiling, trying not to laugh aloud and scare Jerry. "I'm a good one to talk, aren't I? Let me clean up my hand and then I'll come get the glass."

15

Like magic—spilled milk and spilled blood—the anger was gone. When she'd washed the cut and put a Band-Aid on it Mom came back with the dust pan to sweep up the glass shards. I had mopped up the milk, poured Jerry more, and put the glass in the center of the table, far from the edge.

"Here." Mom had wet a paper towel and dabbed at my face. "Damn, look at the time. I don't want to leave you—"

"Mom, it's fine." I pushed the towel away from my face. "Don't worry about it. Put your sneakers on and go to work. It's fine."

"No, it's not." But she sat down opposite Jerry, pulled on a shoe and began to lace it. "There's stew or ravioli for dinner. Try to have some salad with it, will you?"

"Sure." I pulled my binder from my backpack and looked over my assignments. When her shoes were on and her jacket slung over her arm she stopped behind me and put her face down next to mine.

"I love you, bud. Even when I screw up, I love you." She kissed me.

I felt her hovering there, warm and anxious. "I know, Mom. Love you too."

When she was gone I looked up to see Jer watching me. Looking at me. Then Jerry got up and went to the window and began to play air guitar.

I did my algebra assignment first, then the English. I didn't care whether David Copperfield was the hero of his own story or not, but Mr. Wiczisky did, so I was plowing through it, hoping I'd remember what I was reading. Now and then I looked up to see Jerry, still at the window, still playing imaginary music.

Then something loud happened outside, loud enough so the curtains didn't muffle it. I didn't have time to figure out what it was—a car crash or construction accident, whatever—because Jerry lost it. He began to flap his arms; he kicked at the couch,

16

overturned the end table, swept pictures from the wall and books from the shelf. His eyes looked like he was being tortured, his mouth opened in a big O; high, frantic *ah-ah-ahs* spilled out of him.

I tried to get to him. Touch helps, Mom said. But Jerry was frantic, his arms flailing, beating. I couldn't get close.

"Jer! Jerry! It's okay." Keep your voice steady but not loud. "Jerry. Be cool, now, man. Jerry, it's okay." On impulse I began to hum, very low, the tune I dreamt Jerry playing. Whether because my voice reached him or he just ran out of panic, Jerry began to settle down. I could put my hand on his arm, then on his shoulder, then get him to sit down on the couch where he rocked the rest of the panic out. "Shhhh, Jer. It's okay, right? Chill." As I was talking I looked around to see what the damage was. Broken picture frame. Some bent paperbacks, one with the cover half torn. The TV had been shoved to one side on its cabinet and the VHS tapes were spilled all over the floor; one of them had been stepped on.

It could be worse. I could get it cleaned up and fixed before Mom came home. Jerry had stopped rocking and slumped back on the couch, his eyes closed. Sleeping, maybe. I closed my own eyes, as tired as Jerry, as tired as Mom.

"Man, I'm so sorry," Jerry said. He was holding a yellow-faced acoustic guitar with a braid of rosy inlay around the sound hole, playing something that sounded classical but restless, with a high insistent rhythm. "You okay, bro?" He gestured to me with his chin. "Is that blood? Did I do that?"

"What? No. You never touched me."

"Mom, then. Crap, Sammy, I'm sorry."

I thought back; Mom didn't hit me hard enough to draw blood. "It's hers. She cut herself. Not your fault."

"I dropped the glass."

"She put the plate on the table too loud."

The music went on, anxious, fidgety. "Sam, this can't go on. You guys can't go on the way you're doing. You can't."

"What do you mean? We're getting along. I just gotta help Mom more—"

"More? How? You're twelve, man. You're a kid, it's not your job—"

"Then whose job is it?" My voice sounded loud in the open air. "Mom has to work. I have to take care of you—"

"I'm sorry." Jerry sounded like he meant it. He ran one finger crosswise down the neck of the guitar, making a scoop of sound from low to high. "You got a crappy deal, bro. But you don't need to try so hard all the time."

I felt my face get hot. "What the fuck do you know? Mom's stressed out, she can't do everything, take care of you—"

"What if I give this up?" Jerry stopped playing. The silence was filled by ocean sounds, bird sounds, the whickering of breeze in beach grass. "Will that make it easier?" His long face was filled with all the expressions he never showed elsewhere: love and humor and regret and resolution. "Mom won't worry about this—" he waggled his fingers the way Mom had done. "If she's not worrying, she doesn't hit. She shouldn't be hitting you, kid."

I ducked my head. "She hit me before you started playing guitar."

Jer nodded. "But it isn't helping." He sounded sad. "Listen." Jerry started to play something different from the Flamenco piece he'd played before: a gentle run of notes like cold water over pebbles in a brook. The moving shadows in the distance—they were people, and they were coming this way—stopped for a moment, as if the new music surprised them. Then they started coming again. I wasn't sure why they were coming, but if they liked the music that was a point in their favor. The song sounded like flight, and hope, and sun and the way a smile feels on your face. All that.

"That's beautiful." The word should have sounded sissyish, but it was the truth. "You shouldn't stop, Jerry." I couldn't find the words I wanted.

"It's the only way to fix it." Jerry ran his hand up the guitar's neck. "What else can I do?"

I got up and went into the bathroom. Jerry was right: I had a smear of blood on my cheek where Mom had hit me. I washed my face, then started picking up and putting back. There was a dent in the back of the couch where Jerry had kicked it; I rubbed the spot until the fabric evened out a little. I put the books away, shoved the TV back to the center of the cabinet, put all the stuff back on the end table. Jerry sat there, his eyes not quite closed, breathing. Not playing air guitar. *What else can I do?*

Mom dressed to go to school with Jerry the next morning. Jer moved through breakfast like a robot, like a suit of armor without anyone inside. I had never thought about it before, that however sealed off he was, there was a person in there. This morning Jer ate his cereal and let Mom put his jacket on him, he was cooperative and slow and his fingers did not pluck at imaginary strings, but he wasn't there. After school Mom told me the meeting had gone well, had been quick, and she'd gotten home to nap afterward. "And Jerry's calmed down," she said, looking over where Jer sat, thumbing the X-Men in his lap.

But it wasn't just calm. Did she not see how *gone* Jerry was? I nodded and unpacked my binder and let Mom tell me about dinner and eating salad before she left for work. Jerry read the X-Men, then read it again. His shoulders were slumped so far that his backbone made a dinosaur ridge in his T-shirt.

When Mom had gone, I sat down next to him and took the comic book from his hands. "Jer, you want to play something?"

Jerry didn't move.

"Mom's not here, she won't worry. Go ahead." I nudged him.

Jer shook his head. He looked up, past my shoulder. His mouth worked, but no sound came out, not even a high wail of denial. What was it like to have things to say and no voice to say them?

"For fuck's sake, Jerry, tell me something. Play."

Jer stayed stubbornly silent, stubbornly unmoving.

I closed my eyes. All I saw was the inside of my eyelids. I opened them again and shoved Jerry roughly. "Tell me something."

I closed my eyes again.

Birds wheeled overhead, breeze ruffled the beach grass, the ocean shushhhed behind them, but Jerry said nothing. An electric guitar, ruddy red with a black plate, rested against the rock Jerry sat on. The shadow people were close enough not to be shadows any more. They were climbing the dunes, moving toward us.

"Who are they?"

Jer shrugged. "More shut-ins."

"Shut-ins?" I thought. "People like you?"

"I guess." His voice was flat.

"Jer, play," I urged.

"It's not a good idea," Jerry said. "If I start again, I won't stop."

"Why do you have to stop?"

"We've been through this. For Mom. For you. It makes things too complicated." I must have looked blank. "At home."

"So you're going to walk around like a zombie for the rest of your life? Like this morning?"

"Is that so different from the way I usually walk around?"

"Yes!" I shouted it. The approaching wave of people stopped, looking up at the ridge where we stood. I think I scared them. "Before, you didn't have this. You didn't know you could do this. I didn't know—"

"What?"

"I didn't know *you*."

"You knew me. At least you didn't treat me like…" Jerry's mouth twisted into a sorry grin. "Like a potted plant."

"But you're not like that. Not here. You can't give that up."

"It's one or the other, bro." Jerry looked at the Stratocaster at his side. "You help Mom all the time. Giving this up is the only way I can. That way I can stay with you. " He shrugged. "I love you guys."

All the anger I felt a minute ago oozed out of me.

"Listen," Jer said. "You're not supposed to be here. Let it go, bro. I love you." He ran a finger along the guitar's neck absently, the way Mom sometimes strokes my arm. I wish I understood this, I thought. I wish I did.

"What happens if you keep playing," I asked. "If you let us go?"

Jer thought. "I don't think there'd be anything left of me there."

"You'd die?"

"I don't think…die. But if I stayed here…" There was longing in Jer's voice. "I think I'd be gone there."

"Like a zombie? Like those guys?" I pointed to the walkers.

Jerry laughed. I'd never heard that before. "Zombies? Dude, they're just coming for the music. But I guess I'd just be…not there. Like in a coma or something."

I thought of it. Mom wouldn't be able to keep Jerry at home if he was a vegetable. He'd have to be in a hospital. Relief, then guilt, rolled over me like tidewater up the beach.

"It'd give Mom a rest." Jerry looked out over the dunes. Wind ruffled his bristling hair.

Give Mom a rest. I thought of that, the line between Mom's eyebrows that never went away. I thought of Jerry's laugh, and his music. "Jer, if it weren't for Mom and me, would you keep playing?"

Now it was Jer who looked guilty. He nodded.

I took a breath of salt air. "Look: we'll be okay. Whatever happens. Here—you've got fans, dude." I pointed down at the approaching people, close enough so you could see their faces, climbing the dunes purposefully. "You don't want to disappoint them."

"Mom—"

"Mom and I will be okay," I told him. "Pick up the guitar, Jer. I want to hear you play."

Jerry reached out and put his hand on my head, not ruffling my hair, just touching me like he was giving me a blessing. Then he took up the electric guitar and began to play. The first notes shimmered in the air as if you could see them. I watched Jer's fingers flex and slide on the strings. For a second I had this weird double vision: Jerry fluttered upward like a kite, like a bird, to wheel among the birds overhead. At the same time he was sitting in front of me, picking out a complex cascade of blues. The song was as full of heart and longing as the sound of the ocean. When I looked down the dune I saw the people scaling the final rise, smiling, swaying to the rhythm of Jerry's guitar.

Chopin, Fiendishly
– Patricia V. Davis

Author's Note: "Chopin, Fiendishly" is part of a longer work featuring the character of Zara, who first began germinating in my mind when I was in the ladies' room at a concert hall in New York. An amazingly beautiful woman, dressed to the nines, was staring at her reflection in the long row of mirrors. She opened her evening bag, took out a small jar of cream, scooped out some of it with her finger and then patted it around her eyes. She stared at the results for a moment, then pulled out mascara, lipstick, eyeliner, blush and redid all of her make up, which was already flawless. Something about how she went about all this was...disturbing. She kept scrutinizing that reflection, looking dissatisfied.

I saw her again as we were leaving after the concert, held tightly to the side of a man who was no less beautiful than she. He was staring down at her with a look of total absorption. They made for a breathtaking sight, but she still did not look happy, and I was intrigued with why that might be, what the man meant or did not mean to her, and what had brought them to the concert that night, which was, as I'm sure you've guessed, a concert featuring the works of Chopin.

Chopin, Fiendishly

Her face would create her destiny. That, and her music.

She understood that the year she turned seventeen. Until then her mother's incessant, simpering coo of, "Practice, Susan dear, practice—you won't regret it" was enough to make her want to crush her own wrists so she would never have to sit at a Concert Grand again. But when her parents insisted that she play at yet another of their oh-so-tedious Connecticut dinner parties, designed to impress Daddy's clients, she decided to rebel. Down came the French braid that her mother had woven tightly against her skull, so that all that loosened, honeyed hair tumbled softly against her shoulders and back. The clear pink lip gloss was replaced with a color that made her mouth look like a plump, ripe cherry just ready to burst, and the conventionally cut suit in a color the designer called "cappuccino", but which was really just a fetid beige was thrown aside for a midnight blue silk dress that shimmered to mid-thigh. Her descent down the stairs into their Thomasville appointed dining room was timed deliberately too late to be sent back up again to change, and as she greeted their guests with a little half smile at her mother's quickly masked shock, she thought, Now. Now they'll finally see the real me.

A trivial teenage mutiny. It was meant to be nothing more.

As she'd been taught, she sat elegantly at her piano and began to play one of her favorites, Chopin's "Nocturne Opus 55 No.2." Wrapped in the melody, she was wholly unaware that she had everyone's mesmerized attention, not necessarily because she was playing more brilliantly than ever, but more because of the abrupt, startling appearance of her ingénue beauty. The combination of that and the sounds she created with her graceful, competent fingers flooded her audience's senses. They could hear only her music, they could see only her, and there were those among them with the sudden craving to touch, smell, and taste only her. All of the women, including her own mother, felt an inexplicable fearful urge to flee, while the men watched her the way a snake watches a rabbit. Or was it the way a rabbit is mesmerized by a snake?

Eight months later, she played again at what she couldn't know would be her last dinner party with her parents. Her father's boss, a man fifty years her senior, stood up at the finish of her "Fantasie Impromptu Opus 66." Swaying on his feet, a sickly pallor to his skin that had nothing to do with his age, he said, "I love you, Susan," in the same somber, matter-of-fact tone he used when he addressed board members at corporate meetings. Then, in front of the twenty horrorstruck guests, he drew a gun from his suit pocket and blew out his brains, his blood spatter permanently soiling her mother's antique Belgian lace doilies.

Susan had met him only a half a dozen times, and each time she'd said no more to him than, "Hello, Mr. Sanford."

As it happened, Mr. Sanford had no heirs. This was just as well, because he'd bequeathed Susan his entire estate—millions of dollars in property and stocks—to be held in trust until her eighteenth birthday. When that day came, she collected her fortune and left home for good, leaving her mother sobbing and her father furious and mortified.

25

By the time she was twenty-five and at what one might assume was the peak of her beauty and talent, she'd changed her name legally from 'Susan' to 'Zara', and had already developed an international following. One night, while playing at the Salle Pleyel in Paris, she captivated a French viscount, who, like the first man who'd been enslaved by her, was also more than a little older than she, and also more than a little affluent. Zara and the viscount eloped within the week. Conveniently, he died early on in their marriage, when his heart failed while watching his wife play a duet—Chopin's, of course—with a handsome young Italian newcomer. The Italian had been paired with Zara for "The Wish" because the concert organizers thought they looked so dazzling together.

Now Zara's inheritances included a villa on the Côte d'Azur, a townhouse in Upper Manhattan, and a mansion on the San Francisco Bay. With these resources at her disposal, she traveled widely, learning to speak several languages, performing in many more magnificent concert halls, accruing much more money, and inadvertently causing the deaths of many more men. With that reputation growing, the men might have been a bit more wary around her, but they weren't and you couldn't blame them. How could they help but be besotted by her worldliness, her riches, her virtuosity, and by what had now become her staggering good looks?

The women she encountered were another story. They were fascinated, too, but most of them were also intimidated, and curious. You couldn't blame them, either. How could they help but be curious, and madly so, about a face and body that were still as luscious and nubile as on the day she'd buried that French viscount, more than sixty years before?

Zara was 85 years old, yet every year she'd only grown more beautiful. When asked about her age, she was charming and gracious. She never tried to hide how old she was; in fact, she seemed proud of it, but those who hoped for some revelation of her beauty secrets were left disappointed. The swing of her hair, the sway of her hips, the lilt of her eyes were all as timeless as the music she played, and no one but Zara knew how that was so. During every media interview, no matter how blunt the interrogation, she smiled a smile as white and serene as the keys on her piano, and said nothing.

With every decade she remained the same, the speculation and whispers grew. It was certainly true that with her vast funds, she could consult the best cosmetic surgeons and buy their discretion. She was also known for maintaining a diet and exercise regimen that even the most determinedly vain found rigorous. Nonetheless, every woman who saw her was certain that resolve, money and science simply could not be all there was to how she'd remained so vital for eight decades and counting.

They were right. Zara did have a beauty secret—a terrible one which delighted her. Her beauty was nurtured by the anguish of others. When women were near her, their anxieties about their own desirability in comparison to hers was so palpable, it made the air surrounding them sigh like the saddest notes of a song in the key of A minor. And when men were near her their longings echoed endlessly, like the deepest thrum of a bass cello's strings.

The pining of those who watched and listened to her only increased as she played, and their torment seeped into her pores, revitalizing her. It was her elixir, her fountain of youth, and because she'd somehow figured that out, she played with all the black passion of her merciless heart, almost always Chopin, enticing every drop of agony and desire from her listeners. A man in the third row, who'd just been married to the love of his life, forgot her very existence next to him as he heard and watched Zara. He never saw his lovely bride in the same way again. An actress celebrated for her beauty left the opera house, went home and promptly slashed up her own face.

Others left Zara's performances both elated and shattered. Lying in their beds that night, the splendor of her face and music still clawing at the essence of their very being, they shivered or sweated, or made love wrathfully while thinking of not their partner, but her. The next day, every one of them swore they'd never go back to see her play again. Yet, all of them were compelled to go back. They went back and went back, listening, watching, wondering and wishing. Their frail human lives went on without them ever knowing. They went on and grew older and eventually died, while Zara played Chopin to a packed house every night, forever and forever, youthful, lovely, magnificent still.

She was a sensation.

Ibiza
– Sam Cutler

Author's Note: I lived on the island of Ibiza for many years, and return to visit regularly. This piece is the first chapter to a book on the island that I never quite got around to finishing. I currently live on a bus in Australia, and am of "no fixed abode."

Ibiza

In Barcelona, Spain, I boarded a ferry for the ten-hour journey to Ibiza, the small island that was to be my destination.

From an upper deck, I watched as the boat slowly eased its way into the harbour pointing for the open sea. Below me, on a lower level, the passengers were crowded at the ship's rail and throwing streamers to people waving farewell from the dock. The boat captain let off several merry departing farts of the ship's horn as it maneuvered slowly away from the wharf.

People were screaming farewells in a striking babel of different languages and frantically waving to their loved ones. The last streamers were being thrown, falling short of the dock and landing forlornly in the water. With no words of farewell for my benefit, the departure of the vessel had made me feel sad and I headed for the bar. This was to prove to be an interesting mistake.

I ordered a coffee and a cognac and surveyed the scene with the practised eye of a man who has crossed the English Channel many times. I happily absorbed the usual chaos of people and belongings and too few tables and chairs. There were children getting lost and grandmothers getting irritable. The waiters were viewing the whole caboodle with contempt, and hovering above the chaos was the indescribable cacophony of a thousand tongues. Above the cacophonous noise, the steady throb of the ship's engine gave a reassuring pulse to the proceedings and I decided it would be enjoyable to studiously fall apart on Veterano, my favourite Spanish brandy. It is said that with three Veteranos a man will feel like a Matador, with five he becomes a King; with any more he can be whoever he wants.

I was feeling tipsy and decidedly regal when I first noticed "Juanita" sashaying into the bar. She surveyed the proceedings with a jaundiced eye and, with effortless panache, pushed a child off a chair and snarled abuse in guttural Spanish to its mother, who apparently felt powerless to intervene. She then plumped herself down on the commandeered chair with dignity unruffled and, tossing her hair defiantly, she thrust her ample chest at the hostile world. Having created something of a stir, she attracted the attention of a disinterested waiter who stood beside her with haughty disdain. He stared into the middle distance and asked to nobody in particular what she would like. "*Un sol y sombra y un cafetito*," she demanded, and fixed me with a baleful and insolent stare, as if to ask "what's it to you?"

I perked up immediately. This was my kind of gal. She had ordered a lethal mixture of cognac and anis to be accompanied by a small black coffee. The lady had style. We began a halting conversation in my poor Spanish, her inadequate English, and our competitively atrocious French. She told me an impossibly elaborate tale.

Her lover in Barcelona, it seemed, was an eminent plastic surgeon who had not only constructed her breasts but also shaved her Adam's apple and "done down there." Juanita was on her way to Ibiza to join him for a vacation. I was intrigued and, with me trying not to appear rude by staring at her alterations too closely, we became simple and immediate friends.

31

Her drinks arrived quickly and, as if on a signal, by the time she had finished her second cognac a man appeared beside her with a guitar case. He looked exactly as one would expect a gypsy guitarist to look: stereotypically dressed in black, and blessed with a face that screamed of what the Spanish call *mala leche*, bad milk. He stood sourly by the table and called out rudely to the waiter, who had not bothered to come over. Beer!

Another child was removed from a chair, and the guitarist elaborately arranged himself in front of us on the newly vacated seat. No one from the child's family dared protest. The man finished his beer, called for another one, and removed the guitar from its case. Juanita prepared to sing.

The whole of the bar took not a squint of notice, but this changed abruptly as soon as the woman opened her mouth. *From out of the strong there flowed forth sweetness*, the Bible would have us believe, but upon no critical examination could Juanita's opening salvo be described as "sweet." A piercing and unnatural falsetto of startling volume transfixed the passengers and, with shameless abandon, Juanita launched into an old music hall song. With a practised and ferocious intensity, the languorous guitarist became suddenly animated and the people stared and were shocked into silence.

Most of the audience knew from the voice that this was no woman, for surely no woman could or would have chosen to sing in such a manner. People smiled gently and found it amusing, with the German passengers the most wildly enthusiastic, trying to beat time with their hands on the tables. The first song ended to thunderous applause from one part of the crowd and with bemused silence from the other. I could sense mothers wondering whether their children should be actually witnessing this impromptu show and then resigning themselves to their predicament; there was simply no other place on the boat to sit but the bar.

Juanita stood for a song and took the shawl from her shoulders and provocatively draped it around her hips. I imagined her practising the move in front of her bedroom mirror. Accompanied by the Gypsy, she sashayed between the tables and belted out a song, which sounded like a mixture of Catalan and Arabic influences. It was dreadful. The words were indecipherable and sung with the same abandoned howl as before.

People began to get the joke. "Incongruous" is the word that springs to mind, and I could see it written on the expressions of the passengers, who began to clap wildly in time. To raucous cries of *Olê!*, Juanita brought the performance to a close and the guitarist proceeded to pass round the hat. I was enchanted, and getting very drunk.

Soon Juanita began eyeing me provocatively, and the guitarist shuffled away. The bar had settled down, and people were snoring uncomfortably as they tried to sleep in their chairs. The ship proceeded gamely through the gentle swell and the monotonous throb of the engines subdued the children. Outside it was dark, and the lights in the bar had been dimmed.

I wanted to sleep and, with Juanita generously offering to share her cabin, we stumbled along numerous alleys and passageways, until we came to her door. The cabin had four bunks and a small washbasin in the corner; through the porthole, I could catch a glimpse of the phosphorescent sea. I lay in her arms and contentedly fell asleep and woke with a splitting skull, stark naked and unsure of where I was.

There was no sound and no movement from the vessel. My clothes were on the floor of the cabin but my companion of the previous night seemed to have vanished. I dressed, painfully aware of a raging headache, and checked my pockets. My passport had been thoughtfully left behind—on the cover was a crude heart, drawn in lipstick.

I was smiling grimly as I poked my head out the cabin door.

The boat seemed deserted. Nauseous and deflated, I stumbled through corridors and staircases to the upper deck, emerging into brilliant sunlight to the surprise of a couple of sailors lounging at the rail. I was in Ibiza.

I walked unsteadily down the gangplank to the dock and headed for a bar, realising that I had no money. Mariano's was the same as it had always been, with Mariano serving his customers slowly and methodically at his own pace. I hadn't been in the place for almost a decade.

The owner recognised me immediately. He grinned contentedly—"*Que pasa, hombre?* I not see you long time. Where you been?"

"America," I replied.

I pulled out the linings of both my pockets to show the proprietor that I was stone broke. He grinned and told me to sit down, asking me what I would like to drink. "*Un sol y sombra*," I replied, "*y una cafetito.*"

Mariano looked at me thoughtfully. "*Mala suerte?*"

"No, not bad luck. Just a woman."

He laughed. "*Cuidado con las chicas, hombre.*"

Watch out for the girls: ironic advice, all things considered. Juanita's favourite drink cured my hangover within minutes. Cognac and anis: a sucker punch of a drink if ever there was one, and I was certainly a sucker.

I tried to recall what had happened that night on the boat. What her breasts and her poonani had looked like. Nothing. Simply nothing would come to mind. That disappointed me, for I would have liked to remember the results of the surgeon's art.

Most men have a morbid curiosity about seeing what a penis that has been turned into a vagina actually looks like. The very thought of such an operation, of the pain that must be involved, fills them with deep and disturbing fears. I'd had the opportunity, but was too drunk to remember a thing.

I smiled indulgently. All was right with the world; I had simply been protected by some superior magic from an experience I was not yet prepared to embrace.

I sat contentedly in the morning sun, ruminating on the nature of my peripatetic existence. I'd got to America with nothing; now I was here with nothing. Same same. In the midst of plenty, why concern myself with what I possess? I've arrived in Ibiza, a magical place, and I'll probably leave here with nothing too. What is there to worry about? We come into the world with nothing and we'll sure as eggs is eggs leave the same way. Naked in, naked out; we simply borrow some belongings for the journey. Trust and the world will provide.

In the Calle de la Virgin, the shopkeepers were beginning to open their stores. A lone priest walked thoughtfully down the hill from Morning Mass at the cathedral. I wondered if he was thinking "rich or poor, it's all the same in the kingdom of Heaven." At least Juanita hadn't stolen my passport. The lipstick heart made me grin. Relaxed and content, a reassuring voice in the back of my head crooned softly, "this world is a beautiful hotel." At that moment, it was as if the great chain of causation which accompanies all human foolishness gave a generous and knowing smile.

Barry the Jeweller materialised before me, and in a broad Australian accent asked, "Where the hell have you been?"

"You know, getting high and getting by ….. going with the flow," I replied modestly.

He studied me for a nanosecond, and sat down with a grin. "You just got off the boat, didn't yer? Welcome home."

Didn't You Used To Be Somebody?
– Erika Jahneke

Author's Note: This story had several unique inspirations: the work of Teddy Pendergrass (my mother exposed me to "For Ladies Only" at an early age). Though I had intended to write about a "Pendergrass character" for some time before the legend's death, this particular story took the shape it did because of some tributes I read in The Guardian online. They were well-meaning and respectful, but it was hard to ignore that they looked at his life from a very able-bodied perspective. My injury is different from Darnell's, but in some ways I feel more connected to the ways he would look at life. Maybe I'm wrong...we're quite different in many other ways, but writing about this character has been a unique exercise in walking in someone else's shoes, so to speak.

Didn't You Used To Be Somebody?

For the first time since right after my accident, I had that dream about the tree.

Initially, it was an actual tree, although even that image had been altered by my memory into something green and lush, not the leafless cluster of sticks Nature would insist upon late in November. In my dream, I remembered the smell of snow and the lack of feeling in my limbs. Some nights, I dream as if it were all new, rather than the battle scar carried through two decades, carried because of the appetites of my younger self.

I have plenty of ordinary dreams, in which the chair is as close to unremarkable as it will ever be: dreams of missed flights, forgotten lyrics and going with Norman, my attendant, to pick up my kids at their mother's house, or tasting some recent loved one's juices upon my tongue.

Be careful as you write this part, miss. You might be young and blonde, but all reporters seem to be after the smutty angle these days. I include it to rebut those claims that by including love songs on the albums I put out after the accident, I was "attempting to hang on to past glory" or whatever that snot-nosed white

37

boy wrote. In many ways, I love more fully now, although some of the variety may be gone.

I suppose reading that made it easier to abandon even my small attempt at touring-while-quadriplegic. A tour is a lot of work even at the top of your form, and my new circumstances added tons of new details and time constraints. Still, I might have continued, if I had been treated more as an artist and less like a museum relic that reminded people how things used to be, sort of like living bell-bottoms. There were things they didn't want to be reminded of, though, like how fragile human bodies are. Fragile gifts from our Creator. The fact that I could sit there, and more than heal, actually sing, seemed to confound everyone, and they couldn't hide it. I do wish I could visit France again.

I decided to stop, once and for all, one morning in Chicago. A tourist approached me in a hotel lobby and asked "Excuse me, didn't you used to be somebody?"

I gave her a small version of that old smile. The full-strength version, back in the old days, might have been enough to make her take her panties off in the elevator, but I had grown up a lot and she wasn't my type at all: mom hair that looked like she cut it herself, zinc-oxide nose and a Cubs hat. No harm in giving her some of the old charm, though. Didn't cost nothing.

"I like to think I still am. You know?" And I leaned back and tried to look as if my wheelchair was some kind of chaise and any minute now some lackey was going to bring me my favorite travel drink. I think then, that was margaritas on the rocks...it wasn't too long after that that I gave that up too; there's something accidentally sobering about getting hammered in a special cup, through a straw. I did it a few times to show myself how little my life was going to change.

Instead of some game with sidelong glances and flirts, Cubs Mom blushed violently and painfully, as if she were a lobster in a pot. "Uh, sure, of course you are...I didn't mean...I just meant like from television or something like that."

It wasn't a great save, but she suffered over it so much it was easier to be the big person. "I was on Soul Train a few times," I told her. "But I'm not sure you ever saw that. Of course, there was a lot of coverage of my accident."

I extended my hand a little to show there were no hard feelings. "Darnell Watkins."

"Lois Smith. My sister Franny will be so tickled...she always liked the black groups and that...is that okay, that I called them black groups...should it be African-American?"

"Say 'soul' or 'R&B', but it's true...we are a black group. I wouldn't have that any other way, either, ma'am."

"Of course not," Lois said, and she nodded so emphatically that the damn hat bobbed. "I think that's just super...your attitude is just super-great. Franny will be glad, too. She thought you died."

For a minute, that sentence sat between us as if it were a title in a French film like the ones my first manager liked dragging me to. She thought you died. To avoid reading it again, I studied the garish lobby carpet in a way nobody with eyes had studied it since some pencil-necked geek in a far-away office had selected it, or at least, that's what I figured. It was all different shades of pink with flower bouquets on it. I never want to meet the person who can sign the check for that in good conscience.

"As you can see, ma'am," I told her, all hearty and shit, "I'm still among the living. Just got beat up is all." And I was reminded of my son. Junior had just turned ten, and hit his first real smart-aleck phase...what was that sound he made non-stop? Duh, that was it. Like you were too stupid to waste any more than a grunt on. I hated it; it seemed so disrespectful, but this woman just kept on cataloging dead brothers she might have gotten me confused with: Brother Sam, and Otis, and Marvin Gaye, and she was trying so hard to be friendly and decent and

39

Get it Right, and all I wanted to say was "Duh!" I even shaped my mouth around it, but in the end, performers' instincts die hard and she walked away smiling at my not-really-a-joke about passing news of my survival to the recording industry.

It was true. A lot of cats I thought of as friends-for-life had stopped returning my phone calls, beyond telling me they were "So sorry, man," and making sponge-bath jokes. Occasionally, they sent nuts-and-chews, which I passed around my floor at Rehab.

There is magic that happens between a singer and a willing crowd, that rivals some of the greatest highs on Earth. Much of the debauchery of my previous life was just a sad attempt to hold onto that magic. Still, the thought of facing potential millions of those conversations between now and the time I turned my numb toes up, made me come back home eagerly and start building a home studio. Sales of the post-accident albums were never what the earlier lover-man tracks were. Sometimes, audiences never forgive you for getting serious, even if you didn't almost die. George Harrison had some lean years too.

Much as I might have wanted to, I couldn't deny things were different.

I had the time to think about everything in ways I hadn't, ever before, and so it seemed impossible to document another Everyman's romantic high or low...my life had been bisected, like the tree in my front yard, and I felt like describing the weird terrain on the other side as I discovered it. I did it anyway, even if the people in charge only found one single in it, and that one the goodbye to the old life that made me famous. In a way, I understand, and yet, who wants to feel that his life isn't commercial?

Oh, well, water under the bridge now. Time passed, and my writing partner's oldest daughter turned from a clever and inquisitive little girl to a robot in a grey suit, spouting recorded messages about market share, per-unit sales and the internet. She is known everywhere as savvy and fearsome, and, in my view, has changed for the worse; she is no fun at all. She has made us all rich, and there is no question she has made the business sit up and take notice, even during times like these. I wouldn't need to record anything, not in that old "rent due," way that sometimes made us so desperate. Back then, brilliant shit would pour out because we needed it. Before I get too romantic about those old days, I should remember the more thoughtful pieces that never got their due because we flew by the seat of our pants so much. Not that need ever had much to do with the impulse to sing and play…those of us that do, do it anyway.

But I wondered what happened to the little girl who was so thrilled to show me fireflies. I suppose worrying about the latest cover art for some compilation is almost the same, but I dreaded it anyway when she leaned over my desk with four disc-cover versions. I hesitated over one because it was a picture of me and her father, about fifteen, trying to look as if we knew everything. We had no idea what was waiting for us. Lawanda— she cut off that first syllable first chance she got, trying to be sophisticated; maybe we're not that different, after all, pounced. "So, Uncle Darnell," she said, in that cement-mixer style of talking she brought home from that business college, "Is that the one you like?"

"I like them all. Give me a minute."

"We need to decide by the end of the week." Wanda looked prepared to sit with her arms crossed, watching, the whole time. Eventually, I knew something would just hit me the right way and I would know, but I didn't say that to her. Wanda liked to plan everything, and if the need ever arose, I could eat off her desktop.

Sometimes I needed to work up to that gleam in her eye, and that's the God's honest truth. I pressed a button on my chair, and made a project of adjusting myself and pulling my reading glasses out of their case. Sometimes this was enough to make her go away; she has the clearest memory of Uncle Darnell walking and having fancy cars, including the miracle of German engineering I wrapped around the tree. Without realizing it, I must have stepped on some kind of Deadline. I tried to look contrite, but the truth is the girl loves Deadlines like most folks love cake. If I didn't screen some out, I'd be sweating something all the time. Add in that PowerPoint, and to Wanda, it's like having the circus in town. I don't understand.

I leaned over and looked at some of her other choices, including one that looked like a kid could have painted it. She beamed when I touched it and seemed to admire its watery colors. By not saying anything, she was bound and determined not to influence me, though it seemed too artsy and more like the cover of an Enya CD than one of mine.

"Oh, you know me, La, uh, Wanda," I corrected myself just under the wire. "You know so much more about sales and stuff than I do."

"That 'stuff' isn't just about sales," she lectured me. "It's about Protecting The Brand."

"Please, dear," I begged her. "Please don't show me the chart again."

Wanda seemed stricken by another impulse then, and headed for my bathroom. It was a strange sort of turnabout: she was inside and I sat outside, wondering if she needed help.

"Wanda...are you all right?"

And I heard it, returned like a catchy hook for a pop song, or a jingle from when I was young and commercials had jingles. *Didn't you used to be somebody?* I thought about bursting in, but it was the adrenaline talking.

I heard a quick rush of water as she flicked on my modified faucet. "Yeah, fine, must be something I ate. Maybe yesterday's shrimp wasn't fresh."

It's not like me to get up in grown people's business, but she sounded strange. And it was almost like she had the shrimp line in place, ready to use, if this should happen. Besides, we all ate the shrimp. "You sure?"

"What else would it be?" Maybe you didn't plan everything, LaWanda Mae.

"Yeah, probably shrimp." I considered saying something snappish about nine-month doses of food poisoning, but I figured she'd have to work it out on her own time and I wasn't going to interfere with that.

Suddenly, bits of life that had seemed puzzling until that moment found themselves assembling, like lyrics and melodies often do, and I understood. In a flash, it made sense why it had been hard to get Norman, my trusted live-in attendant, when I needed assistance at night these past few weeks, after years of service. I thought one of the voices in his room sounded familiar, but I guess I chalked it up to déjà vu all over again, as Mr. Berra said. Sometimes, it was hard to see where Norman ended and I began, and at times like that, the separate life I tried so hard to protect just evaporated.

I wondered whether love had ever made Wanda loosen her grip, but maybe she'd left her briefcase under someone's bed overnight. "You sure you're all right?"

Only a slight shine on her forehead was left to show me this wasn't an ordinary meeting, as Wanda flipped open her laptop. A few moments passed and she seemed buried in work. Apparently, I was the only one preoccupied with the new life within Wanda.

She surfed to our website, where she was greeted by the tinny opening bars of our biggest hit.

"We should release 'Muriel'," Wanda told me. "The fans seem quite taken with it."

"Sure," I told her. "If you can find it."

"What does that mean?"

I was getting irritated with her busy-professional act and the fact that she was poring over everything as if her world had shrunk to laptop size. "What do you think? Literally, I don't know where all the tape is." If I could have, I'd have pounded my fist on the table, but it doesn't work that way anymore. Norman would have to do it, and I was almost glad I'd sent him away for the afternoon.

Knowing Norman used to feel like knowing my own hand, especially after he made such a seamless transition from roadie to attendant. Maybe I blocked it out because it made me uncomfortable to know how much was going on without my knowledge—especially sexual intrigue. Time was, if anyone was creeping from my house, it would have been me.

Somehow, sleeping through it felt like being catapulted instantly to old age. I sifted the thought in my brain for a moment, and rejected it. Talk about non-commercial. "I still want you to look into those house rentals."

Wanda snorted. "You still on that?"

"Just for the winter...I'll be back by the time you have the...shrimp."

"Look, you know, I understand," she continued, "How hard it must be to pass by that corner every day, with the anniversary coming up, and..." She paused helplessly, spread her hands, and gave me that famous "Listen to reason," face.

Sometimes, I think it's a pity some folks grow up at all. Eight-year-old Wanda would have understood exactly why I wanted a change of scene, or at least, would find crossing the country a great adventure. I would have bought her some Indian earrings and she would be thrilled.

"Wanda, dag, it's been twenty years. I hardly think about that anniversary stuff anymore. But there's a transplanted trumpet player there that's been writing to me and your father. I thought we might do some work. New Orleans has great trumpet players, even if they do end up drying out in Arizona. Maybe I'll talk to the boys while I'm there."

She sensed my excitement and softened a little. For a moment, I could see a trace of the girl she'd been. She looked like her mother, whom I met first and chased after, but once she met him, Irene only had eyes for my knuckleheaded drummer friend, Parsons, who was suddenly older, grayer, and a family man, doing some kind of business in New York.

"I'll talk to Daddy," Wanda said, finally. "It might be good for you to go away and clear your heads. But that is a lot of money to spend on tomcatting. Also, those boys may be your nephews, but they aren't worth a damn."

I'm sure my look said things I didn't trust my mouth to say, because she turned away with a flush in her cheeks. "Nice of you to give me permission to live my own life, when I've known you from the moment you first drew breath. Maybe I'll move there…how about that?"

"It's like, Cracker Central," Wanda pointed out. "You know you couldn't stand it."

"Probably not," I admitted. "But it's really not your decision to make."

I hadn't gotten that far yet, just up to sun in the winter and sitting by somebody's pool as it gleamed like a diamond without a setting, playing a little music, looking at some fresh scenery. I couldn't admit it after talking so tough, but I did notice as the accident anniversary drew closer, I got a shiver down the parts of my spine that still got shivers. It had faded over time, but twenty years was quite a milestone. It seemed that, in honor of it being t-minus-ten-days-and-counting, every one of my favorite restaurants and stores seemed freshly stocked with eager young counter help guaranteed to make me think *You weren't even born the last time I could stand*. And, of course, the same tree was right outside my window, ready to hold my mood hostage on the one night a year an elm tree wasn't just a tree. I would really feel better once these travel arrangements were finalized, and my neighborhood was in my rear view.

"I'm just looking out for you." Wanda's expression was full of love, which was great, but her tone was patient, which wasn't. "You're the one who said you don't know where your most famous tape is. I just don't want you overtaxing yourself."

"It was a different time," I explained. "People didn't think this stuff would last. And, I know I have a lot of limitations; I also have intimate knowledge of them. And did you ever think that, if it wasn't for it being rare, nobody would even care about an album I dedicated to my mother?"

I could feel myself flushing at the memory of trading one of the masters to my dealer. I got my head up before a show and really felt that I had gotten the better end of that deal until recently. As for the other copies, who knew? Maybe the dealer snagged two copies. Maybe the bassist's guru got in touch with his coyote-trickster spirit.

"It's all ancient history," I explained. "It was…"

"The seventies," she finished, sounding like a bored teenager being asked to tell what she did on her summer vacation for the thousandth time. But there was a tiny indulgent smile lifting the corners of her mouth and for that, I was glad. She was about to have enough problems.

"I know you weren't there." I'd tried to explain the heady blend of optimism and fear that surrounded those years that were her early childhood, but it doesn't matter now. Wanda's thinking is a strong, bright line. There is no erasing it or crossing it.

Alex Parsons didn't fight me on the winter-in-Arizona plan, at least not as much as I expected. "Sure," he said, with that slow smile I'd known my whole life, "What the hell… let's do it."

That instantly activated all my doubts, but it wasn't as if I had a crystal ball, or my objections would have been stronger.

"Really? I thought you wouldn't…well, never mind," as inarticulate and dithery as a comic-book housewife. Any minute, I thought, my chair tray would be replaced by a frilly apron. "Just because I broke my back doesn't mean you gotta agree with me."

"You won the argument, fool. Don't you know to quit when that happens? Yeah, you know, Arizona isn't my dream come true…"

"Cracker Central?" I offered.

"Yeah, partly that, but you know too much sunlight depresses me. I must be part polar bear or something. But it'll be nice to hit the road again. Especially now that we can park wherever we want."

Alex liked living out of suitcases, which always looked perfect despite being thrown together in two minutes. His sudden burst of interest in my winter plans gave me a pang of guilt about how much our close partnership had held him back. He had written songs for other acts, but he always made it clear that our work together was the top priority. I felt myself well up a little at the thought."

"If you'd like to be alone to write this in your diary, I could leave."

I snapped out of it, cleared my throat, and looked away. If I had known the clock had started winding down on our lifelong friendship, I'd have hugged the son-of-a-bitch and dared the world to write whatever down-low mess they wanted. Not that they would have; I'd been downgraded from pop act to survival story, any scandal wiped out in the snap of my spinal cord. Anyway, these young folks coming up put us to shame. So I don't know why I snuffled and said "Allergies," only it satisfied him and he gave me this little nod, as if it were all forgotten.

I suppose I should have known something was up when I got a

47

call before noon, although morning calls didn't give me an automatic jolt of fear since my mother passed.

"Mr. Watkins? This is Detective Ken Ingram from the Phoenix Police Department. I need to talk to you about Alex Parsons."

I honestly expected Alex, loopy from being up all night, to sing me some "great harmony" that he found in his head after five Coca-Colas, and, even when the flat-voiced detective identified himself, I only thought that there might have been more involved in the burst of creation than Coca-Cola, in which case I'd be more than prepared to hound the backsliding motherfucker. Having made the resolution to start right then, if need be, I straightened my spine and said "Could I talk to him please? If he needs a lawyer, I can handle that..."

The cop coughed, and sighed. I figured he must not have been doing it long, if they let him make human noises. "Sir," he told me patiently, "That won't be possible. Mr. Parsons was fatally shot. His body is at the medical examiner's office."

All the air seemed to go out of the room in one big burst, even though the loft was mostly empty. I started keeping track of my breathing and thinking of times tables, trying to keep my grip. The last thing I needed was to faint or get dysreflexia.

The feeling passed. All better. Except it wasn't.

I had almost forgotten the cop, until I heard his tiny voice in my speakerphone. "Mr. Watkins, sir, are you all right?'

"As well as expected...medical examiner...that's the morgue, and all that, right?"

"Yes...the morgue, right." Suddenly this young cop sounded like he felt bad telling me uncomfortable things. Maybe he was a fan. But, if so, he would definitely be classier about it than the star-struck orderlies in my mother's hospital room. Mostly, I had enjoyed fame, but that still left a sour taste in my mouth.

"What happens now?"

"Well, someone has to identify the body, then my partner and I start to investigate."

"Give me an hour." Even inside my own head, my voice sounded hoarse, as if I, rather than Alex, had gone back to old habits. Out of the corner of my eye, I spotted the crumpled green top of a pack of Salems peeking out under the couch. I guess Alex's smoking isn't going to kill him now.

"You don't have to do that, Mr. Watkins. I'm sure given your…special circumstances, you could send a family member. Take it easy on yourself." The detective's voice sounded younger and friendlier, the kind of voice that made me think of words like 'wholesome.'

"The man was like my brother. You don't need to concern yourself with my…circumstances." I was sharper than I like to be with a white man I don't know, but somehow the idea there was an easy way out of all this got my back up. The cop seemed to understand. After that, he was all business.

"Since you'll be in the area, would it be convenient for me to take your statement? When it comes to these kinds of cases we like to be efficient whenever possible."

"Fine. Of course,"

Until I left that morgue, I wanted to believe some terrible mistake had been made. It hadn't.

On the way back from the police station after giving my statement, I was halfway recognized again. This time, my questioner was a young woman who once would have filled my requirements in every way…my dream girl, circa 1975, only with more disciplined hair. She studied me like I was a new sample from her stamp collection.

"Do I know you?" She sounded abrupt, the way women her age always do.

"I hardly think so." I was not in the mood to offer anything else.

49

"Maybe not recently…did we go to high school together or something?"

The chair hung between us. "Unless…" I gestured to include it.

"Not that I know of," she told me. "But accidents do happen."

"That's for sure."

"I know I've seen you before…" she said. "This will bother me all day. Did you used to be somebody? Like on TV?"

"No." It hit me all at once; the strangeness of being in this bright and sunny city on one of the darkest days in my life. "No, not at all."

Saint Rufus Fair

– Barbara A. Denz

Author's Note: This story is a retelling (with many changes) of the Scottish historical song, "MacPherson's Rant." If you recognise the original in it, I'll be surprised. This is what SHOULD have happened!

Saint Rufus Fair

On the road from the high country in the west rumbled an ornate carriage with the blue, green and black ribands and flags of Clan Grant. It was followed by six horsemen clad in the colours of the region's Laird and riding even with the carriage's pace. A dark-haired girl pushed a fine curtain aside and leaned out, eyes closed, breathing in smells of dust and meat pies and apples and hay.

Fiona opened her eyes and saw the town of Keith's Saint Rufus Fair spread around her. It filled the market square with fishmongers hawking their wares, brightly-clad tinkers banging pots to draw attention to their trade, jugglers tossing balls to the cheering of children young and old, and pipers tuning wayward reeds. The autumn-morning sunlight dazzled on silks and satins in shades of gold, green, blue and red. Local clan tartans were held in place by coin-filled sporrans and long broadswords, their owners swaggering about the fair with wives, children, mistresses and servants in tow. Off to one side near their brightly-coloured wagon, a Gypsy fiddler held a crowd in thrall while his band's harmonies tightened a spell woven by the haunting fiddle notes of a Highland aire.

"How much longer, guardian?" eleven-year-old Fiona asked the finely-dressed man seated across from her. Her black eyes sparkled in the sunlight and her curls bounced with the ride of the carriage and the breeze. She squealed her delight at the sound of bagpipes skirling to life.

"We're here, child," answered the Laird of Clan Grant. He, too, leaned out the window, telling his driver to stop near the gypsy band's wagon. "There's someone here I want you to meet."

"In Keith? We had to travel to the fair to meet them?" she asked.

Her guardian laughed. "Yes, child. Jamie MacPherson is the pride of the Fair. You'll see." The carriage stopped. "Now, Fiona, you may step down."

The tune stopped and the crowd was laughing and throwing small coins into the open case at the fiddler's feet as the coachman opened Fiona's door. A few paces in front of her, the fiddler leaned over and retrieved the coins, settling the fiddle into the case and turning it toward him as he chatted with the crowd, flirting here and laughing there.

The coachman held out his hand to help her down, but Fiona jumped to the ground and slid on the cobblestones in her new boots, coming to a stop with her hand on the fiddle case on the ground at the fiddler's feet. A large hand reached out to steady her. It had rings with dragons and strange sigils on most fingers, and three different coloured layers of cuffs at the wrist. That was all Fiona noticed. Her eyes and fingertips were drawn to sun-bright yellow, cobalt blue, and carmine red paint. She pulled her arm free from the large hand and knelt down on her fine dress, completely absorbed by the brightly-painted flowers, sigils and vines on the fiddle case at the large man's feet.

Too swiftly to be stopped, Fiona picked up the less ornately-painted fiddle from its ornate case, and cradled it in her arms, gently touching the strings and humming a tune the fiddle's strings echoed. As she reached for the vine-painted bow, the long-fingered hand grabbed her small one and squeezed until she winced and looked up.

"Just what do you think you're doing?" a black-eyed man in his mid-twenties hissed at her, leaning a few inches from her face. She leaned back onto her heels at the sound of the Scottish dialect her mother's family spoke. She had not heard the melody of that phrasing in the year since her mother's death. It was the Gaelic of the Travellers—the people known in local and legal slang Romanichal or Gypsies. Her people. She blinked back a tear, still staring into those black eyes.

The stranger held her gaze as he pried her fingers from the fiddle. His index finger nail flicked lightly across the strings, inspecting the tuning and never taking his eyes off her. When he finally looked away, he put the fiddle and the bow lovingly back into the case, latched it closed, and slipped the case strap over his shoulder.

"Nobody touches Jamie MacPherson's fiddle unless he invites them to do so." His eyes held hers again, and she could not move.

"I ... I ... I," she stammered, "I meant no harm to the fiddle, sir. She's beautiful and I just wanted to touch her." Fiona blinked.

"*He's* my fiddle and not for the likes of children," Jamie laughed. "Isn't that right, boys?" He released her gaze and looked over his shoulder. Fiona blinked. His band was made up of three tall, young, slender, dark brightly-dressed raggle-taggle Gypsies, one of them holding the pipes she had heard. The pipes wailed their dying-pig sound from the bag under the piper's arm as he bowed to her.

"Jamie," the Laird said warningly, "let her be. You're scaring her and I brought her to meet you. Her mother has passed and the child is my foster now." The Traveller looked at the Laird, bowed, and winked.

54

"I'm not a child," Fiona countered forcefully, not hearing. "I'm eleven!" Then she dropped her head shyly.

"Then meet her I shall, old friend." Jamie smiled, and bowed to Fiona, who looked up cautiously. "Young lady, bright and beautiful as this autumn day, I'm Jamie MacPherson, swordsman, Traveller, horse-trader, tinker, occasional thief of women's hearts, and general wanderer." He laughed. "But mostly, I'm just a fiddler and a dancer." He leaned close to her and whispered, "Don't listen to anyone who says otherwise."

His hand swung in an arc toward the band beside him. "Angus is the piper, Donald is my brother and the whistle player, and my cousin Peter plays the strings I don't play." Each of the young men bowed as he was introduced.

She curtseyed to each politely, and then turned back to Jamie. He smelled of onions and flowers and something Fiona could not identify. Whatever it was, it made her hungry for his fiddle's music, but she didn't dare reach again for the instrument that kept calling to her.

The Laird of Grant put his arm around his ward's shoulders. "This is Fiona. She's a daughter of the dark people on the lands of Clan Grant—her mother was a princess of that tribe and a dear friend of mine. You might have known her."

Something passed between Jamie and the Laird that Fiona did not comprehend, but when Jamie looked back, it was with a warm smile.

"The daughter of a princess. And eleven. I was in your country when I was not much older than you and I did know your mother. She was... we were...," he stopped, raised an eyebrow at the Laird who responded with a nod, and kissed Fiona's hand. Then something caught his eye. Around Fiona's neck was a necklace bearing the same sigil as that on one of his rings and on his fiddle case. He lifted the necklace and traced the symbol with his fingernail. The necklace glowed purple in his hand. He stared at it as the purple light faded and then let it drop. Jamie looked back into Fiona's eyes.

"Follow with us," he said finally. "It's time we made our march around the Fair." Jamie took his fiddle and bow out of the case, latched the case, swung it over his shoulder and strutted away, fiddle to his chin. "Let's let everyone know that Jamie MacPherson and his Travellers band are here."

"Go ahead," the Laird laughed as her eyes begged to follow. "Just make sure you stay with them and don't wander off. Jamie will get you to our dwellings before evening falls."

Fiona lifted her skirts and dashed after the musicians. Angus the piper led them through the Fair past ancient wooden carts filled to overflowing with breads and dried fish and trinkets. He was followed by Donald playing the tin whistle, Peter strumming a strange round plucked-string instrument Fiona had never seen before, and, finally, Jamie, towering over his bandmates and those they passed. The crowd parted as the musicians strode by, and then closed around them and followed along. Fiona struggled to keep up as the band held the followers in thrall.

She was being pushed back further from the music, and having trouble seeing where to go, when Jamie called out to her. "What's wrong, lass? Can't find your way through the crowd?" He laughed. "Let her through, good people. She's with the band." And a path parted for her. Jamie winked at her and, laughing, lifted his fiddle again and picked up the bright, fast dance tune and the band danced through the crowds.

From aire to strathspey to reel to jig, Angus piped the fiddle along. Back to their wagon with its makeshift platform, Jamie pulled his bandmates up next to him and launched into a fast set of jigs.

From the edge of the market away from the Travellers' Highland home, five horsemen tried to push their way through the crowd, but the crowd knitted itself together into an impenetrable mass of humanity until the leader began using his riding crop on the people around him.

Jamie's eyes narrowed and he quit playing. He nodded to Angus to play on. The front of the crowd looked around, released from the spell of the fiddle.

"Why are you beating these people, Duff? What have they done to you?" Jamie growled, as five armed men on horseback pushed the crowd aside and reined in at the wagon, horses flecked with sweat and stamping the flint in the cobblestones to sparks. Alexander Duff of Braco, a balding man with a silk-covered round belly that bespoke his rich tastes in food and clothing, did not deign to answer the musician.

Calmly and smoothly, Jamie swung the fiddle case off his shoulder and placed his beloved fiddle inside, latched the case closed and swung it back over his back, its long leather strap crossways across his large chest. He crossed his arms.

"Let's see what they think they have on me this time, shall we?" He grinned and the crowd roared laughter.

"Jamie MacPherson, you are a plague on this region and I'll bet we can find those you have stolen from this day," Duff shouted over the crowd.

"And since you've just arrived, who exactly am I supposed to have wronged?" Jamie asked amiably. He sat down on the edge of the wagon's back gate, his long, muscled legs dangling and swinging. His bow hand had landed gently on the hilt of the huge sword he carried loosely at his side.

"Draw that sword here in the square, MacPherson, if you dare!" Duff leaned forward and threatened through tight lips and fiery eyes. "Just give me the excuse I need to hang you!" His horse tack jingled. Jamie lifted his hand from his sword hilt.

"I'd not give you the satisfaction of enforcing laws meant only for my kind," Jamie smiled sweetly. "It would make this game of ours much too easy. It is my goal to remain a musician and free

57

and yours to deny me both. I'm just a better man at achieving my goals and confounding yours."

Duff's face contorted in rage and he pulled his sword from its scabbard.

"THAT'S ENOUGH," shouted the Laird, striding from the back of the crowd, his armed guard behind him. "Put that away, Duff! You have no jurisdiction here and no proof of any wrong-doing by these Travellers."

"I don't need proof. I just need him to draw that sword and I have him. Besides, everyone knows you finance his exploits, which makes you his accomplice to whatever wrong he commits! Or perhaps you have Gypsy blood, too." His voice ascended into its highest register.

"Watch yourself," the Laird said ominously, eyes narrowed and face flushed. Even his red hair seemed angry. "You accuse your Laird! If you have no proof against any of us, then you need to go. I see nothing wrong in what he does today."

"You never do!" Duff spat. "He will pay!"

"Perhaps," Jamie countered quietly, "but not now and not at your hand."

Duff pulled his horse's head around and rode away, scattering the crowd as he passed. The others followed.

"Come, all," Jamie said amiably to the crowd. "Let's dance to something bright and cheery while you return to your day," He nodded to Angus and his brother and cousin as he unpacked his fiddle again, struck up a lively reel set, and danced along with the crowd.

Fair stalls were closing and vendors were wheeling carts away to prepare for the evening's entertainment as the autumn day-light waned. The band sat again on the edge of their wagon, munching harvest bounty gifted them by the vendors and chat-ting with those women and girls who had stayed behind with their food gifts, hoping for an evening's dalliance with the fiddler. Fiona had been watching Jamie from a bale of hay to the side of the square all afternoon.

The Laird sat down next to her and handed her a hot meat pie and an apple while he drank from a flagon of ale.

"He's an interesting sort, isn't he?" he asked her.

"Why would that Duff man come all the way from his home to argue with Jamie?" she asked between mouthfuls.

"Alexander of Duff is a jealous man…," the Laird began, choosing his words carefully for her ears as he watched Jamie eat and chat with his bandmates. "Jamie has a habit of taking Duff's women and his pride. And Duff is not a man who lets affronts go easily. I fear for Jamie. There's only one way that a Traveller can be hung without cause and Duff seems bound to take advantage of the old laws before we can change them."

"What would happen to him?" Fiona asked quietly.

"He would be immediately hung," her guardian responded, hugging her close. "But never fear. Jamie is wise to Duff's tactics and would not be drawn in by them. He much prefers his fiddle to his broadsword!"

They watched as two young boys used long sticks to pretend at sword fighting. Jamie slid off the back gate of his wagon, tousled the bright ginger hair of one of the boys, and combed his fingers through his own black curls as he started toward the Laird and Fiona.

"Hey, you, fiddler," came a sultry voice from a window above him. Jamie stopped and looked up. In the window was a well-dressed woman of some years, breasts mostly exposed as she slid out onto the window ledge, her lap covered in a blanket. "Wouldn't you like to come up here to fix my pots this evening?"

"Well, I am not primarily a tinker," Jamie laughed. "But give me a few moments, madam, and I'll come plug any holes you need mended."

Jamie did not see the flash of metal from under the wagon. Instead, it was the desperate notes from the fiddle on his back that warned him of danger. He whirled to face the foe and saw the blade below him in time to draw his own. He hacked at the blade aimed to hobble him, and connected with its owner's wrist. Hand and sword clattered in the night and the owner cried out in pain.

"Jamie, no!" yelled the Laird, rising to his feet and looking for his own sword as he called for his own guards and ran toward his friend. "Put the sword down!"

Jamie ignored his mentor and protector, and yelled "Keep my fiddle safe, daughter," lifting his fiddle off his back and tossing it toward Fiona. Three sigils came alive in bright red—the one on Jamie's ring, the one on the case and the one at Fiona's throat. The case and its contents flew into her hands. Fiona gaped, but held the case tight to her chest and scrambled back behind the hay bale.

From the corner at the edge of the market road, Duff's men spilled onto the square, swords drawn and screaming. It was a well-planned and well-executed trap. For a few seconds, Jamie was alone, backed against the wall. The woman above tossed the blanket from her lap out the window and it descended like a falling fog onto Jamie's head.

Now all except Jamie could see that the woman was wearing the tartan of Duff's clan. From under the blanket, Jamie fought fruitlessly to free his head and sword hand, but Duff's men were upon him, shouting for all to stand back. Six more of Duff's men grabbed the rest of the band and one held a sword to the Laird's throat.

"Treachery," the Laird yelled. "This is treachery, Duff, and you will not get away with this!"

Jamie's anger was answered by the fiddle in Fiona's arms. It sounded like the strings were being played by his sword and the sound rent her heart. Fiona tried to run toward her father, but the Laird grabbed her and held her fast. Fiona tried to scream her father's name, but a woman's voice in her head sang "Do not move. Do not help. I need you. He needs you. We cannot go on if you are killed, too."

The fiddle's strings kept playing the melody of those words and it held Fiona immobile. By the time Fiona could focus beyond the melody's spell, Jamie's struggle was over and he was in irons.

Duff raised his sword to the dark heavens above.

"You, Jamie MacPherson—Musician, Traveller, and Gypsy, by the laws of our land, are to die for pulling a sword." Duff was rage-faced and shaking, laughing maniacally. "I've got you, you bastard, you foul son of MacPherson by that Gypsy witch. And there's nothing you or that foul Laird of yours can do about it!"

As Duff's men pulled the blanket off Jamie's head, the disheveled musician, though shaking with anger, said evenly, "What? You don't like my music?" He laughed mirthlessly.

"Laugh all you want. You will hang for this. And no one can save you." Duff's seething face was so close to Jamie's that the Traveller winced at the assault on his ears. Four men held him from behind. Two others held Duff.

"My music always saves me," Jamie said calmly, pushing his long nose closer to Duff and staring straight into his eyes. "And you can never understand. Nothing you can do will kill my music. And where my music lives, so does my independence and power."

"TAKE HIM AWAY!" Duff's face contorted and turned a splotchy red-blue. He whirled on his Laird, who now stood holding the shaking Fiona, "You cannot stop this. We are off to my home and the Sheriff there will hang him as fast as we can arrange it. Do what you will. This Traveller is dead."

Fiona tugged against her guardian's hold, tears bright in her eyes. "It's alright, child," Jamie consoled her. "Bring my fiddle to the gaol when they finally get me there."

"I promise," she said softly, the fiddle crying a mournful tune that only she and Jamie heard. And she and her guardian watched as Duff's men dragged the tall, sturdy, cocky young Gypsy away. Fiona started after them on foot.

"Wait," said the Laird, pulling her back. "Don't worry, child. I've already sent riders with a plea to the Marquis to spare Jamie's life. He is a friend to the Travellers, Fiona. He'll send word in time and Duff has to obey him or risk the noose himself."

"But I have his fiddle. He needs her and she needs him," she pleaded.

"We'll follow on and see if we can't try to fix the damage his sword has caused. Then we'll get him and his family back into the music that seems to keep them safe. That's all we can do," he said, lifting her into the carriage and signaling to his driver.

As his carriage raced over the rolling road toward Jamie's gaol in Banff, the rising harvest moon lit their way over the rich farmland. Fiona sat as tall as she could in the carriage, still holding the case close to her. Inside, the fiddle cooed quietly, but Fiona's whole body ached with stronger music. Beside her, the Laird cleared his throat. She looked at him through tear-clouded eyes.

"What did your mother tell you of your family?"

"Only that both she and my father were Gypsy royalty," she said quietly.

"Jamie has now named you daughter." The Laird seemed to be choosing his words very carefully. "Your mother was a princess among her people. What you do not know is that Jamie does indeed come from royalty on his side, too. He is a prince. And your mother believed that you were destined to be both a queen of the Gypsies and its lead fiddler."

"Me?" gasped Fiona. "Girls don't do that! How can this be?"

"I don't know. I only know that your mother foretold this day. She said that at the Saint Rufus Fair you would begin a new path."

Fiona stared straight ahead. "What do I do with your fiddle now, father?" she asked her absent parent. And only the fiddle answered with a quiet buzz of strings.

In the waning hours of the night, the carriage pulled up to the gaol. Whispers from the case awakened Fiona. She sat up and rubbed her eyes. The Laird sat next to her, his brow furrowed and his sword loose in his hand.

"What's wrong ...," she asked, but he held up his hand for her silence.

"You stay here. I'll be back as soon as I can," he said as he stepped out of the carriage. "Don't go anywhere! It's not safe for you here!"

She nodded, knowing full well that she had no intention of obeying him. After he had gone, she pulled her cloak tight around her and stepped quietly down and slipped down a side alley. The fiddle buzzed.

"Hsst. Child! Fiona!" she heard. She froze and looked around. It was Jamie's ringed hand poking out of a dungeon window next to her feet. "You have my fiddle. I don't go anywhere without him. Everyone knows that. I need him and he needs me." It was bluntly, though plaintively put and invited no rebuttal. He reached out his huge hand.

Fiona lifted the case off her shoulder and stretched it out to Jamie. From inside the case, the fiddle jangled and the case seemed to narrow itself so it could slip between the bars.

"SHE told me you needed us here. So we're here," she whispered.

"The fiddle speaks to you?" Jamie asked from the darkness.

"Yes, she does now," Fiona said quietly. "She told me her name is Magda and she's very old. And she wants to be with my father until she can't be any more."

Jamie's chuckle echoed in the walls below. "Then so he ... she shall." Jamie scowled at the case in his hands. "So you speak to my daughter, too, do you? Since when do you speak to anyone but me?"

The fiddle was silent.

And then he was gone from the window, fiddle in hand. Soon, the town was filled with the mournful mountain aires of Jamie's Highland home. And all the bustle of the new day melted into a vague sadness for life that had passed by. And no one knew quite why.

During the night, the town had filled with all the Travellers who had attended the Saint Rufus Fair. Their wagons gathered at the edges of the town, and those Travellers within them were brought to the town square, surrounded by hostile Sheriff's men challenging one and all to draw a sword. None took the bait. With them came the smells of strange meats cooking, and the soft burr of the Traveller Gaelic. They brought instruments of all kinds. They carried or rode strange animals. They played games with the children and entertained the crowds quietly.

No matter what the guards did to silence Jamie's supporters, his fiddle still played. But it was never in his cell when guards went to search, although they beat him horribly to get the wretched sound to stop. It was said that a Gypsy ghost was playing the fiddle, for no one had seen him since he was locked away. No one, that is, except his daughter. Sheriff's men searched for any who were helping Jamie, but no sign of any of them was found, even when the men marched within a whisper of where Fiona lay. And the Traveller Gypsy members of the crowd who could see her were not about to give her away. She lived in a new world now. And she couldn't have explained exactly what she was seeing or feeling. Although alone, she never felt afraid. Jamie had the fiddle, but the case had come back to her, wards from the triskele of the sigils keeping her from detection and harm.

When the morning light crested the hills, the fiddler stopped and the Laird found Fiona next to the gaol window, surrounded by candles and Travellers holding vigil. At her feet was the brightly painted fiddle case and in her arms was the fiddle. She was sound asleep, holding her father's broken hands. The Laird joined those sitting in awe and lifted her sleeping head into his lap. Fiona awoke as sunlight washed her face. She let go of her father and closed the fiddle into the case.

None knew that their beloved fiddler's fate had already been decided within the thick stone walls of the Sheriff's Hall without the accused ever being brought to testify in his own defense. As the sunlight spattered its rays on the scaffold, Jamie emerged, battered, bruised, bloody, but not chastened. He was held by two of Alexander Duff's men and surrounded by four of the Sheriff's men. A low rumble began through the crowd that rapidly became a cry for Jamie's release. Duff raised his hand for quiet.

"The Traveller Gypsy Jamie MacPherson is a plague on our lands," Duff yelled as the roar of the crowd tried to drown him out. "He is a thief and a musician of ill repute and a rapist and so much more, but the crime for which he is to be hanged is that he pulled a sword at Saint Rufus Fair in the town of Keith, and his kind is hanged for bearing arms in public." As soon as Duff finished speaking, the Sheriff stepped forward and raised his hands for quiet. It was not granted. The crowd was rapidly becoming restive.

"The trial of Jamie MacPherson, Gypsy Traveller of this region is complete," he began. This was greeted with outrage. He raised his voice and continued.

"SILENCE," the Sheriff shouted. "Jamie MacPherson, you are found guilty of being Gypsy and wielding a sword in public, and causing harm. I hereby judge you to be hanged by the neck on the cross of this town square until you are dead. Now!"

And Jamie was escorted up the stairs to the noose hastily thrown over the town's cross. His eyes remained defiant as he called for quiet.

"They may call for my life, but they will never silence my music!" he yelled. The crowd cheered.

How Jamie's bonds were freed and the fiddle left her care and appeared in Jamie's hands, Fiona could not say. It was on her back and then the weight of the fiddle was missing while the case remained. But she heard Jamie's familiar tone from his broken body, and his tunes played out and no one stepped forward to stop him. For the while, the waiting crowd was held in the thrall of the solo fiddle.

The hangman ascended the steps next to Jamie and put his hand on Jamie's bow arm and the music stopped. Jamie looked at the quieting crowd.

"Will any man here take my fiddle to play her?" he called. Fiona smiled at the fiddle's new gender. No one responded in the hushed crowd.

"None?" he said. "Then she is mine to destroy!"

He lifted the fiddle so quickly that all Fiona could see was a blur. She heard the crack of wood on stone and looked up to see splinters in his hand. The fiddle was no more. And the hangman slipped the noose around Jamie's strong neck and before anyone could move, pulled hard. Jamie's feet kicked, but his eyes fell on Fiona as they faded, and the smile never left his lips.

The crowd collapsed in cries and tears. Only Duff, the Sheriff and their men cheered as they swaggered triumphantly away to the local pub.

No one could say when the sigil ring left Jamie's hand and appeared, perfectly sized, on his daughter's hand. Nor could they say the exact moment she wore the bright colours of her people. Fiona stared at the ring in awe and looked up with tears in her eyes into the lifeless eyes of her father. Then she looked around at the Travellers who had gathered around her. Donald, Peter, and Angus started a familiar Highland aire of Jamie's. They were joined by other Traveller musicians in the crowd. The Laird's men cut Jamie's body down from the scaffold and the crowd followed behind the Laird and the girl to the edge of town. There they lifted her onto the wagon that belonged to the band. Her band.

Fiona lifted her head high, tossed her dark curls back, and opened the case, as the fiddle within called to her in Jamie's voice. She raised an eyebrow at that, but just chuckled. She checked the tuning as she had seen her father do and picked out a new version of the aire.

"We are one, now, my beautiful child," the fiddle sang. "I will help you find your voice. And someday you will be able to be proud to be Jamie MacPherson's kin and will carry his last song to the world. We'll call it MacPherson's Rant, shall we?"

"I'll take my own voice now, father," she whispered. "But you can help me whenever I feel like it."

The words to the new song rang clear in her head and she lifted her young voice and sang it out, playing her fiddle in the low, dulcet tones of its now-male voice.

"You are definitely my daughter," it said to her, laughing. "You have my ego!"

Fiona giggled and changed to a light, fast reel. And as her own eyes filled, she played tears into the eyes of those who watched her become one with her father, her fiddle, and her band.

Fancy
– Brett Milano

Author's Note: Two things conspired to cause this story: I got hold of some Australian reissues of Bobbie Gentry's albums, and was reminded of how beautiful and evocative they are. This also got me remembering seeing her TV special when I was seven; I recall that the first scene had her singing "Chickasaw County Child" in silhouette against a dark Delta scene—the mystery was enhanced by our tiny black & white television. Around this time I heard a new album by the excellent songwriter Jill Sobule, which contained a song called "Where Is Bobbie Gentry?," so I decided to come up with an answer. Some of the details in this story may be true; the rest of course is fancy.

Fancy

Wanda knew what happened to Bobbie Gentry, and she wouldn't tell a soul.

The whole thing was a responsibility she'd never asked for. But, when a childhood friend—one she'd always worshipped from afar, if truth be told—came looking for solace, she was glad to open her home. That was thirty years ago, during which time the world had caught few glimpses of Wanda, to say nothing of Bobbie.

Taking care of a beautiful, damaged recluse for thirty years isn't easy, but Wanda had known what she was getting herself into. She was already pretty good at hiding from the world. She'd been the plain one, the one without talent or glamour, the one who'd never needed to leave this wood house on a dirt road. Nobody had ever suggested that she become a professional singer, though she grew up with an abiding love for music. She also grew up with a soft heart.

Besides, Wanda was in love, or something close enough to it to find the romance in this secret cohabitation. Since Bobbie's disappearance, Wanda got to be the shoulder to cry on, the hand to hold, the quiet companion on long nights listening to crickets and staring into the river, under those overhanging trees that she'd always found so scary as a child. That, more than the money she never felt much like spending, had made it worthwhile—all the time Wanda spent sifting through legalities, keeping the music catalogue in order, getting the royalties off to the proper charities. And most of all, dealing with Bobbie's cultists.

It took many years before they started showing up. Like the rest of the world, Wanda had been in awe when she saw Bobbie singing "Ode to Billie Joe" on TV, thrilled to see her flowing hair and smart prom dress, against a Delta backdrop that looked like the one Wanda knew. But it seemed the world's interest had ended there: Maybe the world wasn't ready for a song like "Fancy," one of her follow-up singles, in which a proud Delta woman escapes family poverty through prostitution. Bobbie Gentry made a few more albums, uneven affairs that alternated her own wise and nuanced songs with pop hits of the day. After that, by all accounts, she simply walked away.

By the time Bobbie disappeared in 1978, she hadn't had a hit in nearly a decade, and hadn't recorded in years; the TV specials and the Vegas engagements had fizzled out. Wanda had remained a fan, and she thought that people didn't know what they had: Bobbie was a storyteller, a natural star with a soulful Southern voice, and people were writing her off as a one-hit wonder. She'd pour her heart into a concept album, and they'd still call to ask her what Billy Joe threw off the TallahatchieBridge.

Wanda still got that question. Usually, she'd just say "His laundry" before hanging up. There were still DJs who played "Billie Joe" on oldies stations, usually saying something like "Boy, I wonder whatever happened to her." Wanda was only too glad to make sure they never found out. But she had to admit, the gentleman callers (and they were nearly always gentlemen) were getting more creative. As the years went by, they got caught up more in the mystery of Bobbie Gentry; they played the records, found the video clips and fell in love. The albums that didn't sell first time around were now "cult classics." They were finally figuring out that Bobbie had written most of her own songs and filled them with the mood of the strange, secluded places she had seen in her childhood and in her imagination.

The intrepid ones consulted the internet. They learned about her disappearance in 1978, how she'd walked away at the height of her career, how there'd been no more music and hardly any sightings. There would always be young men who believed that they could rescue her, win her favor or at least an autograph. To them, Bobbie would always be the siren on the 30-year-old album covers, with the flowing dark hair and the layers of eye makeup. Wanda had a soft spot for these poor searchers, and she tried to let most of them down gently.

Finding the house wasn't hard. Anyone with some motivation and an internet connection could find out where Bobbie grew up. That led them to the house deep in Chickasaw County where her family had lived, and where Bobbie was said to spend time when she wasn't being a star in Los Angeles. Wanda had to head them off, and sometimes she wished she didn't. They were getting younger and more charming; they wouldn't call in advance but simply show up, usually in the early part of a Saturday evening—in formal dress and bearing flowers, looking for all the world like they wanted to take Bobbie to a debutante ball. Wanda would have gladly sashayed off on the arms of a few of them.

Of course, they never paid attention to Wanda. Usually, she sent them off, told them the house belonged to a distant branch of the Gentry family, told them the famous singer had rolled through town in 1971 and they'd had a grand old time. She saw their faces fall, and watched them carry their albums and their bouquets back to their cars. And yet...Once in awhile, it would

71

happen. The most sincere ones—the ones who knew how much it meant, the ones who wouldn't sell any stories to the press—would get a glimpse of Bobbie. This would be one of those nights, assuming the singer was willing to grant it.

There were few stirrings from Bobbie's room nowadays; not like their early years together when Wanda would be able to give solace, before the withdrawal and the general ennui had taken over. But Wanda wanted to make a play for Keith from Massachusetts. He hadn't called, of course; but Wanda read those internet sites too, including the fan chatboards that linked to Keith's blog. So she knew that he had begun driving south nearly a week ago, that he was alone and single-minded, so much so that he'd skipped the popular sidetrack to Memphis and Sun Studios. He'd been posting updates from his trip all week: He'd been to Bobbie's birthplace, and spent hours driving in the country with the top down, as he imagined she'd done forty years earlier. According to his recent updates, he'd be getting into town in about three hours.

"Have you sounded him out?" It was unquestionably the voice from those records Wanda loved so dearly, the one she'd consoled herself with over time. And after all they'd been through together, the voice still made her heart flutter. Yes, she said, Keith was young and sincere; he wouldn't bring any photographers, and he'd know how much it meant. "Okay," came the response from behind the locked door. "I can do it one more time."

Keith arrived as expected—flowers in hand, earnest expression on his face. Unlike some of the callers, he showed no disappointment when the non-glamorous Wanda answered the door. She liked him immediately, offering him tea and slipping a bit of bourbon in without his asking. Hearing his story, she felt for him and his frustrated affection.

"I can't tell you how much Bob—how much Miss Gentry means to me. Nobody makes records like that anymore. Here, the band I was in with my old girlfriend...we covered 'Fancy'. It's nowhere near as good as hers, but it did well for us, got us gigs across the Northeast and even got us some airplay. Our singer was such a fan that she even copied the hairstyle. Don't worry, I have a good computer job now and haven't played in a couple of years. I don't need her to make us famous. I just always dreamed that someday she'd hear us play it."

"Oh darling, I wish I could hand it to her now." Wanda allowed Keith to step into the doorway while she put his homemade CD on an end table, covered in what looked like an ancient bit of crochet. She watched Keith take in the badly-lit living room. It hadn't been redone in decades; the TV and stereo were the same clunky old models that were around when Bobbie was recording.

Wanda gave Keith a kind smile and refilled his teacup, but stopped short of inviting him inside, letting him linger by the doorway.

"Now, you're a very sweet young man, and I know that Bobbie would appreciate your coming. But you know, we like to live quietly out here. Yes, she does come around and I certainly look forward to that, but I never know when she's coming or for how long. Sometimes it's only an hour or two. She'll sign some forms, have a cup of coffee and then she's off again."

"What does she do in between?"

"Oh, she lives. Drives her car up and down the coast. Once she sang 'Billie Joe' with a bar band in Petaluma and came back laughing about it— told them she was a retired rodeo singer and they had her back up doing Patsy Cline songs all night. Says she's been writing, but nobody's heard whatever it is. If you want to know, she seems much happier now than when she was famous."

"Does she have any boyfriends?" Keith blurted out, hoping he didn't look as embarrassed as he now felt; but how could he leave without finding that out? He realized how hopeful he sounded, like he was about to apply for the position himself.

73

Wanda just smiled. "That's a question a lady doesn't ask or answer. Now, I'd invite you to stay but I usually start getting ready for bed about now—I'm not as lively as I used to be, you know. Look, I'll make sure she gets this. You probably won't hear from her, but I can promise that she'll hear it. And I know she'd be grateful for your time and your courtesy. Anything else I can help you with before you go?"

By now Keith knew he'd only get one more question, and for years he'd chide himself for resorting to the most obvious one: "What did they throw…"

Wanda cut the question off with a patient smile and a wave of the finger, as she had many times before. He ventured another thanks as he made his way out the door.

Keith had already heard about Wanda. The fans he'd corresponded with online were full of information, rumors, tidbits—she was close to Bobbie after all, so he'd been looking forward to meeting her. Who wouldn't welcome a friendly face in the middle of a long pilgrimage? But he also knew what he might see if he was one of the lucky ones. He knew where the best vantage point was, across from the rear yard—If you thought you saw the light upstairs you could go ahead and wade into the pond; it would be worth getting soaked. According to the posts he'd read, the last person who'd gotten the glimpse was a good two years ago.

And, oh my Lord, the light was really on up there. His heart jumped as he went running, not even bothering to remove the shoes—of course Bobbie's room would face out onto a pond. So much for staying dry. He ran into the waist-deep muck, tripped over a vine and covered the suit with mud. The one suit he owned was now totaled, to say nothing of whatever money was in his wallet. Not that he cared; the only thing that mattered right now was seeing what was up there.

At first glance, nothing was. The window looked only onto a wall that was barely decorated—some kind of photo maybe, or it could have been a mirror. But hold on, did something just move up there? He grabbed the opera glasses from his pocket, raised them to his eyes, and saw mud. Get hold of yourself, he thought, at least long enough to wipe the lenses.

And yes, he did see something move by the window, a flash of something red—a body in a gown, perhaps? A few frustrating seconds later it came back into view: a body swaying gently in time; there must be music playing up there. And then, if he maneuvered to catch the angle, a face reflected in a mirror.

It had to be her. The hair he'd know anywhere—those endless black curls he'd been so fascinated with as an adolescent—and that dress looked suspiciously like the formal, flowing one she wore on the cover of "Local Gentry." Surely she couldn't still have it after all this time? Her dancing was enticing to see, slow and slinky, the hips swiveling, the head swaying. Did it matter whether the music was really there or just in her head? Keith watched, intoxicated. What was he—eleven or twelve the first time he'd imagined seeing something like this?

She came to the window.

He knew it was her, now. The face looked out over the pond, swept the dark skyline and just for a second, looked directly at him. Keith barely had time to register the face that looked toward him. Still beautiful, he was certain—pale skin, sculpted features, remarkably large and dark eyes. Damn, if only those glasses would stay in focus. But Keith could swear that their eyes locked, just for a second. Could she really seem him out here? Maybe not, but there was something knowing in that glance, something reprimanding but flirtatious as well—a raise of the eyebrows, a sly smile. He watched her hand move, reaching for…a light switch. And just when he began to register the contact, it was over.

People he'd been in touch with had seen the same thing. One guy was certain it was a mirage, the others had assumed she was tragic, left alone with her reverie. But Keith preferred to think she was just stopping in between those adventures Wanda mentioned, still gorgeous and vital. You never knew about Billie Joe and you'd never really know about Bobbie, but seeing her there was good enough.

Keith caught his breath and slogged back to his car. The drive to the next motel would be sloppy and full of swamp water, but filled with the mystery of the singer he loved.

Was that really worth doing, the singer wondered, retreating to a dark room once again? But, okay; Wanda liked the kid and she deserved any favors he could do for her. Besides, the fascination with Bobbie needed to be fueled. It was kids like this who would keep her memory alive. They all thought they loved her. But they'd never know who loved her the most.

The hair, at least, had been Bobbie's: She'd worn it on all the album covers over her own fetching, but much shorter hair ("just a little embellishment," she called it). The makeup was hers too, carefully preserved all these years in a specially commissioned refrigerator. And the dress…A dress fit for a debutante ball, or one of those TV appearances Bobbie loved. But it was the one she had been wearing that night in 1978, the night that had begun so beautifully with their talking on the phone, making plans for another wild escape together. The night when she went driving too late, too dark, maybe too much in love to pay attention. The night she went over the goddamn Tallahatchie Bridge.

A great voice of the South had been silenced that night. And another one had not, at least not by death. But after Bobbie died, he'd never wanted to sing again; he knew he never really could. He also knew that he wouldn't let anyone find out what had happened to her: Bobbie deserved more than an ironic end that echoed her song; she deserved to be the object of mystery and obsession—Let people search and think they could still see her if they deserved it.

Once he'd come out of the initial shock, he'd made the plan, and he'd stuck to it ever since. Covering up her death was easy—greasing the right palms gets you everywhere—and faking his own was even easier: People are always willing to believe that big stars have drug problems and overdose in the bathroom.

He'd loved Bobbie since he happened to tune into a TV show back in 1967. She was beautiful, teased-up like Priscilla, but with that wise sexiness that Ann-Margret had when they had their wild fling during "Viva Las Vegas". People thought they were just acting well when they saw the steamy chemistry all over that movie. That was fun, but it wasn't love; love was what hit him between the eyes when he saw Bobbie, all tall and haunting with that powerfully deep voice on his TV.

He sent the guys out to buy her record that night, and he'd stayed up till morning playing it. Meeting her was the hardest part: She was never impressed by celebrity, not even her own. Winning her over had made him rethink his career, his music, everything. Bobbie played her own guitar, set her own direction, wrote her own songs. He could listen to the records, as he did every night for months, and know it was all her. He strived to do something that good, to at least put across the feelings she'd stirred in him.

She was on his mind when he took control and showed the world what he could do. "The '68 comeback," they all called it. "Any damn thing to get this lady's attention," he knew it really was.

Sending the guys around to bring her to him did no good at all. This one did what she pleased. Finally, she'd shown up in Vegas, just walked up to his dressing room and knocked—something nobody was allowed to do: "Heard you were looking for me?" For the next five years, they'd been together. With each year it got more surprising that nobody found them, but nobody ever did.

They'd always met at Wanda's house, and she was good at keeping things secret. Their conversations were as intense as their lovemaking, Bobbie was the first to understand what celebrity meant and the toll it took. And they'd sung together, done that for hours, just the two of them with one guitar, sometimes just singing along with the records. It was the best music he'd ever made, and it was for them alone. Why sing for the crowd again, when nothing could top that?

He took off Bobbie's wig and packed it away in its box—next to his guitar, her prize set of silver finger picks and the other souvenirs of their short, blessed life together. These days, his drug problems were real. The haze of Dilaudid wasn't as intoxicating as Bobbie had been, but it was as close as he could get. Diving into that well was the only real comfort he got, despite all Wanda's attempts to connect—she was a sweet lady, but he couldn't return that love. What he wanted to do was sink into sleep once again, the room swirling, Bobbie's things all around him, her music still playing in his head.

Bobbie, my angel, I hope you're really out there. I wonder if you're lonesome tonight.

Vampire Fiction
– Rain Graves

Author's Note: The idea of writing about a band called Vampire Fiction has been in my mind some time. The character of Bark evolved from a dark drug-era Peter Murphy, to a post-religious Johnny Cash with June Carter Cash dying on his arm. The unromantic love affair with drugs, the why behind it—which isn't always just your own demons in rock-n-roll—it's everyone around you, and theirs... To the dark and rich history behind the myth/legend of Antigone, and what you dig up in your past and take into battle with you, when you have nothing left to lose. At its core is music.

The hardest part was getting the Roman names right. Roman nomenclature suffers from both redundancy and hubris. What better names for rock stars? Gnaeus Corvinus Cato means "Born (or birthmark), Raven tribe, the Clever or wise." Marcus Lupus Augustus means "Of the God Mars, Wolf tribe, The Revered One."

PS: There aren't any vampires in this story...but there are parasites. If this story had a soundtrack, it would be just four songs: "Caesar," by Iggy Pop. "Cuts You Up," by Peter Murphy.

"Dirt," originally by Nine In Nails, but in particular the version performed by Johnny Cash. And "Vincent (Starry, Starry Night)" by Don McLean. In that order.

Thank you, and good night.

Vampire Fiction

For all intents and purposes, and to the general public, Bark Evans was a vampire.

He liked it that way just fine. He'd made a mistake though, and that had to be remedied. The fans, the cars, the women, and the drugs all were unintended, and leading a life of anonymity inside a giant, surging wave of faces in a crowd was no longer working. Things needed to be done. Egos needed to be murdered. Maybe even his. Definitely his shadow's.

He could go out at night, and not be recognized. He wasn't the singer he was supposed to be, up close and personal with stardom. Fifty million records sold, and everyone thought they knew everything about him. That was okay, though. It was public—an opinion formed by perfect strangers, larger than life and certainly more grand than anything he cared to live up to. On stage he played the part: thick black eyeliner, a brooding, biting stare, velvets and lace. The overgrown, scruffy hair. A clean shave.

But at night, when everyone was waiting for a rock star to slip through the stage door, he slicked back his sweaty hair, put on a low black Stetson, dirty jeans, and a worn cowboy shirt from

1963 he never took off, except for the show. When he left the unmarked dressing room, he looked like a roadie. He was careful not to open his mouth, even partially, in case someone should notice his fangs—a genetic helper in the rock star façade that often got him laid. He'd filed them a little sharper for effect.

He was pretty good at being invisible when he wanted to be. It was the only thing that was truly his. They didn't want him to be that guy sneaking out the back, anyway. They wanted him to be primal, evil, bursting with raw energy and rage, howling and growling and gumming his way—and their way—to ecstasy.

There was much in this life that was a ruse. The echo of his heroin addiction that his drummer, The Fool, had gotten him into one night as a means for "spiritual enlightenment." More's the hurt; Fool knew what he was doing to himself and to Bark—he just didn't want to do it alone, decade after decade. At least, that's what Bark liked to tell himself. It avoided the darker truth: The Fool was the brains behind managing the band, the shows, all the money... and he owned Bark. If Fool wanted him to do something, he did it. In several thousand years, nothing had changed except the venue and pieces of the band.

Heroin was a more mellow high than cocaine for Bark. He avoided coke mostly, because of his own temper. If he did too much, things went bad, especially at low tide and a full moon. Bark paid attention to things like that... doing drugs on a beach under a full moon. The universe was important to him. Gone was important to him. She mattered the most.

People had to be paid off to keep quiet, and it wasn't the tabloids he was worried about finding out. A good story about a bloodless corpse washed ashore at high tide when Vampire Fiction had a gig in town was publicity you couldn't buy, The Fool often said. He encouraged the deviance.

The real problem was more immediate: addiction. Whether it

be to flesh or drugs, he had more than one, and with multiple addictions came great responsibility. To Vampire Fiction, and to Fool. He answered to no one else, not even himself.

He still needed the methadone to get him through the day, though the dose had been reduced considerably. He was less violent and erratic in sobriety, but also less controlled. *Drugs have a funny way of emancipating you from yourself, while enslaving you to your supplier,* Bark thought. The Fool was it. He'd always been that guy. A controlling interest in a dying, preternatural business.

Bark had known him his whole life. A backwoods sort of Alistair Crowley reject-sort with enough ability to conjure threatening things, but in all his sneaky, sniveling ways, Fool would run from a real fight if his magic failed him. That didn't often happen, these days. He wasn't stupid. Fool got his name from the first card in the Tarot deck: the seeker of knowledge. It didn't help that he was older than time itself.

That knowledge had got him control of Bark and the band in the first place. Some time in the 80's, Bark noticed something off about himself, and it wasn't the dope sick. He'd kicked that part in rehab, but something else was stuck to him.

Something dark, and dangerous. He couldn't remember it being there before, all those years ago, getting high. It licked at his heels when he walked, and hissed when he turned corners on the street. It pushed on his back like sunshine during a hangover, even at night, when he couldn't see it. It had a name, deeply rooted in evil, but he knew not what it was. He had no way to control the shadow and, like a puppet painfully aware of his strings, he knew who was conjuring the tether behind the curtain.

It had been a long night. Two forty-five minute sets and an encore had left him exhausted. After a night of howling, singing, screaming, Bark was eyeing The Fool sitting with his shirt off under the harsh florescent backstage lights, pants soaked through in sweat. He seemed to be resting, sticks still in his back pocket. Except there, in the air of tension, Bark could see the tiny crack of his eyelids open, glittering like a venomous snake, watching him, waiting…The Fool was pale, like a fish belly. he winced at the sight of him.

Bark calmly smoothed his overgrown curls back, put his black hat on and tipped it. He spun on his boot heels, out of the room, his opaque shadow clinging, creeping behind, threatening to engulf and become him. He bumped into Million on the way out. She clawed at his chest, red nails sinking into his threadbare shirt. "I've got a rig if you want to get high," she purred. He growled in disgust, shoving her aside. She shrugged and walked into the dressing room, where Fool remained.

It was always the same dream. A thunder in the concrete above, wave after wave of cheering and energy, as the Gladiators were announced. These were not sanctioned events; they did not happen in daylight. When Rome was shrouded in darkness, well-placed, giant torches were lit in the coliseum arena, lighting up the circular ground in the middle. A greedy hum electrified the air with supernatural whispers, cracking whips, and the periodic pounding of drums. Somewhere in the darkness, Gnaeus Corvinus Cato lurked, choosing his paranormal predators to fight the larger-than-life human personas with short swords. Polynices was rumored to be among them, a famous foreigner from Greece.

It started with music in the middle. A warm up band for the main event—beautifully silk-clad women, young boys, and plump, middle-aged men raised their falsetto voices in song. It was eerie and sad at the same time, partly because of the words, which were hard to ascertain if you weren't below, waiting to perform.

If you stood in the center of them, as Bark often imagined

himself, you could look up to see thousands of tiny torch lights glittering in double lined spokes, up through the stands all around, illuminating the treacherous concrete seating for the fans. There were always accidents, up there. Sometimes they fed him and the others the remains.

The musicians, bled into pens on the sidelines during the fight, audibly winced when they dragged the bodies away, if there were parts left. Bark knew Antigone would be among them if her brother Polynices was fighting. He lifted his head to the air, absent-mindedly searching for her scent. He found it; a mix of garlic and roses. Unnecessary precautions that would do her no good if a vampire actually escaped.

There were other things to worry about besides; Succubae, lesser demons, the occasional dragon, and corpses specially risen from fresh graves by curse of their fathers who damned them. They bore astounding agility and strength. Bark and the others were not to touch the musicians, Cato said. They were only there to calm them down.

The night always ended badly. Cato would move one of the chosen predators out into the holding gate and make the announcement, "*Carpe noctum; dulce periculum…*Seize the night; danger is sweet." A gladiator seeking the ultimate glory would step into the ring. Cato never announced the man's name until he won—it was anticlimactic for a human to have such hubris. Instead, as the crowd waited on the edge of euphoria hoping for their favorite villain's name, he would speak it, along with a catch phrase.

Bark was always sarcastically summoned, "*Auribus teneo Lupum*! I hold a wolf by the ears…" The crowd would go wild, chanting, "Marcus Lupus Augustus! Marcus Lupus Augustus!" Both holding him and letting him go would be deadly, under ordinary circumstances. But he was bound by trickery of oath, and the magic that bound his undead soul to that oath. The opaque shadow was cast; he could not shake it, nor elude it for long. The story of how Cato had trapped him one fateful night was the stuff of legendary magic, and venomous fangs that glittered long into the night.

Cato's eyes glowed green, and it was a harvest moon. He hadn't known what overcame him, until the fangs sunk in. The ancient Basilisk gave him a choice that was not a choice: Serve the god he saw himself to be, or forfeit all love, all mating, all nourishment, all time. It was a trick the venom worked on his mind. He actually thought he could break the curse in some quest or with some better God's favor. There had been none, however.

The dream blurred, and the killing and eating seemed more like a prelude to indigestion. It was afterwards, in the first light of dawn, where he always found Antigone wandering the cages, coming far too close to all of them for safety. Tears stained her cheeks, her dress tattooed with blood and dirt. "My brother, Polynices! Where have they taken him? What have they done with his body? They said they would not feed him to you... Did Gnaeus Corvinus Cato feed him to you? I must know!"

But they were not allowed to eat the Gladiators. It was a flesh too prized for slaves. The undead were only given the casualties of the crowd, and other slaves offered by wealthy backers. The Senate did not sanction the night games, and thus, any gladiator caught dead fighting in one was to be left without proper burial, by Roman law. Prized, indeed...to rot under the hot Roman sun, in a public square, their masters, properly chastised in the loss of income he might have generated.

Bark left the confines of the pen to help Antigone find her brother's body, so she could give him a proper burial. The shadow kept him under the Basilisk's control, but not underfoot. Once caught again, he was punished, and amongst the pain of the magical means Cato employed to force him into better submission, he awoke, always, in a muscle-locked, fevered, sweat. *In Somnis Veritas*, Bark thought. *In Dreams, There is Truth.* That was the name of Antigone's favorite song. The echo of her voice rising above the others, before the horror of her brother's death, soothed his pain. It had an innocence he loved very much.

Rehearsal was about to begin, and Fancy was dickering with his Flying V, long brown hair tied back in a ponytail. He was eyeballing Million as she sauntered around the room, with a predatory look she loved to encourage. She was giving out checks to the band again, and why she was on Fool's payroll was beyond Bark's understanding. He wanted to rip his check up, but he couldn't. He owed a lot of money to a lot of powerful people. That was the way his life always seemed to path-out.

"Hey Milly," Fancy said. "What song do you want to hear?" His black eyeshadow made his blue eyes disappear whenever he closed them, and he looked dead already. Bark thought it was a shame that wasn't the case, but silently thanked the Gods he didn't have to spend an eternity with him.

"Play Zombie Kittens," she spat. Bark hated that song. It was about groupies...and she loved it because she was one.

"That's not on the set list," Bark sneered.

"It is now." Fool fingered the edges of his drum kit like some bizarre mummy. His hands were taped up from the burns; magic had its price.

"You want to play it? Go ahead. Do it without a singer," Bark snapped.

Gone had just rushed into the room, late again, and attention was thankfully diverted to her as she carefully stepped around Bark's clinging, opaque shadow. It was better that way. It could cause frostbite in humans, if she lingered too long in it. She picked up her bass, mumbling an apology, never meeting Fool's serpentine gaze. No one seemed to notice the absence of the ring

87

on her finger. Its cylindrical ghost burned like lust in Bark's pupils; a solitary diamond wreathed in pure silver, giving off too much light. No one knew. The stone was now hanging around her neck, in a locket with a lock of his hair.

"Where are we?" she asked.

"Zombie Kittens," Million hissed at her. Gone regarded her with a raised eyebrow, but plugged in and tuned up.

"Hey Milly, I think you'd better check on the sound guy. I hear he hasn't had his daily blowjob for the crack you smoke," Gone said, and the boys sniggered. Even Fancy, as he patted Milly's butt and growled into her ear, sought to shuffle her along. "Let us work, love. We'll make them watch later." Fool clicked his drumsticks, indicating time was short, to hurry her exit. She obeyed, as all addicts do for the promise of their drug of choice, and left.

Today was the day of reckoning, Bark thought smugly. He'd play the songs he'd been forced to write, and then he'd play a new one—his song. He'd let Fancy and Milly go on thinking he was human. He'd even take whatever Fool dished out before the show…but when he hit the stage, it was all over. The door to the cage would open; he would sing beyond the bars of his prison, once more.

Tonight was a full moon, and Bark had found an opening in the cycle of planets that came only once every thousand years. It was a hole in the stars, when, for the brief hours of an eclipse, all magic was rendered useless, and all supernatural powers were null and void. This would leave him vulnerable to brief mortality, but not without the vulnerability of others. As a man, The Fool didn't stand a chance against him. And as a man…Bark could set himself free.

Gone was not fully prepared for what she'd done the day of the show, taking off the wedding ring that she'd been naked without, a gift handed down from countless generations of Bark Evans'

88

family tree. A circle that could be unbroken. As instructed, she'd taken it to a store in downtown Oakland, and had it melted down to form a single nine millimeter bullet.

In somnis veritas, she thought. *In dreams there is truth.*

Stuck in a glitch of reliving a past life over and over, she could not break the cycle. This time it had been her brother Perry on a chopper during a protest ride to free the Egyptian people. Somehow something went wrong; there was a thick fog, and a path was lost at night. When they hit an unseen bump in the road, she tried to hold on to him, but was thrown. The bump had seemed fleshy, somehow.

In the midst of the pain of her injuries, terror crept in, and threatened to overtake her small form. It was not the fear of death that was frightening, but a memory colliding with reality, as a sound emerged from the darkness. Slithering. Hissing. Something wet under her boot, cocked awkwardly over a rock. A bone was broken in her leg, but she wasn't frozen. She began to claw her way through the fog towards the sound of Perry's spinning wheels. For a moment something cold and hard brushed her aside, like so many potatoes in a mottled sack. She groaned under the weight of the shove, and saw two glowing green eyes. An opaque shadow crept over her then, and she knew it to be death. Then the eyes disappeared, and there was nothing but dark matter. Not even the fog was visible through the magic.

Perry's screams were not short-lived. From the hissing and ripping sounds, he was first torn limb to limb before being swallowed by the Basilisk. It saved his head for last, she assumed. The venom had paralyzed him from struggle from the neck down, but it had not limited his brain from sending signals to his mouth to call out to Gone, telling her to run as he was being devoured.

She cried, and cried, unable to move any further.

Bark found her at dawn, broken, bloodstained, and mentally beaten. He hefted her up to try and take her where she could be helped, but she insisted in hysterics that he help her find her brother's body. If she could just see it, she told him, maybe it hadn't been real. Maybe these monsters didn't really exist.

No trace of him was left. Things were left undone; she'd defied law before, in another life—she'd gotten to bury him. She'd paid for that with her life at the time, and was cursed to relive these events in every subsequent one. The Basilisk decreed it so, in reparation.

No matter how many times on tour, when she'd tried to visit magicians to lift the curse, they all bowed their heads, not meeting her eyes, and closed their doors tight. Bark was the only one to try and help…and in that help, there was love.

The Fool tolerated them as suffragettes; he was confident in his mastery of their enslavement, as history dictated. *They owed him,* he thought, for that long-ago night in Rome. The exposure of the case alone had been enough to shut him down. When the money was gone, so was his patience.

Gone picked up her pace as she got into the private car that would take her to the Oakland Coliseum. She fingered the object in her hand, rolling it over her thumb and forefinger, humming the bass line to "This Awful Dream I have," her favorite Vampire Fiction song. When the venue was in sight, she wondered briefly: What had happened to all those other captured undead, who used to fight the gladiators so long ago. Where were they now?

She arrived just in time to change, as the crowd was chanting, "Bite me, Bark! Bite me, Bark!" waiting for the pyrotechnic explosion to announce the first song, and the ruse that was their rock star life. So loved, they were, by their fans. Outside, a full moon was rising, only to be greeted by a rare eclipse. She smiled, thinking of the hole in the stars.

Bark had the small, ornate handgun he always holstered behind his right hip on stage, and now it was leveled at his bandmates from across the room—every one of them—a single bullet in the chamber, cocked and ready to fire. Rage flared his nostrils, sneering lip partially caught up on one of his perfectly filed teeth, making him look a caricature of himself and Vampire Fiction. The show was long over, but the night was not. The timing couldn't be better. The Fool's eyes had stopped glowing, his power momentarily dissolved.

Gone had a ghostly look on her face, looking out the window. Fancy was still fingering soundless notes on his Les Paul. He surmised a wry grin as he said, "What are you going to do, mate? Shoot your fucking band? Who'll play your ego-stroking songs then? Hmm?"

Bark moved the aim of his pistol slightly to the left and behind Fancy, where Milly was hiding her disgust. She said, "Whatever," and rolled her eyes. Only The Fool looked on steadily, a serious, deadly tone in his voice as he said, "I don't think you want to do that, Bark." and he was right. Bark didn't. The hunger in his shadow did. It was as if other shadows, unseen and unpredictable had gathered, watching. If they were there, he couldn't see them.

He wasn't sure if it was the methadone edginess that finally pulled the trigger, or that momentary flash of thousands of years of torture in the light before his eyes. He looked to Gone for courage, and when she smiled, it was done.

A slowly muted firework seemed to cause a great and harrowing silence, followed by the crackle and hum of energy. Stars were disappearing out the window; they reappeared in the room, dripping down from the electric air, and onto the floor, like puddles of silvery-black ink. He saw a ripple in time when the bullet went into his own chest. He'd watched it to see if it would really work.

When he looked up and saw the tears in Gone's eyes, he knew it had.

A bloodcurdling, angry scream died in Fool's throat, even as he outstretched his hands in wizard-like repose, as if to cast a spell that he'd long forgotten how to use. It was no use. The opaque shadow of slavery tethered from Bark to Gone to Basilisk began to coil into knotted threads, then snapped like bridge cables, one by one, as it met the star-puddles conjured on the floor. The Fool was zapped by these, a binding, unearthly chain that glittered black, unlike anything they had ever seen. He was muzzled, then. They could hear his squealing protests no more.

The sudden roar of voices seemed far away and near all at once, just like the crowd had been, an hour before. The music had stopped playing long ago. Now there was only blood where Bark's shadow had been, swathed in long tendrils over the floor. Notes spattered on a page of cold-cuts the band hadn't eaten, in a room too small for everyone. Fancy was spotted with it. Milly was in hysterics.

The eclipse completed itself. It seemed to suck Gnaeus Corvinus Cato into a slither of angry, unnaturally hungry wings, until even the faint glow of his green eyes ceased to be. The air in the room, despite the hover of death, was much lighter.

As Bark looked about the room, it reminded him again of Rome. From the linear cinderblock walls to the curved archway windows, and high ceilings, Oakland Coliseum was as deadly a manifestation of his past, but with a happier ending. A cornered animal with tunnel vision, heels dug into the dirt with a roaring crowd on all sides screaming and yelling for him to come out and play some more.

This time, he wasn't the beast. He was the gladiator. There would be no encore; he had earned his freedom…and Gone's. The curse had been lifted. The spell was broken. He'd found the right way.

He looked at her, then. Her pain was also her joy, and with a mouth full of blood he said, "Wolves mate for life, Antigone."

He dragged himself close to her feet, fingering the casing fragment that was lodged in her boot tip, and she bent down to touch his face. The fur was growing in, and she stroked it. He handed the fragment to her, and said, "Make this life a good one, *ab hinc*. From here on."

On a chair close by, covering a bloodstained set list, was a black Stetson, soaked in sweat. Beneath it she could make out the words, "This Awful Dream I Have," and she smiled, seeing it had been crossed off the list.

Family Values
– Jeannette Sears

Author's note: I've recently written my first novel, *A Light Rain of Grace*, about the life of a female rock star circa 1966 to the nineties. In *Family Values*, the protagonist of the novel, Emma Allison, is hanging out at a Sausalito, CA restaurant, The Trident, in the mid-sixties. It was a time and place when you might be dining in the same restaurant with Janis Joplin, Jimi Hendrix, and members of a popular English band on any given night. In this short story, rock star Emma gives the reader a peek at the San Francisco Scene at the height of its golden years. It's also a peek into the psyche of a talented and beautiful but highly erratic young woman who, with the best of intentions, gets herself into the craziest and often most hilarious situations.

Family Values

I was with my manager, Herbie, at the Trident in Sausalito when I noticed a guy sitting at the bar with some other musician types. Probably what drew my eye to him was that the waitresses were doing the hover dance that meant the cat must be worth checking out. Herbie was hunched over the table like a gargoyle, blah blahing about the record and trying to get me to agree to another tour over the holidays.

"Emma, baby, be reasonable. Sixty-seven has been a great year for us; you're already a star, but I promise sixty-eight will shoot you into the galaxy."

"Jesus, Herbie, you're turning into a poet...into the galaxy, yeah, just what I need...get a little spacier." I threw down a shot of tequila and beckoned a waitress over. All the waitresses in the Trident were gorgeous hippie girls, very natural, no make-up, wearing jeans or mini-skirts with lacy see-through blouses and no bras, of course. Many of them wore the flowing vintage clothing that I favored. I fit right in with my boas and furs, my purple velvet and lace.

I wasn't wearing anything see-through that day though; my

Aunt Mildred and Uncle Harold were joining me for dinner right after my meeting with Herbie. I ordered a double cappuccino just to make sure I'd still be on my feet when they got there.

I could sense that people on the scene were aware I was in the room, but they were cool—gave me my space. Everyone except the guy at the bar. He was looking over at me every two seconds and I know he caught me looking back. He recognized me for sure, but it wasn't intimidating him.

The Trident has floor to ceiling windows with the best view in Sausalito. From any table in the room you can see the Golden Gate Bridge spanning the Bay, and Alcatraz, and the skyline of San Francisco. A tourist's dream, but the Kingston Trio, who built the place, catered to the counter-culture—artists, hippies, and musicians. Hand-carved redwood curved around the walls and tapestries draped from the ceiling. The menus were all done out in psychedelic print. Janis had a booth of her own and I had preferred seating too. Everyone from Jimi Hendrix to the Stones passed through the place.

Of course I was going to do the tour—Herbie always got his way—but I wanted to make him sweat for it. I had a reputation to maintain! So, I was listening to him like background noise and trying to figure out what to do. I had told my Aunt Mildred and her crazy Pentecostal preacher husband, Harold, to come on over to the Trident after their visit with my beatnik parents, Ray and Stephanie. My parents live in Sausalito and Aunt Mildred told me she and Harold were nervous about coming to my place in The City because of the hills. Okay, fair enough. If you're not used to driving in San Francisco it can be pretty scary. The Trident was the obvious place to meet.

But as the coffee started circulating through my bloodstream and I looked around with sobering eyes, I began to doubt my judgment about my choice of meeting places. Okay, my judgment is never all that reliable, but the Trident? What was I thinking!

Aunt Mildred and Uncle Harold live on the East Coast and I hardly ever see them. There is something good about Mildred in spite of her dogmatic beliefs, and I didn't want to blow her away on our one visit per every five years. Stephanie would no doubt have already done a pretty good job of that anyway. I didn't really give a shit about what Harold might think, and anyway, I was much more interested in getting to know the guy at the bar than having my night eaten up in an argument with a right-wing fundamentalist.

My mother, Stephanie, had called that morning around 11:30. She rarely calls that early so I knew something was up.

"Is everything all right?" I sat up in bed and reached for a cigarette. "Did Dad kill Uncle Harold or something?"

Stephanie laughed. "It would more likely be me doing the killing. I can't believe the crap he's fed my sister. We're getting through it though—just staying off any subject of any importance whatsoever. But Em, I thought I better remind you that you're meeting them for dinner at six."

"Jesus, Stephanie, I wouldn't space that out."

"I know, I know, but they're such a bummer. Mildred wasn't always like this, you know. She's gone crazy. Guess what her chief complaint about California is so far?"

"Surprise me."

"Naked babies on the beach! Honestly. We took them to Stinson Beach yesterday and all they could talk about afterward was how many naked babies they saw! Harold said that they'd heard a lot about how decadent California is, but they still couldn't believe that people would let their children roam around naked like the savages in Kenya. You know they were missionaries in Africa in the fifties—it's such a strange mentality...calling people savages...well, I got into it with him—for all the good it did."

"Jesus, it's going to be a great evening." I rolled my eyes and sighed deeply.

"I know you're rolling your eyes, Em. Just remember, it's only one night out of your life, and Mildred does really love you."

"Don't worry; I'll be good. I love her too."

I heard the relief in my mother's voice. "You're an angel."

"You might have a hard time getting anyone to agree on that one." I was laughing as we hung up.

So, I was sitting there in the Trident across from Herbie thinking about the naked babies on the beach and I realized that I'd created yet another recipe for disaster. I couldn't bring my Pentecostal relatives into that place. They'd freak out and run screaming or something.

I glanced over at the guy at the bar, then back at Herbie. It looked like he was grinding his teeth at me. I gave him my most sincere smile.

"Okay, okay. I'll do the tour but I want some time off from mid-December till New Year's Eve. I appreciate everything you do for me, Herbie; you know that. I just need a little time to chill."

"Don't worry; we'll work it so you're happy. I didn't think you were even listening to me."

I scooted round the booth and put my arm around Herbie. "Don't I always listen to you?"

"Save your charm for someone who doesn't know you," Herbie said, but he was smiling.

We both got up to hug goodbye. Herbie looked me in the eyes. "Take care of yourself, beautiful. Don't burn the candle at both ends."

As I hugged Herbie, I was looking over his shoulder at the guy at the bar. He was looking back.

I slumped back down into my booth and sat with my head down, trying to recoup and figure out what to do. It was too late to ward Aunt Mildred and Uncle Harold off at the pass. They were due to show up in five minutes so they would already have left my parents' house. Obviously, I was going to have to meet them outside and suggest we go elsewhere. But before I left, I wanted to make contact with the guy at the bar and let him know I'd be back later. Easy enough, I thought—just sashay over there and tell him. I was in the process of gathering together my things to leave when this voice with a strong English accent got my attention. I looked up and the guy I'd had my eye on was hovering over my table.

"Hey, Emma Allison, right? We have mutual friends, but you're more gorgeous than their description. I'm Jimmy; may I join you?"

I laughed. "You can sit for a minute, but you wouldn't want to join me where I'm going—trust me."

Jimmy slid into the booth beside me. "Try me, love. I'd throw myself under a lorry for you."

"That won't be necessary; but do you think you can wait a couple of hours for me? I'm meeting some people. Should be back by eight or so."

He leaned in close and whispered, "Take me with you."

I could just imagine the look on Uncle Harold's face when he got a load of Jimmy—tight leather pants, hair down his back, shirt open to the waist and long, colorful scarves billowing. Plus, the way he moved oozed sex appeal…I'd been responding to it from across a busy restaurant…and up close, well, I thought about blowing old Harold and Mildred off. But I couldn't do it. Crazy religious fanatics or not, they're family.

I reached up and stroked Jimmy's hair, just a quick caress. "Listen baby, wait for me, okay? You can't come with me. I'm meeting my relatives from the backwaters of Maine. You'd give my uncle a coronary. Take my booth; have some dinner. I'll be back." I slid around to the other side of the booth and stood up before he could protest any further. "Nice meeting you, Jimmy," I said over my shoulder as I walked away.

"You better come back or I'll hunt you down," he shouted after me.

I liked a guy with nerve. He was a musician; that was obvious. I thought he must be from that new English Power Trio I'd been hearing about.

Even the parking lot of the Trident is a trip—always a dozen or more hip people milling around to see who's on the scene. I tried to sneak out to the curb so I could get in the car with Harold and Mildred before they even had a chance to park, but too many people recognized me and I got waylaid before I made it across the small lot. So, I was standing in the center of a group of friends, fans, and groupies when I saw Aunt Mildred making her way toward me.

"Em honey, is that you?" she called.

Of course, everybody turned around to see who was calling me honey in such a familiar tone of voice. Poor Aunt Mildred gasped as the little crowd swirled toward her. I saw her look of confusion just before she was engulfed by the friendly little mob of freaks.

I swear the whole scene looked like slow motion, and I wasn't even very stoned. One of the junkie groupies draped her arm around my aunt. "Hey lady, where'd you get those shoes? Look, she's got the real thing—genuine granny shoes."

I swooped in and wedged myself between the groupie and my aunt. "Aunt Mildred, it's so good to see you! Come on, let's get out of here." I took her arm and steered her out toward the curb where Uncle Harold was waiting in the car. "Let's go down to the Seven Seas. It's way too crowded in the Trident."

"Were those people hippies?" Mildred asked, looking totally bewildered. "They smelled funny," she whispered. "Was it their perfume?"

Here we go, I thought. "No, Mildred, it was patchouli oil. And no, they're not hippies; of course not."

The hostess at the Seven Seas recognized me and gave us a table that was semi-private. I sat across from Harold and Aunt Mildred, separated only by salt and peppershakers and a candle, but a million miles from their universe. I hadn't seen Mildred in years and I was struck by how much she looked like my mother, physically anyway. Her hairstyle, clothing, and expression bore no resemblance whatsoever. She still had that furrowed brow I remembered.

Uncle Harold leaned across the table first thing and glared at me. "Emma, were those your friends in the parking lot?"

I matched his glare. "Yeah, I guess so—some of them anyway."

He was wearing this big old-fashioned suit and his balding head seemed to be sprouting from his collar. I watched as he fumbled through his jacket pockets and pulled out some pamphlets. He cleared his throat and went into preacher mode. "Emma, you need to ask yourself: Are you leading your friends to Jesus or are they leading you away from Him?"

I attempted a smile. "I never really thought about it. I don't think any of us are leading anybody anywhere…we're just winging it—taking it step by step and letting where we end up be a surprise."

"Well, I can tell you right now that with that kind of attitude where you're going to end up is hell." He plunked his pamphlets down on the table between us. "You need to repent, little sister."

"Could I do it after dinner?" I asked. "I'm starving."

While we waited for our meals to arrive I thumbed through the pamphlets he kept insisting I read. I found them incomprehensible. They all seemed to be mainly about how homosexuals were ruining our country and corrupting young boys. I held up one particularly offensive one and waved it in Harold's face.

"You've got to be kidding. ALL homosexuals are potential serial killers? What? Are you crazy? Who wrote this shit?"

Aunt Mildred piped in. "Watch your language, young lady. Your uncle is only trying to help you. We noticed how so many of your male friends were dressed like girls."

"Like girls? Really?" I tried to remember who was in the parking lot—what they could be talking about, but I drew a blank.

I was tempted to order a drink just to get through the dinner, but I knew they'd really raise holy hell if I did. So, I stayed calm. "Okay, I'll play. What was this girlish guy wearing?"

Aunt Mildred spoke through pursed lips. "One was wearing red velvet girl's pants and women's scarves. And I saw another one with a puffy-sleeved girl's blouse...and all the men had long hair like a girl's."

I couldn't keep from rolling my eyes. "Jesus you guys, you're not in Kansas. What the hell!"

"Language!" Aunt Mildred snapped.

All my earlier thoughts about her being a good person at heart were rapidly fading. I had told myself it was just Harold who was the judgmental jerk, but the loving aunt I had fantasized about was nowhere in sight. She had been replaced by a tight-lipped alien who found naked babies and longhaired guys offensive. I could only imagine what she was thinking about me. What the fuck, she knew I was a rock singer—why should I be trying to conceal my life style to please her.

Nevertheless, I took another stab at trying to win her over. It wasn't like I had a lot of aunts to choose from. She was my mother's only living relative, and I felt I owed her some respect. "Sorry Aunt Mildred. I really am. It's so good to see you." I flashed what I hoped was a disarming smile. "Have you been having a good time? I remember last time you were here you came to see me in my school play. I'm still performing."

She returned my smile, but it seemed condescending. "Yes, we heard. Stephanie told us all about your career. You have a wonderful opportunity to spread God's message of love, but you've got to be careful that Satan doesn't use you. I'm sure you didn't mean to be rude to your uncle, but you should know that he wrote those pamphlets you've shown such disdain for. He has your best interests at heart."

I felt the air leave my body as I slumped down in my chair. "Really Aunt Mildred? Do we have to talk about that again? We're never going to agree. Can't we just live and let live? I was really looking forward to your visit."

When our food finally came, it was a huge fucking relief. We all focused our attention on eating and actually managed some small talk that wasn't about who's bound for hell or anything. I was never so happy to see the end of a meal, that's for sure.

Harold and Mildred offered to drive me to my car—didn't want me walking around with all the strange, dangerous people in the area, I guess. A naked baby might attack me, or something. I assured them my car was nearby and I'd be fine, and then I hightailed it back to the Trident. Mental note: Family or not, that was our last visit.

My best friend, Carol, was sitting at my table with a bunch of our friends. And yes, the guy was there too. I hoped he wasn't flashing out on Carol while I was gone—easy to do, but he was on his feet the minute he saw me.

"So, you did come back, love." His accent was irresistible—not that I had any reason to resist.

We had a few drinks with Carol and company, then headed out for my place in the City. As we drove out of the parking lot, the junkie hippie girl who had freaked my aunt out waved good-bye. I waved back.

Hey, so maybe you can't choose your family. You can choose your friends.

Ten O'Clock Again
– Clea Simon

Author's Note: "Ten O'Clock Again" is part of a larger work in progress examining death and secrets among a group of music fans. Although I've covered a lot of big acts, what really intrigues me is the tribal nature of local club scenes and how it persists or changes over time.

Ten O'Clock Again

Ten o'clock, and the opener will be on soon.

Opener! She laughs. It's only the Craters and the Whirled Shakers tonight, and the bill was probably decided by a coin toss between them backstage. It's the Shakers she came to see, their psychedelic pop still gets her going, with its tambourines and the beat. But maybe she'll stay for the Craters. Depends on how tired she is. Depends on the crowd.

There are only about thirty people in the room, but after a long day at work, Tara is glad enough for the company and for the empty chair by the table up front. Beer in hand, she settles in, waiting for the music. Thirty-seven, she counts. A good house, really, for two bands that have been around twenty years. Then again, most everyone here has been, too. She knows most of them by sight, if not by name, and when she closes her eyes she can place them in the Rat, the Channel, Oakie's, Jumpin' Jack Flash. All the great old clubs, closed now. Those cavernous rooms and black-painted basements are what she thinks of when she thinks of the '80s, back when she, the bands, and everyone here was in their heyday.

She opens her eyes to a bit of a shock. The women are all thirty pounds heavier than in her mind's picture. Or they've gone thin, like she has, a little drawn, a little leathery. The men have fared better. Gray, if they have hair, and some of them have gone from motorcycle tough to resembling the butchers, delivery men, and press operators they are during the day. But mostly they're in good shape, if a little rough. Besides, it's her crowd and nothing new sounds as good.

Twenty years ago, the Shakers wouldn't have been playing a pub like this, as much a burger joint as a music room. But twenty years ago, they'd been rising stars, the best of Boston. There'd have been half again as many label scouts among the fans.

"Hey." Tom pulls up the chair next to hers, settling his shot glass on the scarred wood table.

"Hey." Tara had never known Tom well, but he still feels like family after all this time.

"Good crowd, huh?" They smile and nod, both happy enough to be out, and just then the Shakers take the stage. The guitar and bass bash out the first chord. It's loud and fast and Joey, the drummer, jumps in with a fill, kicking everyone up to speed. More guitar and Phil, the singer, has grabbed the mike. He's smiling, too. Glad to be on stage. But that soon gives way to a rockstar grimace, eyes squeezed shut. Then he's prancing, the guitar taking over the song and his body with it, and he swings the mike stand high. Stadium moves. The guitars crash again over the driving beat of the bass. Joey solos, fast and neat, and the guitars are back. Phil is singing his heart out, and just like that, the song is done.

"Awesome." Tom could be speaking for both of them. Twenty years ago, ten even, Tara knows she'd be up on her feet, dancing, in front of the stage. Maybe up on the table. Maybe next song. Joey leads off the next tune. "One, two, three, four!" and the guitar-bass unison cranks up the pace before Phil joins in. Tara drains her beer. Maybe she will get up, dance right in front of the band like she used to.

She looks around for Min, knowing that she's not likely to have shown up in the five minutes since Tara last surveyed the crowd. Min would've liked this. The band sounds good, everyone seems mellow. Not that Min's been out much recently. Unlike some of their old friends, the ones who've moved on to have families and buy houses out in Watertown or Medford, Min hasn't really replaced the rock scene in her life. But she's grown tired. Tired of the scene, of the music even, if what she says is true when they meet for lunch the next week. Min works at the hospital a couple of blocks from the paper. She's got forty-five minutes, most of which she uses to go on about how sad it all is.

"How's it sad? Nobody's pretending we're twenty." Tara is used to the usual complaints from Min. "We're having fun, and we still like the sound."

"It's just kind of pitiful. The dwindling crowd and all." Min always shakes her head at this point, which makes Tara a little angry.

"It's just the same as any other pastime. We're a group of old friends." Even as she says it, Tara knows it's not entirely true. She and Min are friends. They've spent time together outside the clubs. Gotten to know each other. Helped each other through break-ups and miscarriages (Min's) and divorce (Tara's). But Min has never had quite the feeling about the scene that Tara has, that it's her family, her only real home. Looking around the room tonight, Tara shakes her head and pities her friend. This is something real. Maybe they are all outcasts, but they found each other, didn't they?

"Hey, kiddo!" As if on cue, Gina is there, collapsing into the one chair left. "Don't they sound great tonight?"

"Killer." Tara knows Gina drinks too much, knows that she's never gotten over Phil, even though the singer has moved on to a wife and two babies. "What's the news?" It cheers her to see how Gina brightens, her one claim to fame being her connection with the band.

"They're talking about going into the studio again. You'll hear, they're going to do some of the new songs. They're really great." Okay, so maybe Min has a point, Tara tells herself. They're all a little lost. But isn't it something that they found each other? That they have the scene?

"I'll listen for them." The next tune has started and Gina is up again, shaking it in front of the tiny stage. Looking at her, her too-tight mini-skirt making indents in her waist and thighs, Tara thinks twice about getting up to dance. But just as she's reconsidering the evening another song kicks in, a repeated guitar riff she knows in her sleep. It's "World Enough," their 1986 hit. The song that almost got them onto a major label, out of Boston, out of all this. The bass joins in, four fast bars of building beat. Then the drums. Screw the years, it's time to dance.

If we had world enough, world enough and time...

Time's played them all for fools, but they're still here, and Tara loves it. In a minute, it's 1986 again. She's bouncing around, shaking it with Gina. For a moment, the years, the dinky pub, don't matter. She remembers descending into a humid basement club, working her way through a packed house, and hearing this riff, this command to dance.

I love you baby, and you know that ain't no crime.

The lyrics are inane. Tara knows that, and sings along anyway, shouting into the PA's roar.

World enough and time!

With a crash, the song ends, and Tara heads for the bar.

"You hear about Frank?" Gina is leaning over toward her. Gina always knows what's going on. Tara holds up her empty bottle—and two fingers—for the bartender. She's feeling generous.

"No, what?" The beers arrive, and Tara slides one over to Gina.

"He's dead," Gina takes a swig. "Some kind of accident."

Band and beer forgotten for a moment, Tara stares. Dead?

"I heard he fell down a flight of stairs." Gina fills in the blank. "They're saying it could be suicide."

"Shit."

"Yeah, really. You know about their daughter, too, right?" Tara nods. She'd heard that Frank's daughter had some kind of health problems, that her son—Frank's grandson—hadn't been right since he was born.

She takes a pull from her beer, tries to think of something to say. But Gina is gone, back on the floor for the next number. One of the new tunes, it sounds good enough but Tara has lost the urge to dance.

Frank. Shit.

Maybe Min is right. Tara used to think of this crowd as the lucky ones. The runts who'd survived. They were rejects and outcasts, and she included herself in that crowd, but they'd bucked the curse. They'd all been lucky enough to find each other, to find their own world, here in the club scene. She'd never been able to explain it to Peter, her ex, but she'd always felt lucky to be included. He'd insisted that her outsider status was a choice, that she could join in the real world whenever she'd wanted. He hadn't understood, and had gone on without her. Now, she wonders if the luck has run out.

We are truly runts, she realizes. Gina, Tom, the band. And now Frank. We're sickly, we have fewer successful marriages and happy families. Too many of us have died.

"Why the long face?" Robbie from the Craters has pushed in beside her, an amber shot of whiskey in his hand. "It's Friday!" It's too loud to explain about Frank, about everything. So she nods and clinks her bottle to his shot glass. Turning to the stage, they watch the Shakers doing their thing, same as twenty years ago.

The Blue Firebird
– Charles Shaar Murray

Author's Note: The first version of this story was written in the mid-1970s on an acoustic typewriter in the kitchen of my first wife's family home during a snowy winter in a very remote part of Scotland once immortalised in song by Paul McCartney. It then mouldered in a filing cabinet for three and a half decades, only to be substantially revised a few months back when the formidable Ms Grabien requested a story for this collection. I was under the impression that the heroine was entirely imaginary until I met someone very much like her (except that she played bass rather than guitar and only had blue skin on very cold days) a few years later and somehow persuaded her to become my second wife, though not to remain so.

I'm still waiting for a blue Firebird.

The Blue Firebird

I could hear the music wafting from the club almost before the airtight gateway to the Survival Zone had hissed shut behind my battered skimmer.

New Rome was not a place for the gently raised or the faint of heart. It wasn't the absolute meanest of the various badlands, by any means, but it definitely placed somewhere high on the list. Whoever named it either had a puckish sense of humour or a profound ignorance of Earth history: anywhere less like the original old Rome would be hard to imagine. The pockmarked little asteroid in the back of beyond, with nothing marring its uniformly charred grey surface other than the five-mile blister of the Survival Zone, New Rome housed its transient community of miners, spacehopping hoodlums, and assorted interstellar flotsam passing through on their way from one nowhere to another. Decent folks rarely—if ever—set foot on New Rome, which didn't bother me particularly. It had been quite a long time since anyone had numbered me amongst the decent folk.

Topdogg's Bar And Grill was where most things happened on New Rome. It was the centre of the colony's social and cultural life: post office, diner, supermarket, hangout, city hall, concert hall, crashpad, trading post, employment agency, courthouse and quite a few other things, which made Topdogg himself a combination of mayor, bartender, guru, sheriff, commune Big Daddy, banker, arbiter of disputes, hanging judge, occasional executioner and mostly-benevolent despot. If you wanted someone killed or you wanted someone prevented from killing you, you went to Topdogg. If you needed some emergency maintenance work done to keep a skimmer or shuttlecraft flying, or if you needed to get rid of some weird new kind of clap nobody had ever heard of before, you went to Topdogg. He'd help you if he liked your face or your rap or if it wasn't any trouble or if the price was right.

Behind the club were the various facilities which made up the rest of New Rome. They were as unconditionally Topdogg's domains as the bar. There were machine workshops, markets, hotels ranging from near-flophouses to almost-luxurious, storage warehouses—some refrigerated, some superheated, the priciest offering time stasis for exceptionally sensitive commodities—a state-of-the-art hospital specialising in combat medicine and the treatment of exotic diseases and, most important of all, the hyperconductor-driven generators which powered the atmosphere and climate controls.

Officially—according to the duly-constituted authorities—New Rome and Topdogg's Bar & Grill didn't exist. Semi-officially, the asteroid and everything on it were off-limits to all traffic, without exception. Unofficially, Topdogg did what he liked and anybody he permitted to touch down on his well-protected turf was free to do whatever they wanted provided they didn't contravene Topdogg's rules. Topdogg was well aware of who amongst the powers-that-be required carrots, and who required sticks. He knew full well where most of the bodies in the sector were buried. After all, before he'd finally settled down, he'd buried a fair few of them himself.

112

I was on New Rome to see Topdogg but, just for a change, this time I was the one doing him the favour.

I locked up the skimmer, armed its defences, hefted my bag and walked over to the club, towards the music. It was sweet, salty, stinging guitar blues, with a girl singing. The handscrawled poster in the window said, "LYNX."

Topdogg was leaning his furry bulk against the bar, swapping affectionate insults with the tall dark-skinned woman with the pile of gold dreadlocks behind the bar serving beers to the clientele—pretty much the usual wreckage. New Rome was a short warp-hop from most of the bigger asteroids where miners from all over the sector worked in the transmium pits, blasting out the toxic stuff which powered hyperconductors. Hyperconductor-based technologies had changed the energy game and made it possible to infect so much of the once-sterile galaxy with the human virus. Transmium also made it possible for most of those who'd stayed Earthside to lead lives of luxury unimaginable a century or two before. The trouble with transmium was that prolonged exposure to it did scary and sometimes highly infectious stuff to human DNA. Quite a few of the miners would have been wealthy beyond belief had they been permitted to return to Earth, but only a very lucky few remained sufficiently unaltered—and non-contagious—ever to be allowed back.

Candelle saw me first, and nudged Topdogg. I'd always thought she had too much class to work shifts behind the bar, but—like Topdogg himself—she seemed to feel that there was some ceremonial purpose in personally serving a few drinks once in a while, like it kept the pair of them in touch with the grassroots of their business. Some said she was the brains of the operation and her partner the muscle, but I always figured that Candelle—they called her "Roman Candelle" when they talked about her outside New Rome—and the big guy pretty much had an equal allocation of both.

Topdogg spun round with a big grin oozing through his stubble. "Heyyyyyyy, Jackie boy!" he bellowed, lumbering over to engulf me in a suffocating bearhug, swinging me clean off my feet.

"Just call me Sandstone for now," I mumbled into his sour-smelling shoulder. "You can put me down now, okay?"

"Sorry," he said, sounding not the least bit contrite, but nevertheless returning me to ground level more or less undamaged. "How ya bin, anyway?"

"Just fine," I lied, and jerked my head towards the back room. He nodded and led the way. Candelle popped a beer, handed it to me and blew a kiss. I followed Topdogg through the door marked "Private."

He slumped into his worn leather armchair, cleared some space on his cluttered desk and unscrewed the top of a fresh bottle of Campbeltown Malt whisky. Splashing a pair of generous slugs into a couple of only slightly smeared glasses that apparently resided permanently on the floor next to his armchair, he gestured grandly at the matching chair opposite his.

"You got?" he asked.

"I got." I opened my backpack, pulled out a small green packet and slit it open with my buck knife. He watched intently as I tapped a tiny pile of purple crystals onto the steel mirror waiting on his desk and chopped it into two neat lines. Next to the mirror was an ancient silver Tiffany's straw. I handed it to him. "Check it out. The rest's in the skimmer."

He put his head to one side, and raised an eyebrow. "You may be losing your touch, Ja … Sandstone. I'm not. After you, Alphonse." He handed it back.

I raised my glass. He raised his. We clinked and drank. The Campbeltown was as richly endowed with smoky goodness as ever. I leaned over the mirror, put the straw to one nostril and snorted my line.

Topdogg's face went soft and then everything turned a grainy black and white. I experienced a succession of lifetimes: as a peasant girl in 15th-century France, a commissar in the October Revolution, a centurion in ancient Palestine, a bodyservant to Mohammad, a Republican congressman under Ronald Reagan … and dozens upon dozens, fucking regiments of others. I was father to a hundred children, mother to a thousand more. I was born, gave birth, was bereaved and died, over and over, I buried my parents, and my children. I was oppressor and liberator, victim and saviour. I was hero and nebbish, rescuer and bully. I was the idol of millions, and I was unknown to even my next-door neighbours. I was the subject of endless fascination to entire galaxies, and infinitely tedious even to myself, sometimes in the same incarnation. I was titan and pygmy, giant and dwarf. I was fit, healthy and strong. I was crippled and mute. I was beautiful, charismatic and desired by all and sundry, I was ugly and universally derided, I was mediocre and universally ignored. I was brilliant. I was cretinous. I was worshipped. I was mocked. I understood everything. I understood nothing. I controlled nations, entire planets. I was weak and utterly helpless. I was a man, and hundreds of men. I was a woman, and hundreds of women. I was a member of numberless species in which gender either didn't exist or was entirely irrelevant.

The spectrum seeped back into blues and purples. My face was wet with tears. So was Topdogg's. My whisky glass was full again. Topdogg must have refilled it before he did his own line of Real-Time. According to the clock on the wall, just over eighteen minutes had passed since I'd snorted mine. I sipped appreciatively at my whisky and waited for him to come back from his other lives. It took around a minute and a half, my subjective time. Probably around two thousand years in his.

"Nice," he said eventually. He wiped his eyes, and blew his nose into a scrap of cloth I'd've been reluctant to use to wipe my boots. "Best RealTime we've had in a long while. There'll be a bonus."

He locked my backpack into his wall safe, loaded a credit stick into a microterminal, tapped a few keys and handed it to me. I slipped it into an inner pocket of my old leather jacket and chased the malt with the remains of my beer.

"You wanna hang and see the show?" he asked. "Girl we got playing tonight's seriously good."

"I'm sure she is … and it's always a pleasure doing business with ya, 'Dogg, but I've got places to see and people to be."

"Jac … Sandstone," he said. "I mean she's seriously good. Check her out. What difference is another coupla hours gonna make?"

It didn't seem, at the time, to be a life-changing moment. I was nicely high. I'd just made some very decent money. I was among friends and comparatively safe, which is not a circumstance encountered too often in my profession. And the music coming from the stage sounded very cool indeed. So I let Topdogg lead me back out into the club, hand me a freshly-uncapped beer and park me at a table near the stage. It hadn't been unoccupied when we arrived, but for some reason the guys already sitting there seemed happy to give up their seats and watch the rest of the gig from the bar.

The girl whose voice I'd heard from outside was still singing her blues up on the cramped little stage. I shouldn't have been surprised to find that she was also playing that tough, sensual guitar, but she was indeed. Female blues singers weren't that rare, but women who played the deep-down dirty blues on guitar were still nowhere near as common as I'd like them to be.

She was perched on a high barstool, picking the living daylights out of an odd-shaped blue Gibson guitar with one pickup and two knobs, an olde-skoole black cable running into a tiny little tweed-covered amp beside her. One of the reasons so many good musicians liked playing Topdogg's—apart from access to a big-spending captive audience, that is—was that behind the

116

stage's shabby backdrop was a veritable mountain of preamps, power-amps, digital simulators, modellers and effects processors, connected to a massive array of speakers and accessible either by traditional cable or by using wi-fi. That meant that virtually any player on just about any electric or electronic instrument could get straight up on stage and achieve just about any sound that he or she wanted.

And yet this girl was disdaining the house set-up and using an amp of her own. It was so ancient that I was amazed it still worked, let alone sounding as good as it did. Just about every outlaw musician who'd ever passed through the badlands had played a set on Topdogg's stage at some time or another, but even by this club's standards she was ... hot? She was a nova-espresso superheated to go.

She seemed dangerously thin under her dark loose jumpsuit and her pockmarked skin had the blueish tinge that folks from the thin-oxygen atmospheres get. Her black hair, way past shoulder length, was as ragged and uneven as if something had been chewing at it, long pointed ears poking through the sides of her mane. Her eyes, black and incandescent, raked through the crowd as she sang. The nails on her left hand, where she worked the strings on the guitar neck, were bitten short; on her right hand, where she plucked them, the nails were long. Her lips were a dark indigo against the paler robin's-egg blue of her face. She was easily the most beautiful woman I'd seen in the last ten years.

She was singing the old stuff. By which I mean: the real, real old stuff, the classics from way, way back in the olden days. Songs like John Lee Hooker's I'm Mad Again, Bo Dudley's Who Do You Love, Jimi Hendrix's 51st Anniversary, The Rolling Stones' Honky Tonk Women, The Clash's Should I Stay Or Should I Go, stuff like that, and she handled the razor-fight jive of the lyrics with theatrical relish and a wholly credible menace. She sounded

117

like she meant those words and knew that she had what it took to back them up. Her voice snaked out like a whiplash, she slammed chugging jolting funky rhythms out of her Gibson, and when she played a solo it was brief, witty and savage. She was absolutely sensational. I decided that what I'd thought was going to be my last beer was actually my last-but-one. I was glad that Topdogg had arm-twisted me into staying to listen to what was exactly what I needed to hear. Right mood, right place, right time.

"She's great, isn't she?" Topdogg rumbled behind me.

"Damn right. Where'd you find her?"

"She found me. Came in a coupla days back asking if I knew anyone could give her a lift outta here. I thought of you, of course."

"Of course."

"She had that guitar with her and I asked her to play me something." Topdogg hauled a fat joint out of his shirt pocket, lit it with a lighter made out of some luminous purple metal, and passed it to me. "She did Long Distance Call and I booked her into the first free night."

I took a poke on the j and passed it back. "What's her name?"

"Didn't you see the sign? Her name's Lynx."

"I'm drinkin' TNT, I'm smokin' dynamite," sang the girl on the stage. "I hope some schoolboy start a fight, 'cause I'm ready, ready's anybody can be … I'm ready for you, I hope you're ready for me."

I sat and thought about that for a while. Lynx.

"Speakin' of names," Topdogg growled, "What's with this "Sandstone" biz, Jackie? I mean, you can call yourself what you like in my place, man, but …" He let the question hang in the air until it shifted and settled with the smoke.

"Jackie Diamond's a little hot right now," I told him finally, "but I still need to operate and to operate you need a name. So for the time being I'm Sandstone. All right?"

118

"Sure … Sandstone," Topdogg said. "Any particular reason for using that name?"

"Yeah." I didn't elucidate and he didn't ask me to. We sat and smoked, listening to Lynx as she rode into the last chorus, digging her phrasing and inflection and timing, and joining in the crashing applause at the end of the song. I couldn't remember the last time I'd seen Topdogg applaud. If he'd really gotten off on a performer he usually just muttered, "Ya done good, kid" as he charged up the credit stick at the end of the night.

Lynx was taking a swig on her beer before starting the next song, and that was the moment Jupiter Eddie picked to start getting mean.

Jupiter Eddie wasn't actually from Jupiter. No one was. I've never been there and neither has anybody else, but since Jupiter is a very high-gravity planet, folks who come from the more habitable high-gravity planets—and who are therefore built very close to the ground at around four and half feet tall and four and a half feet wide—tend to get called "Jupiter." They're very good mineworkers and much in demand, because they also tend to be strong sonsabitches, but a punchout with one of them tends to be like fighting a cross between a demented bulldozer and a rhino with crabs. Since their physical construction seems to affect their brains, they're usually slow-witted and aggressive, which is a hell of a bad combination. Hence Eddie.

He'd been sitting down the front with a couple of his friends from the New Siberia mine, all of them getting progressively more and more bombed, but he'd seemed to be happily digging the show right along with everybody else until that last song, which seemed to have twanged some atavistic primeval chord in his grotesquely foreshortened cortex. He banged his almost-empty bottle down onto the table and yelled up at Lynx, "Play some chick songs!"

She shielded her blazing black eyes from the stage lights and

119

peered down at the bellowing barrel at the front table. "Heeeeeeyyyy—an intellectual!" she crowed. "You think that one up all by yourself?"

The room went all quiet and strange. No-one talked to Eddie like that when he got his mad on—no-one who still had all their own teeth, that is.

"Those are men's songs you're singin'," Eddie said, very even. "And that aunt right. Why don't you sing some chick songs?"

The retro fashion for mid-20th century American culture—of which, broadly speaking, I heartily approved—sometimes brought with it certain mid-20th century American values, of which, broadly speaking, I didn't approve at all. Eddie didn't seem like the kind of guy who'd appreciate having his attitudes challenged. This didn't seem to bother Lynx as much as it possibly should have. Casually, she undid her guitar strap and shifted her grip on the Gibson so she was holding it right where the neck joined the body. "Why don't you stand on the guy next to ya so we can see you, fatso?" she sneered.

Eddie put his bottle down on the table. "How come no-one ever taught you any manners, chick?" he asked.

"How come your parents never had any kids?" Lynx snapped back.

Eddie let loose a wordless roar, kicked back his chair and started to clamber up onto the stage. Before he could get more than one leg up, Lynx gave him the business end of the guitar— the one with the stud for fixing the strap—right in the side of the neck. Either Eddie was seriously off-balance or she was a hell of a lot stronger than she looked, because she sent him straight back into the table.

Eddie careened back into a pile of furniture, bottles and broken glass and—being Eddie—got right back up again, roaring even louder. He and his friends—neither of whom looked anywhere near as mean as he did but still quite nasty enough to be

120

going on with—advanced on the stage. Everybody else backed away.

"Let's go, Sandstone," Topdogg said. "Who claimed the age of chivalry was dead?"

Candelle tossed him the pain inducer they kept behind the bar. He caught it deftly and, with surprising agility for a dude his size, vaulted onto the stage where Lynx was kicking Eddie's main sidekick, Ugly Harry, in the balls, sending him up against Eddie and giving Topdogg and me enough time to get to them and join in.

I wasn't crazy about rough-housing in a heavy badlands bar. Basically, I'm a dealer, not a fighter, and while any dealer who expects to stay in business needs to be able to bring enough mean and enough nasty to protect his stash, his bankroll and himself, I generally prefer to stay cool and take a little shit here and there, or even a minor humiliation now and then, rather than do too much fighting. Still, sometimes it's a-man's-gotta-do-what-a-man's-gotta-do time, and on those occasions I just try to do as much damage as is necessary to resolve the situation more or less in my favour and then GTFO with person and possessions at least semi-intact.

I latched onto Ugly Harry just as he bounced off Eddie and gave him the heel of my hand under his jaw as hard as I could. On the offchance that I hadn't broken his neck, I drove the points of my stiffened fingers into his adam's-apple. If he lived, he'd be cursing my name—one of my names, anyway—in a croaky whisper for at least a year. I'd only been Sandstone for three days and already someone was going to have a brand-new grudge against me. Oh well. I sidestepped as he went down and looked around for the next contestant.

Topdogg was squaring off against Eddie, pain inducer at the ready, which was just as well since I don't think anybody else in the joint could've taken him. Those of the clientele who enjoyed watching two extremely big, mean, powerful guys getting ready to try and kill each other were slavering at the mouth. Me, I was seriously wishing I was somewhere else—curled up with Candelle in the skimmer finding out just how far open her "open" relationship with Topdogg was, for example—rather than playing patacake with a bunch of vicious drunks on a brightly lit stage.

Eddie was advancing steadily on Topdogg, who was zapping him repeatedly with the pain inducer—fzzzt! fzzzt! fzzt!—to little appreciable effect. Eddie's other pal had pulled a knife on Lynx, who was facing him off with the blue Gibson in her left hand and her right in some kind of martial-arts claw. As he lunged at her, she blocked the knife with the back of the guitar, stiff-armed him in the nose and kicked him deftly and surely in the crotch. She seemed to like doing that, and she did it with what seemed like the skill born of long practice.

He folded up slow. I aided his downward progress by bringing both fists down on the back of his neck and scooping up his fallen knife, since he seemed to have little further use for it.

That was pretty much it except for Eddie. Topdogg was running out of backing-away space and the pain inducer seemed to be running out of battery-charge. It looked like Topdogg wasn't going to do too well in a fair fight, so I slid up behind Eddie and reached around him, holding the edge of the knife to his throat.

"You can't do twice as much drinking with two mouths, Eddie," I said in what I hoped was a quiet, reasonable tone of voice. "You've lowered the tone of this place quite enough for one night, anyway."

He turned his head a little and I moved the knife closer so the blade was touching his adam's-apple. "That aunt fair, Jackie," he growled.

"Neither's you and two sidekicks up against a chick, big man," Topdogg said. "Let's call it a night, okay?"

Eddie snarled, but he lowered his fists. I moved the knife away from his throat and stepped well back. He shuffled away to his fallen table, grabbed Ugly Harry and the third goon by the scruffs of their necks and dragged them towards the door. Lynx was fingering the knife-gouge in the back of her Gibson. Topdogg stepped up to the microphone.

"Live entertainment's over for the night, messieurs-"dames," he announced. "We hope you've enjoyed the show. Let's hear it one more time for Lynx!" Before the bright shower of applause died away, he signalled to Candelle, who called up a cool-jazz playlist from the sound system to chill the mood before switching off the stage lights.

Lynx rolled up her cable, stashed it in the back of her little Fender amp, carefully wiped her battered blue guitar down and stowed it in the beat-up case at the side of the stage. Once she'd finished packing up her gear, we trooped over the bar, where Candelle had a neat row of shots and beer chasers awaiting us. Topdogg handed her the now-drained pain inducer, and she re-holstered it in its charger. "I reckon it's time we upgrade to the deluxe model," she deadpanned.

"Here's to good blues and good fighting," Topdogg toasted, taking a healthy slurp of his whisky and chasing it with a mouthful of beer. Candelle grimaced, but drank anyway. "Here's to good blues," I said pointedly, and let the drink try to slow my pulse and loosen the knot in my belly.

Lynx didn't drink hers. She twisted the glasses around on the bat with her long nervous blue fingers, making wet ring patterns on the scarred wood. She seemed a lot smaller and less tough without that guitar slung over her narrow shoulders.

"This the guy you was tellin' me about?" she asked Topdogg. "Jackie Diamond, right?"

"Jackie Diamond's so last year," I told her. "I go by Sandstone now."

She lamped me with those scorching black eyes. "Sandstone, huh?"

"Sandstone." I fumbled a packet of cigarettes out of my jacket pocket and offered them round. Lynx and Topdogg took me up on it—Candelle was obviously giving up smoking again—and Topdogg flashed that obscene purple lighter. Shit, I never figured that changing your name was such big whoop, but here I was meeting someone for the first time and here she was using the old name. The last thing I needed was fresh noise about where Jackie Diamond was and what he was doing.

"What can I do for you, anyway?" I asked Lynx, but before she could answer Topdogg was waving us towards the back room. I chugged the beer and followed him. Lynx hefted her guitar case and came after us. She still hadn't touched either of her drinks.

"The guitar'll be safe with Candelle," I tried to reassure her. She shook her head.

"You take that guitar everywhere?"

"Even to the can." She wasn't smiling.

In the back room, Topdogg had laid out three lines of something lighter and less head-rearranging than RealTime and, joint clamped between his teeth, was pouring Campbeltown malt into three glasses—clean ones this time, in honour of a new guest. With a flourish, he relit the joint and subsided into his chair.

"You done good, kid," he told Lynx, reaching for his microterminal and ramming in a credit stick. He tapped in some numbers and showed Lynx the readout. She unleashed a dazzling grin, removed the stick and stashed it in the back pocket of her baggy jeans.

"By the way … Sandstone," he grinned. "I had my boys stash a case of the Campbeltown in your skimmer. They also collected the rest of the consignment."

I raised an eyebrow. "I had it locked and armed."

His grin widened. "I know. Your security and defensive systems were in serious need of an upgrade, by the way. So I had them take care of that, too." With a theatrical flourish, he produced the silver straw. "Snarf up, children. This is nice."

We snarfed. It was nice.

The Campbeltown was a greater gift than Topdogg realised. I knew some folks on an out-of-the-way planetoid I'd encountered a year or two back who got four days" worth of cosmic visions of communion with ancestors and deities when they injected a 4cc ampoule of good Scotch directly into the bloodstream. A dozen bottles of the good stuff, once appropriately packaged, would provide a transcendent collective experience for the entire population and earn enough to keep me in solid fuel and creature comforts for the next couple of years. The rest of the case, of course, I could simply drink. I toasted Topdogg's health with abject enthusiasm, took a healthy toke on the joint, and tapped Lynx on the shoulder.

"Topdogg said you wanted a lift out of here."

"Yeah."

"Where to?"

"Anywhere that's terraformed enough to have clean air, a clean ocean and a nice beach."

"And after that?"

"That'll do fine. There is no "after that.""

I clambered to my feet and stretched. I'd been awake around thirty-six hours on speed and coffee even before arriving on New Rome, and I had a vicious attack of spacelag coming on. What with the dope, the booze and the adrenalin comedown after the brawl, I reckoned I had just about enough energy left to punch a course into the skimmer's computer before I finally crashed out.

"Okay, blues singer, let's go." Candelle wandered in—she'd obviously just finished chucking out the last of the clientele and shutting down the bar—and took the joint out of my hand. She took a hit, bent down gracefully from the waist and gave Topdogg

125

a leisurely kiss on the lips. He clambered to his feet—none too steadily—and swept an exaggerated bow. She slapped him on his massive butt.

"You've had a busy night and you're quite, quite bombed," she said mock-sternly. "Get your fat ass to bed." Topdogg pulled an aggrieved face, but he screwed the top back on to the whisky bottle and switched off the desk light. He put a weighty arm around my shoulders.

"Hey, Sandstone … nice seein' you again, dude. Next time you're up, stick around a coupla days. We can party some, y'know wh'I'm sayin'?"

Candelle looked puzzled. "Why's this drunken clown calling you Sandstone, Jackie?" she asked.

I groaned inwardly. "Topdogg'll tell you later, Cand." I turned to Lynx, who was standing right by the door with the guitar case in one hand and the little tweed amplifier in the other. "Meet you at the skimmer," I told her. "It's the one with the Doctor Strange decal on the door."

She gave me a thumbs-up with the hand holding the amp, and slipped out. I kissed Candelle, bearhugged Topdogg and limped after her.

Lynx was leaning up against the skimmer when I got there.

"It looks kinda beat-up." She stroked the space-weathered paint.

"It generally gets me where I need to go." My voice was crackling with fatigue. I fished the key from my pocket, sensitised it and pressed the ball of my thumb against the screen, opening the portal and lowering the gangway. I offered her a hand up, but she didn't seem to need it. Her grip was unexpectedly powerful, but I should have guessed from the way she'd handled herself during the Eddie fracas.

Inside, she took a quick panoramic look round—which didn't take long—dropped the guitar case onto my bunk, and clocked the bookshelves and the Marx Brothers posters.

"Nice set-up you got."

"I spend a lot of time in here."" I dropped into the console seat and reached over to start the coffee machine. "I travel a lot. My music and movies are all in the ship's memory, and sobs most of the stuff I enjoy reading, but I like having a few dead-tree print books around as well. They're physical objects ... a real connection to other times and places. You know ... I'm the kind of guy who just can't settle down, I'm never in one place, I move from town to town ..."

She undid the catches of the guitar case and took out the Gibson. "Do you play the blues or just live "em?"

I grinned. "Just live "em. I'd love to play but I never learned. They tell me I'm profoundly unmusical. Totally tone-deaf. Can't sing two consecutive notes in the same key. Couldn't carry a tune in a backpack." I gestured at the Gibson. "Looks like a nice guitar you got, though."

She flashed me a warm, spontaneous, nice-kid smile, quite unlike the tough arrogant grin she'd given Eddie. "Yeah, it's beautiful, aunt it? 1963 Gibson Firebird 1. One of the first ones made. Original pickup. Someone refinished it this colour, though ... they never made "em like this at the factory in Kalamazoo, Michigan, USA, Old Earth. Suits me fine." She laid a blue hand across the blue body of the guitar. "We're a pretty good match."

She pulled it into her lap and hit a little riff, then elaborated it, almost like the music had been coming out of the guitar all along but it needed her hands on it before the music could be heard. In the small enclosed space of the skimmer I could hear the notes quite clearly, even without an amp.

"Where'd you get it?" I asked.

"Found it on a beach," she answered in a fairly definite that's-the-end-of-this-part-of-the-conversation voice.

Two could play at that game. "Is Lynx your original name?"

"Almost," she said, "My name's Lynda Xavier. First place I ever played I told 'em just to put "Lyn X" on the poster. Cat who wrote it out was fierce wasted and didn't space the letters out right and everybody thought it said "Lynx". I thought that was kinda hip, so I just kept it that way. And it's a real hassle trying to explain to people that you want to be called something else, aunt it … Jackie Diamond Sandstone?"

I suddenly felt sleep closing in, and I was not prepared to debate the matter. "Look, I need to crash pretty much right now. I'll sleep in the chair, you can take the bunk. Any particular idea where you want to go to find your beach?"

"Earthside?"

I had just about enough energy left to laugh, sort of. "Even with high-charge hyperconductors, this skimmer's pretty much just short-haul. And even if we had the juice to get to Earth, I'm seriously not welcome there. Not even for a picker like you am I gonna be going back for a very long time." I passed her a nav slate. "Hit the database and find somewhere within cruising range that fits your bill."

She looked at the slate, raising an eyebrow. "You still use a slate? Wow, you really are old school. I didn't think anybody used anything but voice communication now."

"Oh, I'm set up for it," I said. "We can do it that way if you prefer to chat with the ship … I just think it's a bit creepy, particularly on long trips. I know guys who end up having their most intimate relationships with their ships" computers … and that way madness lies. As long as I need to type, I still know I'm dealing with a machine. I only use voice in emergencies."

"Like I said … old school."

By now it was pleasantly warm in the skimmer. Lynx shrugged off her baggy oversized jacket and unzipped the top of the jumpsuit, revealing a baggy oversized T-shirt. I turned off the coffee machine and looked at her, sprawled on the bunk with her hands

128

clasped behind her head and her boots on the empty guitar case.

She stretched out a hand to take the coffee cup I passed her. "I'm gonna stay up for a while," she said, "but if you wanna zonk out now I'm happy to mind the store."

I was heading for the shower when the computer dinged and a new window opened up on the visiplate. Sure enough, it showed a beach.

"Susania?" She craned her neck, staring. "What the hell is that?"

I checked the sidebar text. "Planetoid. Not too far. Some rich idiot Earthside had it terraformed as a birthday present for his daughter ... hence the name. Spoiled bitch took one look at the pics, decided she didn't like "em, never set foot on it. According to this, it's still there."

"How far?"

"Thirty-six hours, maybe. Want me to set a course?"

"Sounds like a plan," she said.

I imported the Susania coordinates, made it so and finally hit the facilities. I cleaned my teeth, took a hurried shower and came back to find her cross-legged in my chair with the blue Firebird in her lap. Curled up in my bunk, the last things to impinge on my consciousness before sleep gift-wrapped me was her sharp little profile silhouetted against the visiplate, and the quiet, soothing sound of those long graceful blue fingers plucking improvised variations on Jimi Hendrix's Little Wing from the ancient guitar.

Next thing I knew ...

Rising slowly to the surface, I was conscious first of a gentle blue kiss on my lips and then the smell of freshly-brewed coffee. I ungummed my eyes, uttered the first of my customary early-morning series of croaks and grunts, clutched at the coffee cup like a dying man and waved my other hand about like a drunken hangar attendant attempting to direct traffic. It encountered cool blue fingers and then a lit cigarette was gently placed in its

129

weak kitten-like grasp. I might never know what Lynx was like to sleep with, but she was sure as hell great to wake up to.

I looked up to see Lynx smiling down at me. She looked even more beautiful than she had on Topdogg's stage. I was in love. I felt about eighteen. I felt even more ecstatic than I had the first time I'd ever woken up with a woman. And then I felt totally absurd because I'd gotten all bubbly and adolescent about an early morning smoke and coffee with a girl I'd barely even kissed.

"I let you sleep as long as I could, Sandstone." She sounded almost apologetic. "But the computer says we've arrived."

"It's okay," I told her. "We're hovering in orbit and it's time to take 'er down. No sweat."

I finished my coffee, staggered next door to do my bathroom number and pull on fresh clothes. I struggled into my oldest running-about-on-beaches sneakers and my warmest leather jacket before pulling off a reasonably competent touchdown on the purple grass the coordinates claimed was just a few minutes" walk from the sea.

Lynx's eyes were shining. She shrugged into her jacket and lovingly repacked the blue Firebird in its case. I noticed for the first time that her eyes weren't actually black: they were blue, the darkest possible shade of blue.

The computer confirmed that Susania's atmosphere and climate were still indeed 100% human-friendly, so I opened up, let the gangway extend itself to ground level and stood up to let her pass before relocking and arming the skimmer's defences. On the grass, she moved up to me, slid her free arm around my waist, carefully put down the guitar case and dug Topdogg's credit stick from a jumpsuit pocket.

"Sandstone," she said. "This is for the trip." I started to mutter the statutory aw-shucks-forget-it-that's-not-necessary-and-I-don"t-wanna-hear-another-word-about-it schpiel, but she forestalled me with a gesture. "No, take it, man. I really won't be needing it."

She pressed the stick into my palm and gently but firmly closed my fingers around it. I stuffed into my pocket with the skimmer keys, and we set off towards the beach.

It was early evening, but instead of cooling down, Susania was steadily growing noticeably warmer than it had been when we landed. As we walked I found myself first unzipping my jacket and then removing it entirely and slinging it over my arm. Lynx took hers off too and draped it across the guitar case. When we reached the fine scarlet sand she put her hand in mine. Orange spray was breaking over yellow rocks. The tide was coming in.

Down by the sea, a gentle but insistent breeze was blowing in from the horizon. Lynx led me to a tiny sheltered rock formation, enclosed on three sides, walking as sure-footedly as if she'd paced this beach a thousand times before towards the encroaching tide lapping at the sand. Twenty feet away from the water's edge, she stopped, sat down on the rocks and carefully placed the guitar case beside her. Her face was damply gleaming as if she'd just emerged from the sea, and droplets of water fell from the ragged ends of her hair.

She unpacked the blue Firebird and picked a sweetly sad slow blues, her fingers leaving damp traces of moisture on the fretboard, bent blue notes moaning and crying against the rustle of the surf. Then she put it aside, gently propped against the rock wall and leant over and kissed me, her indigo lips soft and salty as the blues she'd just played.

"Sandstone," she said, a pale and fiery intensity I'd never heard before colouring her voice. "Sandstone. You remind me so much of the boy who left me this guitar."

Slowly she released me. Her eyes locked onto mine as she unzipped her jumpsuit, shrugged its top away and let it fall behind her.

I seemed to hold my breath forever. I couldn't believe how beautiful she was, as beautiful and terrible as an army with banners. At once, she radiated both absolute vulnerability and absolute power. She may have seemed fragile and frail and almost painfully skinny in her baggy shapeless clothes, but naked she was a lithe and slender warrior goddess armoured from neck to ankle with muscle, an armour of plates and ridges and curves that shifted and melted and reformed beneath her azure skin with every breath and movement. Her breasts were small but high and round and taut, and it seemed like there was no other shape that breasts could possibly be in a perfect world. Her nipples were long and thick and the same deep dark blue as her lips.

I don't recall either of us undressing. In my memories, there is no lapse of time between her unzipping the jumpsuit and our beginning to make love, just as there was no distinction between the sounds of the sea and the sounds of our lovemaking, the crash of the waves and the crash of our breathing, the feel of the tides as they gradually advanced to our feet and the feel of her cool wet body on mine. I slid into her as a swimmer slides into the sea, delicately at first and then surging with all the energy of body and mind, her undulating body gripping mine as the sea embraces the swimmer, each thrust and convulsion echoed by the sound of the waves ferociously and lovingly encroaching onto the beach until the waters engulfed us and covered us and she engulfed and covered me and I engulfed and covered her and she and I and the sea and the land were one.

We held each other there in the surf, hugging each other until I felt our ribs would crack and then she broke free of me and we stood upright in the water. By now the sun was down and as the risen moon shone on her skin it caught the highlights as if she was scaled. She gleamed like a fish in the moonlight and I could have sworn that the waters on her face were now joined by tears from her eyes. She kissed me one more time.

"Goodbye, Sandstone," she said. "Goodbye, sweet daddy, I believe it's time to go. Jackie Diamond, you're a hard card to play."

She turned from me and slowly, steadily, walked towards the horizon, further into the sea. By now the foaming tide was up to her knees. I started after her but she turned and waved me back. This time it couldn't possibly be a trick of the light. Her skin really was scaled and her hair had become fronds or tendrils of some kind. With a hand that had become stubby and webbed she saluted me, and now I couldn't tell any more where the water began and she ended because she seemed to be a figure formed of the spray and now the water had reached her waist and slowly the moving spray figure began to dissolve and fall back into the surf piercingly and agonisingly slowly and then she was gone and there was only the sea and the land and me and I wasn't whole anymore.

I sat there on the rock and cried, the tears mingling with the seawater on my face and body and flowing back into the sea around me. For a second or two, I heard Lynx sing the blues again. I felt comforted and then I felt stupid and useless and alone again.

Eventually, at pallid sunrise, I pulled myself sufficiently together to get dressed again, pack up the blue Firebird, and mooch back to the waiting skimmer. I let myself in, turned on the coffee machine and took the guitar out of its case. I remembered the words to some of the old songs Lynx had sung and tried to work out the major/minor shift in A that she'd used in Robert Johnson's Walking Blues.

It was a full five minutes before I realised that until Lynx and I had taken that final walk down to the beach I wouldn't have known a major/minor shift in A from a burned-out hyperconductor.

I put the blue Firebird back in its case and drank my coffee very slowly.

And I wondered how long it would be before I'd realise that the time had finally come for me to take somebody else down to the edge of the sea.

Ghost, in the Key of B
– Deborah Grabien

Author's Note: I've written ghost stories before—the entire Haunted Ballads series for St. Martins Minotaur, for instance—but this is different. There are ghosts, and there are ghosts: what happens when we love the beloved dead so obsessively, we can't let them go? Can you put flesh on memory, simply through feeling? This story—which first appeared in *Membra Disjecta*—leaves the reader to answer the question: is the woman in the story actually complicit in her own haunting by her dead lover, or is she out of her mind with grief? I know what *I* think…

Ghost, in the Key of B

"The Royal Suite, madame. *Et voila.*"

The lift doors opened and she followed the concierge, high heels that had tapped harsh against the hotel's marble lobby now silent, against opulent rugs. He unlocked the doors and stood aside, letting her precede him. He was as sleek and unobtrusive as the rest of the George V, and just as luxurious.

"*Merci, madame.*" He accepted the folded money, along with its implicit dismissal. "If anything is not to your satisfaction, please let me know at once."

"Of course." *Go away, let me lock the door, I know what's coming, go away.* She swept the room, corner to corner, searching for the piano. It was there, a nice Baldwin spinet. Her demand was the same, no matter the hotel: there must be a piano in the suite. "I'll do that. Everything looks fine. *Merci, au revoir.*"

The big doors closed quietly behind him. Another city, another suite, another concierge. Another piano.

Jane's unpacking, such as it was, had become routine. One suitcase, full of clothing she didn't care about, emptied out and hung up, lingerie put into drawers, shoes set side by side on the wardrobe floor. The clothes, the shoes, even the underwear, matched up nicely with the hotel suites; Christian Loboutin and Prada met the pricy flooring of a five-star hotel with ease and aplomb. There were benefits to wealth, not the least of which was the option of buying to fit one's surroundings, thus pre-empting having to deal with other peoples' surprise at how little she cared about what she wore, owned, had.

She wandered the suite, not touching the piano. On the floor beside the piano bench, a small custom packing crate sat, await-ing her attention. She avoided touching that, as well.

Another hotel suite, another city, another world-class view: Geneva, Milan, Athens. The views from her suite in Venice, at the Cipriani, had nearly managed to get her attention. She had stared for a moment across the lagoon, at the spires and roofs of the city shimmering in the near distance, then turned away. Prague had offered her windows framing the Castle, aus-tere and beautiful. It should have soothed her, that blanket of visible history. She hadn't bothered to notice, and she wasn't soothed.

Now, outside the tall windows, the sun washed the Fountain of the Three Graces in the courtyard of the George V. Some-where just beyond her vision, Paris moved along, going about its business, heading toward the hour when the offices would empty and everyone would hit the warm streets, making their way home to the *banlieus*, stopping for a coffee or a glass of wine along the way.

She sighed, a long, complicated noise that had nothing to do with contentment. There was a sterling silver ice bucket on the dining table, with a bottle of champagne cooling. There were also chocolates, the mark of a luxury hotel; in Geneva, it had been cut flowers and fresh fruit in a silver basket.

It took two glasses of champagne before the courage Jane had been waiting for finally kicked in. A chocolate, dark and smooth against the tongue. Another, and she squared her shoulders.

Okay, kiddo. Get it done.

The packing crate was plastered with warnings: *Fragile Handle with Care Extremely Fragile.* On her knees, snapping open fasteners, Jane had a passing thought: *The damned thing's almost as fragile as I am, and almost as easy to break.* Another thought, cutting deeper: *I didn't matter to him. Not as much as this did.*

There were other labels, customs approvals from Italy, England, Greece. It had been her only tangible companion since Richard's death. The piano changed from place to place, but this, the crate and its contents, were constants.

She got it open, unmolding the dense foam, exposing the precious cargo. And here it was at last, two pieces ready to be joined and set where they needed to be: atop the piano, where they had sat for every moment of those six years she and Richard had spent together.

She took the mirror ball and suspended it carefully, delicately, from its heavy stand. A single touch sent it shivering, looking for light to catch and splinter.

He had done that, touched it and sent it dancing, every time he'd sat down at the piano. She saw him, hunched over the keyboard, swearing under his breath as he worked out a riff or a melody line, the mirror ball shining its borrowed light on the man, the instrument, the music. It had been his ritual, perhaps his muse. Now it was hers.

The June days go long in Paris, the lights that spark the night resting and dormant until well past ten. Eventually, the afternoon would slide into twilight, into the dusk and the gloaming, and become full dark.

At full dark, the overheads in the Royal Suite of the George V Hotel would get turned on, and catch the mirror ball, sending its faceted enchantment out into whatever corner of the night held the voice Jane was waiting for.

Long after dark, Jane let herself into the quiet suite. She knew, even as she fumbled the door closed behind her, that there was a confrontation waiting. She could feel it, an awareness of him, the need for him, moving under her skin like a shift in her own blood pressure.

Dinner had been eaten, if not noticed. There had been a time when she cooked ferociously and ate regularly, manifesting through sheer desperation an appetite she didn't possess. It had been her drama, not his: a kind of panic, to get Richard to eat something, anything, trying to guilt him into joining her, to keep him alive.

Those days had become a misty nonsense in her memory. She'd stopped noticing food at all, beyond the bare minimum to keep her going; wine had one purpose, to dull edges grown sharp with loss and grief. Like the food on her plate, its quality and taste had become irrelevant.

Oh, damn.

Soft muffled notes, the barest whisper of sound, coming from the piano and from the air itself. It had to be the moonlight that had done it. There wasn't enough light coming in through those tall windows, from the rooms on the other side of the courtyard, to have been trapped in the facets of the mirror ball. But the moonrise was high and sweet and strong, more than enough.

Hallo, love. Nice posh digs you've got here.

It was a breath, no more, but Jane slumped against the wall. There was no point, hugging the darkness. Light had brought him in, as it always seemed to do.

"Yes, I suppose they are." The white keys on the piano shimmered slightly, calling her over. Almost imperceptible, the mirror ball was moving, catching stray rays and making them into prisms of brilliance in the dark. "What else would I do with all that money? Hire a gigolo? You left it to me, Richard, you tell me."

He laughed. It was an uncanny sound, middle-B on the keyboard, neither high nor low. She felt it down her back, in the depths of her loins. Richard had always sounded like his own piano to her; she wondered if his wife had thought so, but she would never know that. Louisa had been the one subject she could never raise, not in all those years.

So, Paris? Not surprised, not really. Always knew you'd fancy it. Never did get a shot at taking you here, did I? Even on tour?

"No, you didn't." Nails, digging into palms, bringing flecks of blood to the surface of the skin. The wound was an old one, never healing. If the question had come from anyone but Richard, she would have thought it a deliberate taunt, but Richard hadn't had a mean bone in his body. Any cruelty—and there had been some to answer for—had come through inattention, rather than malice. "No Europe for me. You took Louisa, remember? I stayed home in California, cleaning catboxes and being invisible."

Yeah, I took Louisa. She'd have made my life hell if I hadn't, you know? Anything for peace in the valley. You should have raised a fuss yourself, Janeybug. That might have done it. I'd much rather have taken you.

He'd slipped up the keyboard, a sympathetic stirring of string noise from under the lid. It was damped down, as if the soft pedal was in use; the piano's small size kept things manageable. She'd learned that lesson the hard way in Rome, when she'd been given a baby grand. People in the adjoining rooms had complained to the concierge, especially after the night talk had become an argument. In life or death, Richard could get the maximum out of any piano that had ever been built.

"I should have made more of a fuss?" Here it was, the old argument, the one she could never win. She had a moment of clar-

139

ity, as brief as it was tantalizing: *End it. Find a way, just smash the damned mirror ball. Or draw the curtains, don't let the light in. Learn to live completely in darkness.* "I was nineteen, Richard. Remember? You were married, and famous, and I was nineteen and scared shitless that you'd leave me if I spoke up. Besides, I was too busy taking care of you, too busy watching you die slowly. Make a fuss? I didn't have the nerve and I didn't have the time. And you know it!"

Patterns, along the walls and the antique furniture. The mirror ball danced in a revolution like the earth hunting its own gravity, and she didn't know where the light was coming from, but it was here, spattering the walls like the blood of a rainbow, against the curtains and cornices of the luxurious suite rented with the fortune Richard had left her.

There had been no wedding, no vows, no spoken promise involving his worldly goods. That call from his lawyer had been so unexpected, she'd thought it was a mean joke: *Ms. Berg, didn't he let you know? Yes, half his fortune. The other half to his wife, yes, I'd strongly advise retaining legal representation in case Mrs. Halliday decides to contest….*

That will, that will…

Jane had gone into shock, and Louisa had gone berserk. She'd tried to take it, and she'd lost. Richard, even during those brutal final days of intermittent delirium, had been of sound mind under the legal definition. A string of witnesses had proven that to a court's satisfaction.

So, what's on for tonight, love? More arguing? I'd rather have a good long cuddle, but that's not going down. So, what? You still narked at me for dying? Couldn't help that, not really.

The ghostly breath from the spinet's soundbox was tiara music, tinkling and pure: *twinkle twinkle little star.* He'd given her a t-shirt, back when the alcoholism had still been his biggest health issue, back before the stomach cancer, back when he could still walk, go places, make music, make trouble, make love: it had said *I'm With Twinklefingers*. She'd worn it every day for those last two weeks, making it talismanic. The shirt was at home in Sausalito, in a drawer, clean and folded and not even looked at since he'd died…

Right, okay, whatever. Not about me dying. Mad about me not getting rid of Louisa? You ready to cop to that yet, Little Miss Jane of Arc?

"Yes."

There it was, out at last. She'd never said it before, never admitted aloud, to him or anyone else. She didn't know what had finally pulled it free: passage of time, the t-shirt, the opulence made possible by his dying, the fierce intolerable weight of him dying at all.

Or maybe it had been that last thought of his, that little scorpion sting, calling her a martyr. All she was sure of, standing in the darkness and watching Richard's inspiration rotate slowly on its stand, was that, at long last, she was furious.

"You're damned right I am. Why, Richard? I don't get it. I loved you, I supported you, I was there for you. How could you love her more than you loved me? I don't understand. She was only there when she got to be Mrs. Rich and Famous. I never gave a good goddamn about that stuff."

The words poured out, fierce, passionate, buried too long. And something was happening—she heard an echo, bitterness that might have been feeling or sound. Was it coming from the piano, no, that wasn't possible…

Yeah, I know that. I always got that. Took it for granted, I'd say, and you let me, same as you let me do anything else I wanted.

Back to middle-B, trying to calm her. It wasn't working, not this time. She was shaking, long shudders coursing through clenched muscles.

And yeah, I knew you were just a baby, really. But that thing about

141

being nineteen, that's bollocks. Never saw you frightened of anything. And Louisa didn't get the best of me, Janeybug. The music did, and the tequila. You got the rest of it. Couldn't give more than I had, could I?

"Stop it, Richard. Please?"

She was in tears now; the questions had come too late, the answers could never do her any good now, or Richard either. Of their six years together, too much time had been spent in different places. Too many hours of her life had been spent in the kind of paralysis she'd never felt about anything else: *what if I tell him it's her or me, what if he chose her, he would choose her and then I'd die, I couldn't stand it, what if what if what if.*

He was right about that much, at least. She'd given him no reason to think she was afraid of anything. He couldn't have known…

Don't cry, baby, okay? A glissando, high up on the keys, trying to make her smile. *Can't take you crying.*

"Okay." Her eyes had adjusted to the dimness, ceased being dazzled by the shadow and the slow galliard of patterns from the mirror ball. She twitched the curtains open, one window after another; moonlight flooded the room, finding the tiny individual facets.

The ball, it seemed, had been starved for light. The galliard became a faster dance, as the ball picked up speed, revolving, moving, turning the hotel room into a theatre and the walls into a screen behind an invisible stage, powering out rainbows that ran like a river, ceiling to floor.

"You never loved me." She heard herself ask it, heard the question, the one thing she'd never dared allow herself to want a genuine answer for. "Did you?"

The answer was there before he gave it, there in the quieting of the ball's motion, there in the sudden whispers from inside the spinet, dead hands and a damaged heart bringing regret to life, in a major key.

Actually, I did. What, you mean you didn't know? You serious?

"No. I didn't know." The world was moving, not just the mirror ball. The impossible patterns against the walls were lovely things, full of warmth and sun and moon and heart, everything she'd wanted from him and had never had the courage to ask for, or allow herself to believe she had a right to expect. "And I'm not sure I believe it. If you loved me, why did you stay with Louisa?"

Because I'm a lazy sod, that's why. Bloody hell, Janeybug, you knew that. Told me often enough, didn't you?

She said nothing. Too little, too late—but she'd finally got the courage up to ask him, and he'd answered, and that was something.

Of course, it was entirely possible that she was clinically insane, schizoid, whatever they called it. It was possible that his voice was inside her head and nowhere else, that the mirror ball he'd loved was no more than that, a shiny sparkling symbol of her inability to let him go with none of the great questions answered. It was possible she'd lost her mind, gone insane with grief after he'd died in his bed, looking twenty years older than his actual age, down to a hundred pounds. It was possible that all the pianos—Baldwin spinet or Bechstein upright or Steinway baby grand—were silent. It was also possible, she thought, that none of that mattered.

What, now you're thinking you're off your nut? The middle-B, his favourite key in life, faded down the keyboard, a deeper note, discordant in F-sharp. She wondered if she was actually hearing exasperation. *Janey, the only thing you were ever off your nut about was me. Must be why we can't let go of each other, you know?*

"I know." It rose at the back of her throat, love she couldn't relinquish, love she couldn't trust, not then, not now. Tenderness, so much of it. Odd, she thought, that it had all flown one way, from her to him, when they had both been alive to measure it. Now, river and sea were merging, and the flow went both ways. "I have to sleep, Richard. I'm so tired. I need to sleep."

Yeah, you do that. Get some kip. See you later.

She felt something brush her brow, light as a feather falling: a kiss from the air. There were tears in her eyes, but they would dry, as tears always seemed to do.

Love you. No need to ask.

A soft papery ghost of sound, and the piano was quiet. The mirror ball, motionless now at the end of its line, darkened. Paris crept into the Royal Suite, city of light, the here and now, silence and the murmur of another language, another country, a year after death.

The Ballad of Billy Quiver
– Kathi Kamen Goldmark

Author's Note:

You tell me that I'm crazy, that I'm never gonna make it
You bug me!
You tell me that I'm lazy, I'm not gonna take it
You bug me!
Why don't you just leave?
You bug me!

– from "You Bug Me!" by Billy Quiver

The Ballad of Billy Quiver

We were in the men's room watching Billy wash the blood off his shirt when the bartender dead-bolted the lock from the outside, imprisoning all nine members of Lenny's Brain in Marmaduke's Manatee Lounge at two in the morning. I like to think it was an accident, but who knows?

The gig had been bad from the beginning. We'd arrived in our punk regalia to discover that Patcher, our lead guitarist, had pawned his axe and needed to borrow Rocky's spare Strat, which wouldn't stay in tune—not that this mattered so much with our music. So we had not one, but two grumpy guitar players, and it was the contagious kind of grumpy. As the night wore on, it dawned on us that the club had been expecting a country-western band, and we spent the whole evening feeling like that scene from the Blues Brothers movie where John Belushi has to sing "Stand By Your Man."

Billy Quiver, the closest thing we had to our own Belushi, improvised what he thought would be a crowd-pleaser on "Are You Lonesome Tonight." He stepped off the stage, walked up to a woman he'd never seen before, got on his knees, grabbed her around the waist, and begged her to come back to him. This playful joke was not taken lightly by the woman's companion, a Naval officer and a jealous sort, which was why we were all in the bathroom watching Billy wash off the blood when we got dead-bolted inside the club.

Before Billy Quiver, Lenny's Brain had been three girls, Kerry, Corky, and Moonbeam, fronting a five-piece band. Kerry had the perfect look: alabaster skin, jet-black hair, anorexic figure—and a rather high-strung personality. Moonbeam had the sweet, soaring voice. She was pleasant and unflappable, but too much acid had resulted in an inability to remember anything that happened after 1969, including why we were in nightclubs in the first place. A housecleaner by day, she could often be found busing tables and cleaning ashtrays instead of carousing with the rest of us in the band room. Corky (that's me) had the patter and the attitude—a streetwise, gum-cracking, who-cares-if-there's-a-run-in-your-stocking veneer. I'd been in a couple of bands and thought I knew the ropes.

Combined, we would have made one hell of a front-woman. As it was, we got by on goofy charm and cute outfits, with vocals nice and low in the mix.

Everything changed when Billy Quiver wandered into a private party gig in a south-of-Market loft, grabbed Moonbeam's mic, tore up "Good Golly Miss Molly" and poured a can of red acrylic paint over his own head for an encore. He appeared at the next rehearsal with a new outfit for everyone who'd been splattered in the fallout, most notably a pink vinyl mini-dress for me. He stole our show with uninhibited performances of rock oldies and screaming originals. He jumped off the stage onto people's tables. He dove onto the dance floor and lindy-hopped with strangers during solos. He sang Elvis hits in Spanish. He invented a punk-rock Hokie Pokie that brought down the house. He was our ace in the hole.

No one remembers who invited him or where he came from, but with Billy Quiver front and center, Lenny's Brain started getting real gigs at prestigious venues. So what if they were at midnight on Tuesday, and we had to pay to play? We were on bills with bands we actually admired, like the Ruddy Buggers and LWB (for Lame White Bitches). They were famous for booking gigs, promoting them with gorgeous posters, and not showing up. Their catch phrase, "We can't sing, we can't dance, and we've got no soul," made them all the more desirable. They were my idols.

We made imaginative, inventive flyers. We had a small but loyal fan base, an independently-produced single getting a little (very little) airplay on the local college station, and our secret weapon, the inimitable madman Billy Quiver.

We made sure Billy wasn't bleeding anymore and packed up the rest of our gear. It was only when Patcher tried to walk outside to grab a smoke before loading out that we realized we'd been locked in.

"No problem," said Rocky. "I'll climb out a window and pry the dead-bolt. Then let's hope the door opens from the inside." But a look around revealed that the windows were protected with iron security bars—just as every light in the place went out.

"Oh, well, we're fucked."

"Ah geez, the power must be on some kind of timer."

"We are so screwed."

"I had a hot date."

"The babysitter…"

"My dog…"

"I have a mid-term in the morning," Kerry shrieked. "This can't be happening. Somebody do something!"

It was Moonbeam who remembered that there had been candles on the tables along with the ashtrays she'd been cleaning all evening. Patcher found his lighter and I could see well enough to locate a phone behind the bar.

"No dial tone," I reported.

"It's probably on the same timer as the lights, or maybe you need to dial an access code," Harry sighed. "There's a pay phone. Anyone got a dime?"

The pay phone turned out to be broken, its receiver dangling on a twisted cord.

So there we all were, nine members of Lenny's Brain, locked in a bar at two in the morning. Had it been 2011, everyone would have had a cell phone and we could have called for help. But it was 1980 and the world still depended on land-lines. We were, indeed, screwed.

"We could play a game," Rocky suggested. "Two truths and a lie?"

"Oh great. Then it turns into some kind of weird-ass encounter group where it gets revealed that Kerry and Johnny are sleeping together, even though they think no one knows? No, thanks." Patcher lit a cigarette and started poking around behind the bar.

"Hey!"

"We are not."

"Oh come on, everyone knows."

"You think we didn't see you two making out in the alley behind the Philosopher's Club last week?"

"Are you going to believe me or your eyes?"

"Hey, look what I found—dinner."

"We're not, I tell you."

We ignored Kerry's protests and pounced on the packages of Fritos and Slim Jims as Patcher poured us each a shot of Johnny Walker Blue Label. All of us except for Harry, who'd been trying to work up the courage to ask Kerry out, and went off into a corner to mope.

"I'm cold," Kerry whined. Johnny took off his jacket and wrapped it around her shoulders. She shrugged it off, embarrassed.

"I'm still hungry."

"Are there any more Fritos?"

"No, but look—I found a flashlight," Billy said after rummaging around behind the bar.

"I know what we can do," I shouted, suddenly inspired. "Let's run the tunes. We can work on vocals and arrangements even if we don't have power." I didn't tell anyone my fantasy—that we would be like a scene in a movie where the band finds its groove under duress and rises to greatness. But I could picture it so clearly. The transcendence to another level of musicianship; the synchronicity of a big-shot record producer walking by at the right moment, enchanted by what he hears through the window; the fame and fortune to follow.

I used a big purple Ibanez acoustic/electric—I called it the Eggplant—for a couple of our songs, and I pulled it out of its case. Patcher tuned it up and started to play "Look At Me," one of Billy's signature tunes.

"Aw, not now," Billy cried. "I can't do that acoustic. Besides, Billy Quiver don't need to practice."

"OK," Patcher sighed, patience wearing thin. "What do you suggest?"

"Hand me that guitar."

Billy had never played an instrument in our band—he was too valuable as the crazed front man. So imagine my surprise when he started "Hesitation Blues," with delicate folksy finger-picking and perfect timing. I found a harmony, and we sang every verse we could think of, then made up a few new ones appropriate to the occasion:

> Locked in the Manatee, middle of the night
> Johnny and Kerry had a lovers' fight
> Tell me how long do we have to wait
> Can we get out now, or baby must we hesitate

OK, not brilliant. But fun, and it killed an hour or so. We went

150

on to "Dead Skunk in the Middle of the Road," and every old campfire song we could remember. Our band mates fell asleep one by one, heads on shoulders, using jackets as blankets and pillows. Billy had just finished a gorgeous, slow, soulful "Irene Goodnight" when the last candle flame sputtered down to nothing. I heard him rummage around a bit, then saw a beam of weak light—the flashlight—circle the dark room. The beam crossed the far wall, stopped, backtracked.

"Corky, look. There's a door. Let's check it out." A flight of stairs behind the door led to the basement. "Maybe there's a way out down there. You stay here. I'll go take a look." He took the flashlight and disappeared down the stairs.

I found my way back to the others, rolled up my jacket to use as a pillow, and fell asleep at last, cradling the Eggplant.

A key in the lock. Early morning sun streaming through greasy windows. The janitorial crew, an aging Hispanic couple, looked as surprised to see us as we were to see them. But the door was open and we were free to go. In the scramble of collecting gear and loading our cars, no one noticed Billy's absence until we were about to take off. I'd been the last to see him, heading down the basement stairs.

The janitors turned on the lights and we looked in every nook and cranny of the basement. No Billy. The odd thing was, there was no way to get out from down there, either. So we searched the rest of the club—bathrooms and closets and behind the bar.

No Billy.

"He'll turn up," Patcher reassured us.

But Billy didn't turn up. We tried calling, of course, over the next few weeks. His line was busy, then disconnected. Harry and Johnny went by his place a few times, but there was never anyone there.

We pulled off the next couple of gigs without our wild man, but the band broke up shortly after that weird night. Kerry had been accepted to law school and Moonbeam was moving to Mendocino with her kids and her speed-freak boyfriend—that was the official excuse. But without Billy Quiver, we'd all lost heart.

Two years went by. I joined another band, this time country-rock, called Four Shy Guys (actually three guys and two women). I was leaving the house one evening, late for a gig, when the phone rang.

"Corky, it's Billy!"

"What happened to you?"

"I started painting, you know? So I moved to New York to make it as an artist. But it turns out there are a few other people here with the same idea. It's like being on line at the bakery—you have to take a number and wait your turn."

"That's not what I mean. What happened to you that night?"

"Oh Corky, there were so many nights…seriously, it's weird being an artist. I had my first gallery show last week. Instead of applauding and yelling for a Chuck Berry song the audience just walked around looking at my pieces and quietly nodded their heads. So I decided to take requests. Set up an easel in the middle of a gallery. People can yell out 'Hey buddy, know any Matisse?' and throw a dollar in the tip jar. Listen, I'll catch you later. Look me up next time you're in New York."

"Billy!"

He was gone.

He never told me what had happened to him that long-ago night. What happened to me was this: I put down the receiver and changed into my pink vinyl mini-dress. I drove to my gig and plugged in the Eggplant. I told the band to follow my lead, and I played "Irene Goodnight" slow and pretty and soulful, dedicated to my old pal Billy.

It seemed like the least I could do.

The Dead Piano
– Susanne Dunlap

Author's Note: Having an intimate relationship with music and breaking it off can be just as distressing to an artist as divorcing the love of your life. And trying to rekindle it can be just as deceiving and tormenting.

The Dead Piano

The antique store was on the side of the street where the bus let her off to start her four-block walk home. She had a floor of a nineteenth-century brownstone in a decent neighborhood, with two bedrooms, a real kitchen, a living room and dining room. It was plenty for her, especially now that she was in her fifties, and alone again.

That Monday evening, she saw a piano in the window of the store that had previously only featured dining tables, spinning wheels, enormous hutches and other items she had no use or desire for. The shop was closed, so only the lights necessary to deter burglars were lit inside, and at first, she wasn't certain exactly what she was seeing. A wistful fantasy, perhaps, or a wish to be reminded of something she'd lost and not thought about for years.

The closer she looked, the more she realized she was not mistaken. That pattern, the repeated groups of two and three black keys among the white, was more familiar to her than even the alphabet. She had learned their language before she could read. Some people had called her a prodigy.

The piano was not directly in the window—a good thing, since on that side of the street the afternoon sun would beat in mercilessly, damaging the wood and the workings had it stayed there too long—and so her first glimpse was of a half-hidden keyboard, and part of a black case. Behind a forest of chair legs, she could just see one sleek, squared, ebony support, sturdier and at the same time more elegant than those that had only the weight of a human being to bear. It's a grand piano, she thought. Baby? Model O? Model A? Perhaps even the coveted Model B?

She continued on to her piano-less apartment, warmed up leftovers in the microwave, and sat down to watch the news and her favorite game shows. But her mind kept wandering. Why was there a piano that didn't even look very old in the antique store?

That night she dreamed of empty stages and out-of-tune music, and awoke in a sweat, feeling as if she hadn't slept at all.

The rest of the workweek, she lingered at the shop window before passing on to her empty apartment and nightly routine. As merchandise was shifted during each day, more and more of the piano became visible. By Friday, she could make out the name: Steinway.

The blood rushed to her fingertips. Memories of instruments she'd played years ago crowded together in her mind's ear. The feel of real ivory keys against her toughened finger pads. The rich sound, so deceptively simple to produce and yet so difficult to bring to life. Some pianos had a bright, vivid timbre. Schubert, Mozart, Beethoven, passages flying from her hands as she lost herself so completely in the music, she ceased to exist as anything other than a vessel that poured out sound. If you stop to think, you can't do it. The trick is just to feel.

Then there had been other pianos, usually older ones, with a softer, mellower tone. These she loved for Brahms and Debussy. Chopin, Schumann—all the late romantics too. Except Liszt. Liszt needed the panache of a brilliant sound. Sometimes, though, the gentler timbre was even right for Bach. Some people considered it sacrilege to perform Bach on a piano, but she would never have denied herself the pleasure of finding ways to give that cerebral, spiritual music a voice that transcended her own meager talents.

On the Friday night of the same week in which she'd first noticed the instrument, she took a hard look at her apartment. *You should have a piano.* So many people had told her that when she made the move, away from a long and difficult relationship. She'd shrugged and said she couldn't afford one, and in any case there wasn't room. She hadn't played much in the past ten or fifteen years anyway. She'd moved on.

He loved me to play Prokofiev, she thought, a sudden sting of longing bringing the threat of tears to her eyes. Music had brought them together in the beginning. He had had so much talent, but an injury had ended his career as a violinist long before she met him, and he'd become a doctor instead, an orthopod.

She was still performing when they met. She saw him for a pinched nerve in her neck; he prescribed propranolol for her performance anxiety. It successfully steadied her hands, but it made her forget things. Pianists had to play from memory; it was a tradition. And she preferred it. No desk intervening between her ears and the strings and soundboard. Yet memory lapses were the kiss of death, and her memory was unreliable.

The two of them—the doctor and the pianist—became lovers. Times changed. Gigs dried up. Although she reasoned that becoming an academic was a sensible career move that would enable her to keep playing and performing, she knew she was lying to herself. From not thinking about music and just letting it overtake her, she turned to obsessively analyzing it. For years she read, thought—and didn't play. Her dissertation sat on her bookshelf as proof, as much a part of her life now as the piano she didn't have.

But she could change all that. Wasn't she supposed to begin a new chapter, now that she was a working woman again? If she moved some furniture around, there would be room for a piano. Her music was in storage. There had seemed no point in bringing three shelves full of scores to a place where they would never be opened. She would bring them back, if she could have the piano. That piano.

That Friday night, she did not sleep.

What if the piano was in bad shape, and needed a lot of work? She would probably be able to get it for a song, then, and hire one of the piano technicians she knew to bring it back to shape. But such things could cost a lot of money, and once it was done, what then?

Perhaps, she thought, it doesn't have to be that piano. Maybe I just need to go and shop for one, she thought. That piano, the one in the window, could just be a sign that it was time to go back to making music.

Of course, there was the issue of noise. She lived on the second floor. Her downstairs neighbors might object to hours of piano playing. Now she regretted having pounded on the floor when their music got too loud for too long. It's part of living in an apartment. You have to adjust. She should have been more tolerant.

On Saturday morning, instead of going to the antique store and asking about the piano, she decided to try a music store in midtown. She didn't even know, after all, how much pianos cost nowadays. Her stomach tingled while she sat on the subway, like a child going to buy a coveted toy, or to see a magic show, or the circus. It felt good, just to think about the possibility.

When she entered the crowded space of Murray's Pianos and Organs, the smell of wood and varnish assailed her. Everywhere lights reflected the richness of the finishes, polished to a high shine that was as much protective as aesthetic.

An elderly salesman wove his way to her through the throng of benches and music stands scattered among the instruments themselves. "Can I help you?"

When did people stop saying "May?" she thought, suddenly irritated. The man smelled strongly of cheap aftershave. Flakes of dandruff dotted his shoulders.

"I'm just looking." She reached out a tentative finger to strike a key on the nearest piano, a small Baldwin upright.

"For your children? Your grandchildren?" he asked, sensing a sales opportunity, trying to gauge her age and interest level.

"No." Why am I being so nasty? she wondered. She wished she could sit down and play a Transcendental Etude, shock him into awed respect for her ability. But those days were long past. She flexed her fingers, noticing the lack of muscle tone. If she tried to play, he would just laugh.

She wandered around, now and then touching a keyboard, a riff of five notes, like a beginner. She jumped when one of the salesmen sat down at a grand piano and started improvising some jazz.

What am I doing here?

It would take months to get back even a fraction of the ability she used to have. Months of scales and exercises, Mozart sonatas and Chopin studies. And then what? Before, she had always worked toward a performance. It was important to share your vision. Not performing would be like being one of those writers who spends hours and hours at the keyboard, spewing out novel after novel she has no intention of ever publishing—or not enough talent to get published. What is it all for?

She had even stopped listening to music. Once, everywhere she went, she used to plug into her iPod and listen to her favorite artists perform timeless classics. She'd played many of those classics herself, feeling them beneath her fingers as she listened. The sounds soothed away the harsh edges of city noises. But now, she

158

couldn't do it. She didn't remember the last time she'd bought a ticket to a concert.

The old, oppressive mantle of sorrow and regret closed over her as she left the store, not even having asked the prices or sat down in front of any of the inviting stretches of eighty-eight keys. She descended into the subway, empty-handed and hollow-hearted, and transferred to the bus. It let her off right in front of the antique store.

She stopped, and peered inside. The interior was more brightly lit, now that it was daylight. One or two people wandered around among the furniture. The piano was still there, a little farther back, she thought. She walked to the door, and put her hand against it. After taking a deep, calming breath, she pulled it open.

The smell of dust, mildew, and something indefinable that might have been deeply embedded cigarette smoke made her sneeze as soon as she walked in.

"Welcome!" came a voice from somewhere in the back. She heard the sound of scraping against the floor, and then a young man in jeans and a crisply ironed button-down shirt came forward, his hand extended. "What can I do you for?"

She smiled. "I'm wondering, how much is the piano?" Her heart pounded. Five thousand? Ten thousand?

He cocked his head to the side, a puzzled look in his eye. "The piano? We don't buy pianos. Too hard to sell these days."

"But…" She looked over to the spot where she had seen the instrument night after night through the window. In the space where she expected to see the case stretching back, there were only other bits of furniture, some in pieces, some looking almost new.

Suddenly his eyes opened wide in understanding. "Oh! That piano! Follow me."

Together they navigated the hodge-podge of old stuff. Who

would ever want this? she thought, although her own taste was for antique rather than modern.

He led her toward the front, to the view she had had from the window, and there it was.

"Funny thing, isn't it? Some famous piano player used to take it with him when he traveled, so he could practice in hotel rooms."

A dummy keyboard. Someone with a sense of humor had stenciled on the Steinway logo.

"It folds in half and goes in a case," he said, warming to his subject.

"How much?" she asked, smiling.

"One-fifty. One-twenty-five for cash."

She suspected he thought she would try to bargain him down, but she pulled out her wallet and doled out the bank notes. "Can you deliver? I'm only a few blocks away."

She didn't know if she'd ever take it out of its case, which fit perfectly in a corner of her living room. Maybe someday I'll be ready, she thought, as she put on a CD. It was Horowitz, playing Chopin Scherzos. Four beautiful jokes, teasing out the most expression a piano could produce. Musical humor on the deepest level.

Just like her dummy Steinway.

Rites
– Roz Kaveney

Author's Note: *Rite of Spring* is the first of what I hope will be several short stories featuring episodes in the lives of Mara, and of Emma, the two heroines of my four-volume novel *Rhapsody Of Blood*. The first volume, *Rituals*, will be appearing from Plus One Press in the summer of 2012.

Rites

The old man clung the rail at the eastern end of the viewing platform, his stained leather apron flapping in the wind and driving rain. He kicked his feet in an attempt to get a grip on the ironwork, and one of his galoshes came loose and fell.

"For the love of God, Huntress!"

"Which god would that be?" I pulled one of the more delicate of my knives from my hair. I pricked his right index finger with it, so that it would bleed a little. I pulled it up, but not enough to loosen his grip, then patted a square of paper against it, to get a perfect print in red. I had a friend in London who wished such a souvenir for her private collection

"Which god would that be?" I asked him again, in as gentle a tone as I could manage. "The god you hoped to dethrone, or the god Catherine and Mary called to in vain as you gutted them?"

"That was long ago."

His voice was arrogant still, but his eyes could not meet mine. His old arrogance had worn away with the years.

"And yet you wear your apron still," I said. "And I find you in this place of power, with a dead woman at each of its feet."

"They found me." Old Jack was shivering. "They made me do it again."

"And who would that be?" I held the knife to the hollow of his throat to emphasize my words. "Some demon? Some voice in your head?"

"I don't know," he said. "They came to me in the night and held me down while one stropped a razor before my eyes, and shaved my privates raw, and held the razor to my terrified prick. And asked a favour of me as friend to friend, but not as allowing any refusal."

"Men?" I asked him, urgently, for I wished to be done with this. "Women?"

"I know not," he said. "They had black silk around their faces, and were clothed in the night."

"You have lived too long, Jack," I told him. "There was a time when you would not have been caught sleeping. You managed to escape even me, which is something few gods and no other murderers can say."

He had been one of my failures. I had managed to break the power of the Ritual he worked, and put down the thing he raised, and prevent the thing he would have become by killing it. And yet I had lost him in the fog of the streets.

I cannot say I respected him, for I detest all such; but there is a stillness at the end of hunts and stories. My sorrow was for the women I had been too late to save, here and all those years before.

And yet...

"I don't know who they were," he said. "All I know is that I failed them. One of the women below us spoke a prayer as I gutted her and smiled the smile of the saved as I tore the tongue from her throat. I had not only to kill them, but bring them to damnation and despair."

He sighed. "And I faltered. Because my hands and knives are

163

old. Do you never tire, Huntress, with all of your years upon you?"

"No."

"I wish I were as remorseless as you. But you are less vengeful than they will be, I fear. Good luck with stopping whatever it is that they plan." He smiled. "And I choose neither to be their catspaw or your nark. I am Jack. And my dying curse on you and them."

Before I could decide whether I wished to stop him, he released his grip and fell from my sight.

I might have beaten him to the ground and saved him, but I saw little point. And did not wish to. As for his curse, I cared not. Gods and demons aplenty have cursed me down the long years, and yet I still walk unhindered and unharmed. All I knew was that I had enemies in this city, who had planned a working to which tonight's deaths were just prelude.

I doubted whether Jack's slaughter here, or even his death, was intended to be much more than a taunt. I have never met a man, god or demon who was not as obsessed with displays of cleverness as with commission of evil. The small model of the tower I had found among the carved-off hooves and tails among dying cattle in the slaughterhouse of Les Halles, with the slaughterers dead among them, had been just such a boast, intended to send me here just too late.

What they seemed not to realize is that the centuries have taught me a few things, including a measure of humility. Cities fall and people die, and I cannot save them all. Just be glad of what little I can do, to protect the weak against the strong.

I had not been in time to save the four women, but one thing I could do for them. Running through shadow with burdens heavier than their weight, I took each of them to the room full of tables washed by cool water that they call the Paris Morgue, where they would be cleansed and cared for, and those who loved them found. The men and women who attend there know me, as did the monks who did their task a thousand years before, and would not ask questions.

Jack, though...I would leave him to rot where he lay, in the dawn shadow of Monsieur Eiffel's tower.

I had turned to walk away, after coming back for one last look—I admit, one last gloat over a death that was long overdue—when my sandaled foot kicked something that splashed and shone among the rain puddles.

It was a hotel room key, which had perhaps fallen from Jack's pockets or had perhaps been placed there for me to find. Thoughtfully, it had a ticket attached, with the name of the Hotel Aurore, and the room number, 23, printed clearly in indelible ink.

Sometimes, my desire for information exceeds any fear I might have of the few traps that could seriously hold, hinder or injure me. As I looked at the key, the Japanese long sword I call Needful, which was slung at my back with my bronze spear and other weapons, thrummed in disappointment and admonition.

It was right, of course. Dead is a good friend when dealing with such men; but dismembered is a better. I drew Needful, and with my other hand pulled up the head of the smashed corpse.

A single stroke freed it. When I threw it in the river a few minutes later, it hardly made any splash at all. One less possible weapon in the hands of my antagonists.

The room was anonymous. It held little to confirm the identity of its absent occupant save for a leather apron, neatly folded. It had never occurred to me that he would travel with a spare.

Otherwise, there was nothing save the humdrum clothes of whatever his civilian identity had been, and one thing which might, had there been no clue as clear as the apron, have made me doubt altogether that this was his room.

Pinned to the wall was a poster, of an androgyne swathed in

light scarves and wreathes of flowers, with a head dress of the same. Looking closely, I saw the pocking of a thrown knife at its throat, and heart, and guts, and groin; clearly Jack's room then.

The poster read "Theatre of Monte Carlo: Evening of 19 Avril 1911: Ballet Russe".

It seemed unlikely that Jack, or his unseen controllers, were followers of the dance, so it seemed to me that the dancers were most probably their target and their prey. The room yielded no further clue.

I left, not by the door, and came out of shadow some yards down the street in the heart of Montmartre. I soon found a discarded newspaper on a cafe chair and checked the notices: the Ballet Russe had no performances scheduled for three days, after which they would be giving a new ballet. Its title awakened my professional interest. The Rite of Spring? I had known many such, and few of them ended in blossoms and lambs.

The Theatre of the Elysian Fields was a new building, washed by the rain of the night until it shone. It stood a few streets away from the Opera, a building which held precious few good memories for me.

From the noises within—odd snatches of music, the stamping of feet, the hammering of nails and the discord of men shouting at each other in several languages—I gathered that a rehearsal was in progress. Everything was going to be ready, if at all, at the last minute. This seemed to me likely to apply to any planned monstrosity as well.

I took my seat at a cafe some yards away, ordered a coffee and waited for the rehearsal to break up. I sat peacefully, and from time to time a waiter brought me another coffee or a glass of water, and, when I asked for it, a piece of dry bread and some crumbled white cheese.

When he asked me for money, I stared at him and he flustered away. I have no especial objection to paying for food and drink, but nor do I feel any huge obligation. I have saved most cities at least once down the centuries, and the labourer is worthy of her hire.

As twilight fell, an elegant young person in white tie and tails, with slicked back blonde hair and a monocle, and an untidy sheaf of sheet music tucked under her arm, strutted down the street and entered the café's further room. Soon after, I heard the sound of the music I had heard in New Orleans a few months earlier, and relaxed into what had been, for the most part, happy memories.

I wondered who this confident young woman might be, and then brought my mind back to matters in hand.

Now, it had been my habit, these last few decades, to cast a low level glamour when in public, in cities, so that people saw me in whatever they regarded as appropriate dress. I hate squandering on magic the power that I took back from murderous gods, but the necessities of my work had gradually overcome my distaste. Small cantrips are the start of corruption, of course, but I had grown tired of being pointed at in the street by the year of the Great Revolts. A culture of sensibility and manners, backed up by disapproval, had forced me to change what the power of Romanitas and the tyranny of churches had not.

I was used to these small spells working, and so felt some mild surprise when one of the three men who came arm in arm across the road from the theatre looked at me and started to gibber aloud.

"Look!" He pointed, throwing his whole force behind that finger; for a moment, it seemed as if it were feet long. "A witch. Or a demon."

"Vaslav, Vaslav." The largest of the three, an older man with something florid about his features, shook his head. "You must excuse him, mademoiselle. He is a genius and overworked."

167

"Can you not see her?" Of a sudden, I recognized him as the androgyne from the poster that had brought me here. "Dressed in black and carrying swords and spears and knives, as if she were at perpetual war?"

The problem with slight glamours is that they can be seen through by the skilled or by those with the sight, or, and I suspected this was most relevant here, those of doubtful sanity, though a fair degree of accurate perception.

"I've said it before, Sergei." The third man was a dapper young dandy with a receding hairline and pince nez wobbling on a nose that was up-turned with more than arrogance. "Clearly Vaslav is under some terrible strain. His choreography for The Rite is not the brilliant innovation you and the others think, but a symptom. A symptom of madness. We open in three days and we are staring disaster in the face."

"That for your opinion, Igor." Vaslav spat at his feet. "You can talk about dancing when you can dance your Petrushka as well as I can. You have become so arrogant since Nicholas told you that you had dreamed the soul of ancient Russia, hasn't he, Sergei?"

"The whole enterprise is doomed," said Igor. "There is a curse on the whole thing. The theatre manager's secretary falls under an omnibus and the woman who replaces him cannot spell. The whole production is chaos."

"Shhh, my little ones," the older fatter man said. Another man had come up behind them and was hovering. "Trust each other, as I trust you, and it will all do very well. Isn't that right, Nicholas?"

"Yes indeed, Sergei." He seemed distracted. He stared directly at me, and I felt a pressure in his gaze that indicated some degree of power.

"Roerich sees her too," Vaslav muttered, turning to the man Nicholas. "Don't you?"

"I see an elegant young woman with whom I shall talk once

you cease to disturb her," Nicholas said. "Now run along and flirt with the pianist, all of you."

"Such a pretty young man." Sergei was staring at me.

"She's a girl," Igor muttered, and Vaslav nodded.

"As if it would matter to either of you one way or the other," Sergei snorted. "Pay attention to the music he plays, Igor. In a year or two, I shall want you to compose a ragtime ballet, because what Americans listen to. That is the real music of the future. Just wait and see."

Igor fixed him with a stare that was meant to be angry and supercilious, but through his pince-nez seemed merely petulant.

Sergei laughed at him. "Come, my little ones. Let us listen to someone else make music. We are on holiday."

And clapped his arms around their shoulders, hugged them close to him and swept them off into the bar.

"My apologies, Huntress." The man Nicholas took a chair from an adjacent empty table, and sat down at mine. "They are all men of genius, in their way, but they can be tedious in their relaxations. And Vaslav is being driven to distraction by the importunities of Sergei and the jealousy of his mistresses, poor thing. They need to be careful lest they break him."

I enjoyed the way this man talked. As one above the game, who observed and mocked. Of course, I have known many, especially sorcerers, who delude themselves into such an attitude, and they were most of them men who thought themselves immune to conscience, consequences or death. And sometimes I have been involved in setting them straight on the matter.

"Igor?" I asked him.

"A brilliant musician," he shrugged, "with the soul of an accounts clerk and a relentless desire to be more interesting than he is. Sadly, it is only when he is at his desk or his piano, scribbling away at music paper that he is of any interest at all."

"And what is the point of the fat man?" I asked him.

169

"He brings things together," Nicholas told me. "Things happen round him. Art happens round him. He goads men into genius. I am sure you have known many such."

I had, and mourned them.

"Now," he said. "To business. You have heard of our little Rite, have you not?"

"Indeed."

"It really is only a ballet," he said. "Bits of Igor's dream were a little worrying, perhaps. He is a little more interesting, when he is asleep. But I got him to take those bits out, by telling him that they made no sense. And it is quite harmless now."

"It is a death sacrifice, like all spring rites, then."

"The image of one," he nodded.

I leaned forwards across the table to him, as one confiding in a new intimate. "Powers are taking an interest."

"Good god!"

"No." I shook my head. "He has never taken to the ballet; he even goes to sleep when the dancers come on at the Opera. Darker powers. And nameless."

"That's not very helpful, Huntress."

"It means that you can probably rule out the usual suspects. Just go with evil forces you feel must exist, but don't consciously know about. On the other hand, they had working for them at least one of the more famous evil-doers of the last half century."

"Had," he said, in a knowing and conniving tone of voice.

I refused to be drawn. "He met misfortune. But he was more frightened of his masters than he was of me."

"His masters are braver than I, then," said the man Nicholas.

"That fear is your friend." I put my hand on his wrist for emphasis, and felt an expected whisper of power there. "It will wisely encourage you to tell me the truth at all times."

"I grew up knowing that fear." He showed the suddenly unfo-

170

cussed eyes of someone remembering lessons hard learnt, long ago. "Ancestors of mine worshipped the Black God and I heard tales of what you did to him, at my grandmother's feet."

"A job well done, then," I smiled. "So, no problem with your little dance that you know of, then?"

"None—good god!"

There was a noise of breaking glass, and the large man came hurtling through the window of the cafe into the street, with the sleeve of his heavy coat protecting his head, and the dancer Vaslav clutched to him.

"Apaches!" he gasped.

I was puzzled for a second. "Apaches? What…"

"They're a street gang," Nicholas said. "Striped jerseys, pepper-pot revolvers, and knuckle dusters. Sewer rats, pimps and their whores."

"Oh, them," I shrugged. "I've seen them around Paris over the last three decades, but I never needed to know what they were called. I can't keep track of everything."

I drew Needful, and pushed my way into the cafe against the panicked flow of people trying to leave it. I had dropped my glamour altogether, and they saw me as I am, and were gratifyingly impressed. In these latter days, fewer have heard stories of me; nevertheless, the sight of a young girl armed to the teeth and dressed in a black leather shift nonetheless makes an impression, I find.

Several of the waiters lay on the floor groaning. By a back exit, two of the gang stood guarding a retreat. I rushed forward and struck at their hands with the flat of my blade, breaking fingers that I could have struck off, and smashing their weapons to the floor.

I put Needful to both their throats. "Where have you taken them?" I had already noticed the absence of both the piano player and the man Igor.

"To play for us," one of them said.

"At one of our little parish dances," the other giggled. "Our patrons have offered good money for a little spectacle, and made us demand their presence."

More dupes, then. "And if I were to wish to attend?"

One of them made kissy noises with his lips. "We can always find room for a pretty face."

"Between our thighs," the other added.

Such men think all women so threatened by their feeble masculinity that we go all of a vapour or into madness at any sexual reference. It is a sad delusion. And these two clearly wished to defer any questioning by provoking their own deaths. They were to be disappointed. I heard the belated sound of police whistles, and slid Needful back in its sheath, banged their heads together and left them for the gendarmes.

I turned to Roerich. "Is this city as obsessed as it ever was with what lies beneath its streets?"

"I cannot speak for the long past," he told me, "but that would be my impression, as a foreigner."

I seized him by the hand and dashed downwards into shadow. "Well, then," I said, "let us begin our search."

"I have read of this," he remarked, as we passed through lead pipes and ancient brickwork and occasional cellarage. "But what little power and knowledge I have gained in my studies has not taught me of the reality of it."

I stared into his eyes as one recognizing an equal, but one that needed, in this matter, some instruction. "Believe," I told him.

He ducked as our heads passed through the low arch of a sewer junction, "Flattered as I am to travel with you, I am not clear why you need me."

"I do not imagine," I said, "that there will be many pianos being played underground this night. But if there are, I do not wish to waste my time. And you know the man Igor and his music." I paused. "You are probably acquainted with the woman they have taken, as well."

"The beautiful Berthe? Young, talented, a sapphist. Paris has many such, but she may be special. Igor thinks so; she showed him a flute trio that she wrote a year ago, when she was thirteen or so, and he was in an ill temper for days." He laughed. "The female Mozart, if some lover or rival does not strangle her first."

I doubted, though, that those who had taken her cared or even noticed that she was such a paragon. Perhaps they only wanted her to play the piano, but to the tiresomely literal minds of those who perform such acts, she probably counted as a virgin, useful fuel for their ritual. It was with such worries in the forefront of my mind that we dashed through Paris under Paris, parts of which had hardly changed in a century or more. I recognized rubble, and human remains, that were of my own making and had been left to lie.

Suddenly Roerich pricked up his ears—there was a noise of men shouting, and glass being broken, and among it all the surprisingly gentle noise of a piano: a simple tune that felt like a summoning, but which stopped and started again, then a noise of pattering like rain that became the stamping of angry feet, and the summoning of something darker and its arrival.

"There we are," Roerich said. "So fortunate that they chose the piano four-hands version Sergei had Igor write for rehearsals. The fair Berthe will have been needed and so is safe, for the time being, I would think."

He looked at me and smiled. "I have known the odd hero in my time. And you so like to have damsels to rescue. All of you, even one as cold-hearted as my friend Koba."

I know now things I did not know then about Roerich and his heroic friend Koba, whom men would later call by another name: that of Stalin.

He listened a moment longer. "And she plays her half of it better than Claude did, the one time I heard it all the way through. Surprising, given that she must be sight-reading. Perhaps they knew what they were doing when they took her."

We walked quietly, still in shadow, to the door of the underground room from which the music and racket were coming. As we approached, I smelled a scent I had thought lost for centuries. I had done my best to ensure its loss, because of the smoke of which it formed a part—a smoke which the trainers of the arena used to drive their swordfighters mad. And somehow, without the giant wild garlic of North Africa that stung to tears eyes yards away, the concoction of bulls-blood and bhang and the seeds of a blue flower some called Daybreak's Joy had ceased to have a reliable effect and passed out of knowledge.

"What is that smell?" Roerich wrinkled his nose, and made a strangled noise.

I tugged the handkerchief from his breast pocket and stuffed it against his mouth and nose. "Madness and death," I said. "Breathing through silk should protect you. My informant told me that the enemy go veiled and now I know why."

We passed through the wall and into a large room, some sort of cellar, arched and built of untiled red and black bricks.

Igor and Berthe were seated side by side at an upright piano. They wore scarves of black silk wrapped around the lower half of their faces as gags, but also to protect them from the smoke which spiraled from burners in a corner of the room. Two of the figures Jack had described to me stood at their sides, facing the room, with pistols clapped to the sides of the pianists' heads as they played and pistols in their other hands pointing out into the room.

In the middle of the dance floor, two couples, male and female, were dancing jerkily to the music. At first the dance reminded me a little of how the whores of Buenos Aires danced the tango in the early days. One man threw his woman almost into the back of the other, sidestepping the other man's partner as she blew him a kiss. It was a dance that was all sex and threatened violence, even to begin with.

As the music gathered momentum, one of the women reached up and drew her nails down her lover's cheek with a force that laid bare the flesh down to the bone. The other man reached over with a razor and cut two of her fingers off so fiercely that his stroke criss-crossed the other man's cheek. As if unaware of the pain, the first man threw his partner to the floor so that her head crashed and rebounded with a crack, and she moved no more. Her partner reached over, planting a lush kiss on the other man's lips before bringing up a knee into his groin with maiming force. This in spite of the second woman, who had let go of her part-ner's hand and leaped into the air to wrap her legs around the first man's neck with strangling tightness.

The frenzy spread out from them like a contagion. Within sec-onds, all the ruffians and their partners were gouging and scratching and biting and hissing like cats in a bag. It was too late to do more than reduce harm and put a limit to the number of the dead. I drew my long sword and passed into shadow and through the throng to stand in a blink of an eye close up against the two shrouded figures.

"Drop all four pistols," I said. "And you may hope to live through the next two seconds."

"We know you, Huntress," one said in a snarling baritone—this one was male, then. "And your sickly compassion for the in-nocent, and…"

And said no more, collapsing into the gush of blood that came from his wrists as I severed both hands, pistols and all. I turned to his companion, who whimpered a little. "If you use those redun-dant strips of cloth," I said, "you may hope to save his life. My compassion is for the innocent, and them alone."

The other shrouded figure dropped his or her pistols and set to, to tourniquet the wrists. Elsewhere in the room, with the rampaging murderous crowd constantly spoiling their shot, a couple of their companions struggled to take aim at Roerich as he bobbed and weaved through the crowd. He kicked over the burners, stamping at the hot coals with no care for the leather of his boots. He carefully kept his handkerchief against his face.

The two pianists, realizing that things had changed when they ceased to feel pistols against their temples, stopped playing and turned their faces to look at the room behind them. The man Igor at once covered his eyes from the carnage; Berthe, I noticed, stared with interest and a measure of concern.

With the smoke fading into the air, and the music's last clangorous echoes falling from the bricks, the surviving Apaches fell to the floor among the dead and maimed as if unstrung or unsinewed. The two adepts dropped their pistols, and dashed to an alcove at the far side of the room. There was a shelf there, with a small silver box open on it. One of them reached for it.

I had only seconds to pull a knife from my hair and hurl it at him, and my aim was not perfect. I managed only to wound the back of his hand and jar the box a little, so that it spilled silver dust onto the shelf.

The adept cursed and snapped the box shut. Then he and his companion disappeared into the alcove wall. Yet there was no door there. Clearly they, if not their subordinates, had some ability to walk in shadow. And no foolish loyalty to bind them.

Once the person in black had bound their companion's wounds in torn-off scarves, I reached down with the pommel of my sword and clubbed them both insensible, before wiping the blade clean on a scrap of silk I tore from their garments. The sword sang in gratification as I sheathed it.

Roerich moved to examine the powder spilled on the shelf. "Let it lie!" I called to him, and picked my way to it myself. I picked up a few grains in my fingers, and even the touch of it told me what it was. It was the peaceful grazing of cattle and their sudden panic as they were carved alive by men with great curved knives; it was the tiredness of a slaughterman suddenly bleeding on the floor he had so often filled with blood; it was the despair of three whores and the joyful resignation of another. It was the frenzy I had just seen, the passion of the dancers and their innermost knowledge that their wills had been taken from them and that they were being forced to destroy those they loved the best.

It was the best of life, and the pain of its ending.

And it was so much more. It was the rush of power into me that I knew so well from each time I had slain a god. Every time that I think I have finally weighed and accounted for all of wickedness, I am painfully surprised by how little I know.

I turned to Igor and Berthe. "At least you two are safe."

I had been too late once more, but not by quite as much. Dead thugs who had willingly served men they knew to be evil magicians, and found that they were prey rather than minions—I would have saved more of them if I could, but I would not shed tears.

Igor and the woman Berthe were innocents in all of this, and probably, as such, intended sacrifices. All the more valuable, because innocent musicians of genius forced to accompany what had become a dance of death would have ended in their deaths.

There were flavours missing from that damnable dust that evil men and women had hoped to place there: a small victory, but I have learned to value such.

I wished I had noticed that box sooner—or better yet, that I had arrived at Les Halles or the tower soon enough to stop it or its equivalent being used and then taken away. It is bad enough that those with bad intentions and worse deeds take the power of murder into themselves, worse that these seemed to have found a way to gather it and store it and perhaps send it in the mail, or

177

sell it in the marketplace. There was nothing to be done about this for the moment, though.

I gestured to Roerich to place a hand on my shoulder. Taking the two musicians by the hand, I led them from that place of blood and death by the quickest route I could. I noted with some amusement that Igor made sure to grab both copies of the music from the piano before we left.

Sergei and Vaslav had kept vigil at my table. Both of them slapped Igor on the back, and promptly ignored him and Nicholas to concentrate their attention on young Berthe.

"Some brandy for you, lad?" Sergei rested his hand on the girl's left shoulder in a way that skirted lechery, but not by much.

"No, no," Vaslav said. "She is far too delicate for strong spirits. A healthy tisane for the mademoiselle."

He summoned a hovering waiter with a flick of his hand; amid all the bustle and death of that night, I will remember the graceful fluidity of that movement as I do the singing of my sisters dead these many epochs, or the dying sigh of the last aurochs.

Berthe, though, waved all this aside with a toss of her head. She looked at me; she looked through me, almost. I have seen the windows of cathedrals and the lapis jewellery that the Great Inca wore about his neck, and none so richly blue as those eyes.

"Huntress."

She spoke as one who knew every particle of my tale. At such moments I am always torn between being pleased that my legend lives, to warn criminals of their impending fate, and surprise that it still makes its way across the ages.

"My father is a student of Mesopotamian antiquities," she said. "I was reared on stories of you."

"I could tell you more such stories," I told her.

"Indeed, you could, but first I need to speak to Herr Stravinsky." She turned to him. "How on earth have you orchestrated that opening? Those minor thirds?"

178

"Bassoon," he said.

"Oh you clever man," she cried in glee and kissed him, firmly and deliberately, on the nose and then on the forehead, as if a child thanking an elderly parent for a present. Soon their talk was all of intervals and modality, and the moment when I might have talked more intimately with her was past.

At my side, Roerich chuckled. "With artists," he remarked, "the ruling passion to know how a competitor did it will trump gratitude, or even lust. If you want to talk –" he made a sarcastic little sign with his fingers over that word " –to Berthe, you will have to take your turn after the semiquavers and horn calls."

I shrugged. "Now," he said with an insufferable air of knowledge, "about these ninjas."

I raised one eyebrow. "Ninjas?"

"The shadow assassins of old Japan," he said. "I knew them at once by their outfits."

"That's not what ninjas wear," I told him.

"But the black, and the trailing streamers, and the scarves and the hidden faces?"

"Assassins," I said, "do not succeed because they wear strange costumes. They succeed because they know perfectly well that the best way to get close to your target is to look exactly like everyone else. Preferably a someone else that is trusted for her level of access and despised for age or frailty."

Ninjas walked the roads of Japan in the tatters of a poor peasant or the robes of a monk. They did not advertise their presence with elegant outfits in the most expensive of black silk. For one thing, assassination does not pay enough for that much silk. And for another, silk wears well, but not perhaps when your stock in trade is leaping across alleys and desperate fights on lone far paths.

"Still," I said, and watched him brighten, "you may have a point. How do you know about ninjas?"

179

"Read of them, in books of travels."

"Which tells me," I said, "that our enemies read too much and think too little. I am always happy to meet opponents who consider themselves to be clever."

Nicholas looked at me quizzically. "Because," I told him, "they rarely live long enough to consider themselves wise."

I am, for all my years, not especially wise—people have commented on my rashness over the years—and yet I have learned a few things. One of which is always, if I have the luxury, to learn the place on or in which I will kill and save.

I waited while Nicholas and the others slept. Then I had him walk me through the theatre from the cellars where they store as yet unpainted canvases, coils of rope and the torn remnants of dancers' slippers—for there is power in those last which strengthens the ropes, gives intensity to any images painted on the canvases—from the cellars to the high ceilings above the walkways and pulleys and up onto the roof above the great skylight at the centre of the theater's dome, and the gallery beneath it where they wind the great sunscreen across.

"I love these," I remarked. "I always have. Once Vespasian let me wind the windlass which drew the shade across his great arena."

I paid particular attention to the skylight. It was one of the places through which, if that was their plan, our enemies would introduce their drug into the theatre.

I also had Nicholas show me the ventilation system and the hot air vents—this was a new and very modern theatre, with new pipes and ducts all tightly welded and secure. Then he took me to the theatre manager's office, which Sergei had taken over for a meeting, We passed through an outer room where a secretary sat hammering away at a typewriter with her left hand, a room full of mysterious tubes. As I watched, she pulled the paper from the machine, placed it in a cylinder, and put the cylinder into an opening in one of the tubes. She pulled a lever, the opening closed and there was a fascinating whoosh. Human ingenuity knows no end, and is rarely harmless.

In the inner office, the impresario had assembled the theater's ushers and doormen and Chief of Staff, a bunch of tough, old men with the scars of battle on their faces and in their eyes.

"Gentlemen," said Sergei, and I noticed with approval the entire sincerity with which he addressed them and the grunt of respect they gave him for it. It would make my task easier that they did not despise him for being a foreign aesthete of uncertain morals, but instead listened to what he had to say.

"Gentlemen," he went on, "we have a problem. The other night, foreign nihilists kidnapped Monsieur Stravinsky and might have killed him were it not for Miss Mara here, and Nicholas, who managed to rescue him. We believe that they plan to make a nuisance of themselves at the first night. Miss Mara has a certain expertise in such matters."

There is never any easy way with such men, particularly when you walk into a situation and have to rally them round you. I could not be everywhere at once, no matter how fast I patrolled the theatre through shadow, and I needed these men to stand guard at crucial points. Some of them would have to fight under my orders and, in all probability, some of them would die.

Any reluctance they might feel to listen to me was in part understandable, though some of it—probably the most part—would be the tiresome prejudices of such men against short dark women. I dropped the glamour which had presented me to them as a woman dressed a la mode, then snapped it back.

"Nice trick, miss," said the Chief of Staff. "What do you do for an encore, saw yourself in half?"

"No," I smiled. One such man always selects himself as my volunteer from the audience. "I make fat old men disappear."

I picked him up by the throat, carried him across the office, put him outside the door, and closed it. Then I opened the door, shook him by the hand and ushered him back to a place of honour among his men, smiling at him as if we had rehearsed the whole thing.

"Gentlemen," I said. "Criminals intend to attack the theatre tomorrow night, probably by introducing noxious substances into the auditorium."

"Poison?" one asked, making a note in a small book, and in a tone so bland that one might have thought such things a regular occurrence.

"Of a sort," I said. "The sort of poison which leads men and women to run homicidally mad. You've all heard Monsieur Stravinsky's new score?…"

"Bloody travesty," one muttered. From around the room came a chorus of opinions: bloody travesty, horrible noise, I quite liked his Firebird.

"… So you will see that it is the sort of music that arouses violent emotions," I continued. "We just don't want the audience to get out of hand. Last night we saw some victims of the combination, and I assure you that it was not a pleasant sight."

"So what's the plan?" asked the Chief of Staff.

"Essentially, to prevent their gaining access to the skylight, the ventilation or the heating ducts. We will place armed guards— you will be issued revolvers and sabres—and rattles and whistles so that you can summon help. It is possible that they will be dressed in black silk pajamas and veils, more likely that they will be posing as innocent devotees of the ballet. But none of the relevant areas is open to the public—so you will know them by their attempt to gain access."

"And where will you be?" The Chief of Staff's tone indicated genuine enquiry, rather than insolence.

"Everywhere."

They looked at me skeptically, and I summoned just a scintilla of my power. "Everywhere" I repeated and the room became still as a schoolroom when the mistress enters.

With my preparations made, I wandered over to the cafe to take coffee and relax. To my delight, I saw the elegant Berthe eating a pastry outside.

"May I join you?"

"It would be my pleasure, Huntress." She watched me intently, with some amusement in her face. Though she was an adolescent, this was nonetheless a woman of character, who knew her own worth.

"Will you be attending tonight's performances?" I asked.

"I had planned to in any case," she said, "but Herr Stravinsky has been so kind as to give me a seat in one of the company boxes. So much better than where I would otherwise have sat, and a chance to mingle with my betters. Monsieur Saint-Saens, for example, my former composition teacher, who will be so unpleasantly surprised to see me there." There was an attractive malice to her grin. "He really did not like my trio," she explained, "and he tried to have me removed from the Conservatoire as a woman of loose morals."

I did my best to look appalled.

"Silly old hypocrite." she laughed, "when it is well-known to my Russian friends that he shocked Tchaikovsky rigid by taking him on a tour of boy brothels, where he was clearly a regular."

She laughed again, and then looked serious. "Bad things are liable to happen, later, aren't they?" She saw the answer in my face. "I shall be sure to have a scarf handy to protect my breathing, then, and a hat pin and a derringer for self-defense. But I expect you will deal with any problems that arise and I will not have to use any of these things."

"I would hope not," I told her.

"In which case," she smiled, "we will doubtless get to talk further at the after-party."

I was not sure that I would want to attend any such thing. Even to talk to fascinating young women.

Before the performance, I made sure that men were standing guard in the boiler room to prevent access to the heating vents and the ventilation system, which ran off an engine in the same cellar. There was another system of pipes in the room, connected to an engine but with no obvious access. I looked at these questioningly.

"Messaging system," said the Chief of Staff.

"I see," I said, but did not.

My guess had always been that our enemies would come to the roof—they seemed obsessed with theatricals, and something ingenious and showy seemed like a fair bet. Nicholas and I, and a few of the ushers, stationed ourselves around the edge of the vast skylight.

The house lights went down and we were stood in near darkness listening to the strains of music coming up from below. The moon was up and bright, and as silver as the music. It was a sentimental confection for strings and flutes, but I recognized it nonetheless.

"Chopin?"

"Yes," said Nicholas and then fell silent.

"I heard him play, once. In his villa on Majorca." And then I was silent, listening. In the distance, the music was being broken into by the chugging of an engine. It grew closer for a while and then cut out, as if something were hovering. Oblivious, beneath us, a waltz was playing.

The darkness was suddenly covered by a greater darkness— above us was an airship that until that moment had been hidden from us save for the noise of its engine. Magic is surprisingly poor at covering such things. Since most dragons passed from the world, I have become unused to thinking of danger as coming suddenly from what I think of as the empty sky.

With a snake-like hiss, silk ropes spun down from the gondola and men in black silk were clambering down at us. Moonlight glinted from the blades some held between their teeth.

I thought it important to make their task as difficult as possible and leaped for one of the ropes, feeling it slick beneath my hand. Climbing it hand over hand, I reached up and seized the legs of those I met so that I could pull them away from the rope. I did not bother to hold on to them more than a second, but hurled them I cared not where. I protect the innocent, when I can, but these were not they.

One pivoted on one hand. Seizing the rope above him with his feet and dangling upside down, he struck at me with the blade he had worn sheathed across his shoulders. I ducked under his blade and swarmed up under his reach, twisting his neck with my free hand until I felt it crack. He fell away limp, from my sight and my concern.

At the top of the rope, I hauled myself aboard the gondola, grabbing the handhold offered by trailing black silk, before hurling that cultist to his doom as well. Most had descended already, but Nicholas and the ushers seemed to be keeping the upper hand. I had no time to watch, but was impressed nonetheless by the skill with which he employed his sabre and needle-gun.

I reached up with Needful and slashed at the gas bag—this time, I would allow none of them to escape to be a further nuisance to me and to the world. The sword sang to me of its pride in killing so vast a beast.

"Not quite yet," I whispered to it. "There is more killing than that of something not quite alive." I clashed Needful against my spear, and struck a spark, and leapt back down to the roof. The great ship caught with a sudden whoosh. It burned rapidly, but with a flame that only some of us could see to fight by—the glamour that had hidden its approach hid its death as well. Helpless, it drifted away, and I was too busy fighting for some minutes to observe its fate.

It was a silent battle, with music playing beneath us, and then a burst of applause, as the last few cultists, clearly outnumbered, nodded to each other and dived off the roof to their doom. It was just as well; I doubt I would have given them quarter, even had they asked for it.

I turned to Nicholas. "I have committed a grave error. None of them seemed to have about their person enough of the drug to affect an entire theatre, and none of them seemed to be nursing an injured hand." I thought a moment. "Is it likely—because I don't know about such machines—that a woman would be em-ployed as a typewriter who could only type one-handed?" I have lived many ages, and each new thing is, alas!, a source of possible error.

"No," he said, and I did not pause to thank him, but jumped down through shadow into the auditorium, now largely empty for the interval.

I left shadow for a second and sniffed—I could detect nothing, which meant that I was perhaps in time. I rushed into shadow again, and to the ante-room of the manager's office, where the woman secretary, slowed down by her right hand, was placing a glass cylinder into the message system and pressed the lever just before I could put Needful to her throat.

A case lay open on her desk with cylinders in cavities—she had only had time to deploy one. I stepped away from her, and closed the case. As I did so, she lunged, not for any weapon but for a sheet of paper which had lain next to the case.

She stuffed it into her mouth as if to chew and I took her head off with a fast swing of Needful. Pulling her jaw open, I pulled out the paper.

It was a list of names—Princip, Ulyanov, Djugashvili. None of which meant anything to me. Suddenly the dead eyes looked at me and the jaw and tongue spoke without breath. "We sent out the powder," it said. "You will never find them all."

I knew this was true, but I had a job to do here, today. I went to the boiler room, where the Chief of Staff and his men were standing around looking bored.

"They got one cylinder of the drug into the messaging system," I said. "Can you turn up the fans?"

"The performance starts again in five minutes," he said. "We are not allowed to run the fans during a performance. Too noisy."

"So turn them on for five minutes. That will either be enough, or not."

"The audience won't like it."

"They won't like madness and homicidal frenzy any better," I snapped. "If anyone asks, tell them it was meant to put them in mind of the chill air of the Russian steppes in antiquity, and they will think you all terribly clever."

As I dashed through shadow, I heard the fans start up.

In the circle bar, there was a faint smell of the drug, but not the scene of violence I had feared. Voices were a little more heated, perhaps, gestures a little more emphatic. Berthe was there, elegant in a dress that I would have said far too old for her, had it not suited her perfectly. Her eyes were very slightly glazed.

"Hallo, Huntress." She gestured drunkenly to the old and dignified man standing next to her. "Mara the Huntress, Monsieur Saint-Saens."

"The drug?" I said urgently.

"I heard the message tube ring," she said, "and I thought to myself, I thought, that's not terribly likely at the height of the interval. So I turned to my friend Alphonse, who is the chief barman and a lovely man, and I said, let me get that for you. And it was a glass cylinder, and it had cracked in transit and I could smell it, the same as the other night. So I covered my face, and I reached in with tongs, and I dumped it in an ice bucket and I covered it up, and then I went and flushed it all in the lavatory. I think everything is all right, though I feel a little strange."

"Perhaps you should go lie down," I said.

I move among gods and demons and other beings of power. They wonder often how little respect I pay them, and how little vanity I take in my work. And this is why—so much of my work is done for me by weak mortal women and men, helping me because it is the right thing to do. If I worship anything in this world, it is the kind courage of the allies fate throws to my aid.

"I'm perfectly fine," Berthe said. "Right as rain as the English say, I don't know why. Do you. Camille?"

"I hardly think," said the old man, and turned to me. "Mademoiselle von Renssler is clearly under the weather. I don't normally allow my former pupils such familiarity, even the talented ones."

"She is excited," I said, "about Igor Stravinsky's new ballet."

"You'll love it, Camille. There's a bit for bassoon at the start which is obviously a parody of you."

He went very red in the face. He was about to say something, when the bell rang and the bar emptied. He followed them out, muttering to himself.

The bell rang again, and the fans cut out. I hoped it had been enough.

"Whoops," she said, and laughed. "Trouble-making again."

"It's allowed. You did a heroic thing tonight, and managed better than I did."

"The thing about heroes," she said, "is that we inspire each other. Just like musicians."

"Don't you want to go to your box?" I asked her. "And hear the music?"

"It's in my head," she told me, "and right now I feel too sick to move."

She sat down heavily on one of the now vacant chairs and I

sat down with her to see whether she was dangerously poisoned, or would get better.

And that is where we were when the music started—those chords I had heard in the sewers, only played by an orchestra and more evocative even than I had heard them before. Almost at once, there was shouting, and the banging of fists on seats and balustrades and the cheers of some and the boos of others. Among the din, I heard Saint-Saens screaming something about the bassoon, but I could not hear him distinctly enough to be clear what.

After a while, Sergei came into the bar, and ordered a bottle of champagne and one glass. He wandered over to us.

"A scandal, my little ones," he said. "Always better than a success."

"I killed people tonight," I said.

"But only bad people," he smiled, "because, dear Huntress, you are a being of legend, and that is what legends do."

And as the three of us sat in silence, the orchestra and the crowd and the riot and our silence became their music.

Musica Universalis
– Karen Williams

Author's Note: Growing up in Pocatello, I felt like I could reach up and touch the stars, they shone so brightly at night. I wondered what they would say if I could talk to them, and that's where this story came from. I got astrophysics advice from Dr. Dave Clements, but any mistakes are all mine.

Musica Universalis

Clay Jamison loved the stars.

As a boy growing up in the Rocky Mountains, he would stand outside in the black chill air where the stars gleamed like burning ice, spilling out to cover the heavens. Today he stood closer to the stars than he ever had before. He wished he stood steadier on his feet.

The Dark Side Moon Base, nestled in the crater Daedalus, had been built not long after his birth. Inside his cramped cabin, he took small steps in the light gravity, yet he still bumped into the equipment jammed into the tiny space. At least he had his own quarters, even if some joker among the scientists had left a stuffed alien doll for him before he arrived. No one would want to share with him anyway, no matter how special the treatment he received.

His cabin didn't rate a porthole view, though, so he pulled his cube from his pocket and set it to project the view from an exterior camera. He unclipped his boots and plopped onto his narrow bunk, bouncing in slow motion. He clipped himself to his bed and lay back to watch his display of the stars in their splendor. This was his home. Only one thing more would make it complete.

"Play newest, version sixteen."

He remembered a night long ago, when he was a very little boy and his mother had taken him outside to see the stars. She'd held him close and with quick, gasping breaths to hide her tears she'd explained why the other parents wouldn't let their children play with him, how there were aliens and a spaceship, and he had been born to be special. He hadn't listened to her closely. The stars blazed above him, burning down into his soul. His breath had caught in his throat. It was in that perfect moment of calm and glory that he heard the music, if music it was, twisting sounds around rhythms, whistles and pipes and drones and vibrations knitted together, stunning him with their beauty.

Now, almost thirty years later, he knew very well why the regulars stayed away. Only he, of all the children born for the purpose of learning to speak to the aliens, still lived. And soon, very soon, he'd have his chance. He missed his mother, but he still associated her with the stars. He wouldn't forget her. He sank into his bunk, his latest composition beginning. Only he, of all the people from Earth, knew what it meant.

A low rumble felt in his bones, all contrabassoons and double basses. A brass fanfare to stir his blood, as if the bright sea glowing around him and blurring on his cabin walls didn't already burn inside his veins. The strings picked up then, violas and violins and a harp, with the eerie swoop of a Theremin rising above them all, and Jamison melted into the ocean of sound and stars, a symphony designed by his head and his heart. Each pulse of sound met each glowing ball and smoothed pathways in his brain. He—

"What's that noise? It's horrible."

Jamison jerked up, clipping the wall as he fumbled for his cube.

"Stop," he said as he touched the cube, and silence and gloom settled onto his cabin. He turned to his intruder. "None of your business, O'Brien. What do you want?"

O'Brien stood just inside the cabin, the close walls baffled with soundproofing accentuating his roundness. Jamison clambered up out of his bunk, clutching the edge of his desk to keep himself stable. The two men stood facing each other like a pair of bookends too light for the job, each leaning off true.

Jamison waited, turning awkwardly in his heavy boots. O'Brien bounced lightly in place, looking like a beach ball with legs. He'd been on the same shuttle up, but seemed to have his space legs already. Of course he did. Jamison had known him since graduate school, and O'Brien would do anything to show him up. Or maybe he just had lighter boots.

O'Brien licked his lips, tugged at the sleeves of his jumpsuit, then said, "That's it, isn't it? The space music."

"I wrote it," Jamison said, though that wasn't entirely true. He meant it to be what the regulars called "space music." He thought he had come awfully close. He didn't trust the other man, though, or any of the other scientists on the station grubbing for funding. Both men knew he could make millions of dollars if he ever sold a recording.

"Oh." O'Brien looked away.

Jamison had grown used to regulars looking away, when they weren't staring, that is. Thirty-three years ago SETI announced contact, of a sort, and began to build their first transmitters. After the disbelief died down—it never went away entirely—the least hysterical of United States astronomers issued the statement that alien life in some form had arrived in our solar system. Somewhere. And that's all they knew.

Jamison sighed. "Did you need something?" Of course he did. O'Brien always had an agenda. That was how he'd worked his way onto Jamison's project. At least he wasn't an autograph seeker, unlike so many. Jamison wished he would just spit it out. Being this close to a regular made his skin crawl.

"Um, is it OK if…" O'Brien had turned to look at him. "I need to use your scope tonight. Just for a quick check." All in a rush.

Jamison had thought he was going to ask that. Thanks to rich private donors, SETI had a complete array of optical nulling interferometers aimed at the Gliese planets in Libra. Astrophysicists had proved the presence of water and heat sources within the parameters of sentient life when he was just a toddler, and some of them believed that's where the aliens came from. That was only part of the reason Jamison was there, though. SETI had radio telescopes as well, and radio transmitters. They sought, as always, contact.

"I know your first big test is tonight—"

How anyone could not know, between the vids and blogs and taps. But tonight! Jamison couldn't wait. He'd been waiting, literally, his entire life for this moment, his chance with both the stars and his music, and maybe answers. Answers only he could find.

O'Brien wiped his hand across his upper lip, in the slow motion forced by the gravity. Was he sweating? He continued, "—and I turn the collider on tomorrow…" O'Brien paused. He'd stopped looking at Jamison again, instead focusing on a star chart of Libra displayed on one of the cabin's screens. Jamison knew what he really wanted. Jamison's scopes had a special power boost, based in part on the collider's excess energy bleed container. O'Brien was worried, and Jamison wasn't supposed to know. Not that the collider hadn't been a top topic for industry scuttlebutt.

Jamison waited. It was impossible to tap your foot in the light gravity without sending yourself bouncing. He knew. He'd tried.

"I need to use your lab before you start. I have something important to check. With the power bleeds. It won't take long." O'Brien showed his teeth in what Jamison thought was meant to be a smile. "There's going to be a welcome party tonight at dinner. Just take some extra time, meet some people. It's not like your funding is in any danger."

194

Jamison frowned. Of course he wouldn't go to a party. Just the thought of all those milling regulars bumping lightly against each other in this gravity— But...

"No. I can't delay." Jamison hurried on as O'Brien opened his mouth. "Don't you have your own test environment? I know my radio transmitters are using your bleed-off for extra power, but surely—" Jamison paused, breathed deeply. "I need...I need the scopes." The time alone with his stars, the chance to see if his hope about the Libra system was true. He couldn't bear to delay that even for a moment. He smiled, imagining the evening.

O'Brien had stopped bouncing. His voice sharpened. "Chief, it's important. Really important."

Jamison winced at the hated nickname. "What's wrong? Has something happened? I thought your collider project has been going well." Jamison heard voices from the corridor behind the other man. O'Brien didn't appear to notice, but he abruptly relaxed.

"Everything's fine. No problem. You're right. I'll use our test-bed." O'Brien started to turn but added over his shoulder, "Don't worry. Everything's fine." Then O'Brien was bouncing away and Jamison stood alone.

Jamison's smile faltered, but he held down his rising worry. *Nothing will go wrong*, he told himself. He reached into an outer pocket of his station jumpsuit and thumbed his cube, sending the sound to his embedded ear receivers and adding the quiet drone of a didgeridoo to the light reeds. The music teased at the edge of his mind, soothing him

O'Brien's presence had unsettled him. Beyond soothing him, his music meant something, or he hoped it would. He'd worked his whole life to decipher the messages played by the stars into his mind, and written answers as best he could. Soon he would know if his music could be understood by the only people who mattered. His people. The ones who had caused him to be born.

Jamison watched the big man bounce out into the corridor. O'Brien had an ego almost as big as his belly, what with all the press about his big collider project. Jamison didn't see why he needed his lab, though. O'Brien's project dealt with string theory, and the hype, fostered mostly by O'Brien, claimed he'd figured out how to bend space and achieve instantaneous travel. Jamison had doubts, even though his own existence meant something like it had to be possible. Many more prominent scientists than he had doubts, too.

O'Brien planned to put his big new hybrid particle accelerator through its paces later this week. That is, if the sponsors didn't pull the plug. The Asian Union had a point about the danger. Oh, well, that just meant those astrophysicists would complete their research early and go write their papers back on Earth. Their home.

Jamison managed an only slightly awkward glide across the short space to the door. He watched O'Brien and a similarly round molecular biologist, her hair shaved close in the current style among the cognoscenti, bounce gently side by side around the curve of the corridor, deep in conversation. Behind them, two women had managed to style their short locks into tight caps of curls swirling with bright gold and silver highlights. An older man in regulation coveralls scattered with mission patches glided beside them with a jaunty black cap of his own perched on his bald head. The noise from the conversations interspersed with sharp bursts of laughter echoed in the narrow corridor.

Jamison's head hurt. He pushed the button and the door whooshed closed. When he turned back into his room, he caught his rumpled reflection in a wall panel.

"We all look like dorks." He tried a laugh, but his own words stung. He'd heard them all his life, directed at himself. His own locks hung to his shoulders, or they would on Earth. Here they floated gently. He stared at his reflection, comparing himself with the regulars from the corridor. He had thick black hair like his mother, who had been a member of the Shoshone-Bannock tribe. His hair matched the other boys, though it was so black it sometimes gleamed like purple silk. His eyes, so bright a gray they appeared silver, marked him. The space alien doll left in his room earlier had silver eyes and black hair. The stream of shuffling bodies in the corridor could be any of the lines of children walking in from recess to any classroom in his childhood, walking in pairs or groups, laughing or worse yet whispering. He himself had no partner, ever.

They'd lived on the Shoshone-Bannock reservation in Idaho outside Pocatello. The Rez had the best schools and the safest environment in the area, thanks to money from the casinos, so they stayed, despite the questions about who his father had been, despite all the other boys avoiding him. The paparazzi had been kept away, anyway, though that hadn't stopped bloggers, sniffers, satellite imagers, and e-tabloids from filling terabytes about him, or what they imagined about him. He'd quickly been nicknamed "Chief."

"Hey, dork!" His stomach twisted into a knot of pain, and for a moment he thought he had heard his long-ago classmates. Then he realized the sound came from his cube. A reminder from his calendar. "Emily Bork. Emily Bork." She'd asked him to meet her at dinner. She had a question for him.

Almost as long as he'd known O'Brien he'd known Emily, but she soothed where O'Brien rubbed and poked. A psychologist, she studied the effects of isolation in unusual environments, with her specialty astronauts and space scientists. It was that or submarines, she'd told him when he'd asked why. Emily listened to him, and though he'd recognized himself in her dissertation, whether her interest in him was research or friendship he didn't care. He tapped the cube to silence and slipped it in his pocket.

"That's Doctor Emily Bork to you," he said, then laughed at himself for talking to a cube. He wanted even machines to respect her, though. She was Emily, after all. He sighed. He'd miss her, too, when he left.

The music for the last few minutes had switched from deep orchestral melodies to a kind of rhythmic chittering that sounded like swarming bees, backed with a slow thumping beat. He knew it wasn't of his composition, yet it sounded familiar.

"Info, title." His cube stayed silent. He pulled it from his pocket to find it was off, and, he realized, it had been off for several minutes.

Cold slipped down his spine and he shivered. The music faded, and he found he couldn't remember what it sounded like. He shivered again. He really wanted time with his telescopes, but first, dinner.

He brushed at his hair and tugged at his jumpsuit, to no real effect. With the same sigh he used to start his school days he turned back to the door, and with an awkward glide started for the mess. Where Emily would be.

He turned down the corridor, but, trying for a gliding step in his traction boots, he slid straight toward another scientist, Clements, who was gliding up the narrow corridor toward him. The shorter man reached out and grabbed him, and the two men turned smoothly in a crazy waltz until Clements slid out a boot and they slowly skidded to a gentle halt. Jamison wobbled but didn't fall, for the first time grateful for the lighter gravity.

"Careful, um, Jamison, is it? What do they call you? Chief?" Clements, who worked on O'Brien's collider project, didn't look him in the eyes, either, and probably didn't see his wince. Jamison couldn't blame him, though. Of the hundreds of babies born with silver eyes, he alone had survived. Illness, and the regulars' fear, took the rest. He'd been famous forever, it seemed like.

"Jamison will do," he said. "Clay Jamison." He emphasized his last name but he half expected a joke about little green men. He went on, "I can't wait for my first run with the scopes tonight."

"Yes, that's very exciting," Clements said. He gave a little jump, which buoyed him up several feet in the air. "I love being able to do that. But aren't you excited by the harmonics project?"

Jamison flushed. O'Brien's big collider project. He'd be excited if he thought it would work. The new circular supercollider was designed to move particles at a speed so fast that the harmonics generated could reach near-lightspeed acceleration. The particles would also generate enough energy to heat Earth for a decade. Provided it could be safely siphoned to the waiting storage cells, instead of blowing up the moon.

"Sure, of course I'm excited." Jamison tried to sound excited, but inside all he really cared about was talking to the aliens, and finally finding people just like him. With any luck, O'Brien's new energy source wouldn't matter to him. He'd have a new home.

Clements nodded. "That's if it works, of course. There's some question about the stability of the energy bleed. That's feeding in to your project's transmitter, right?"

Another voice spoke from behind Clements. "I sure hope we don't blow up the moon." Jamison found himself bumped and jostled by other scientists, and Clements bounced off with them down the corridor. Clements called back, "See you at dinner. Have fun at the party."

Fun. An hour spent with near-strangers fumbling around in low gravity. No, not fun. He didn't feel like being social and didn't see why he should waste his dinner hour. Just hearing the scientist call him "Chief" made his gut clench.

Jamison tried to push himself off as smoothly as Clements had. He stayed on his feet and didn't hit any of the scientists as he weaved through the maze of the station, though he did clip a puppy-sized cleaning bot just as he reached the station dining room.

He wove his way through the chattering latecomers clustered at the entrance and slid through the doorway's arch into the main mess. The hubbub surrounded him, the noise melting into his skin and oozing down his veins like spicy honey. Dimmed lights let the projected starscape highlight eyes and metal so the room blurred into a hot glow. He lurched into the Director of the Eco-Awareness Unit only to bounce off her into the arms of the tech in charge of radiation monitoring, bumping the tube in her hand, so that sweet goo squirted onto her chin. As he collided his way over to the nearest corner whispers followed him, all with "Chief" prominent. He hoped Emily wasn't there to hear.

Jamison dropped down next to Clements' group of astrophysicists without landing in anyone's lap, though he was surprised he hadn't managed it even with the low gravity. He clipped his boots to the bench. The group had turned inward to have their own conversation, if shouting above the noise in the cramped room could be considered private. He thumbed the menu on his cube to make his choices, and a tube snaked out almost immediately. His stomach growled. He grabbed the tube and flicked off the health cover, then popped the straw in his mouth and sucked. Wasabi and rhubarb, his favorite.

The regulars next to him weren't quite close enough to touch him with their gesturing hands, but their very presence crushed against his skin. He wanted to lose himself in his music, make sure he was ready for his first test tonight. Would he be able to hear his people? As he sucked on his dinner he worked through his planned test, for about the hundredth time, true, but it was important. Tonight he would test just the radio scopes, target different coordinates and gather data. He needed O'Brien's project to complete his, or part of it, anyway. He needed the bleed-off from the collider to power his radio transmitter, fast enough and strong enough to send his own messages back. If he found any messages to answer. If he found the people like him.

"I say it's too dangerous!" Clements had managed to raise his voice loud enough to be heard above the other quarrelers.

Jamison turned away and thumbed in an order for sweet potato pancakes and oysters. He'd just slurped his first slow taste when he heard O'Brien's name from the same group. He shrugged. Probably nothing he hadn't heard before, but he settled in to listen as best he could.

Clements appeared to be in a full-bore rant. "He's disregarding the heat-bleed coefficient. If he doesn't adjust it too much power will be generated."

Another scientist interrupted. "The whole point of building the cyclotron here—" she gestured passionately to take in the moon at large, "—was to take advantage of the space in case this exact problem occurred!"

Jamison stopped listening, stunned by the implications. O'Brien's project had multiple goals, with new energy the primary reason he got funded. The SETI radio boost had always been secondary. And if the collider didn't work, he couldn't talk, for the first time in his life, to people like himself. Suddenly his stomach hurt.

"Clay?" Emily was the only person besides his mother who never called him Chief. She had appeared in front of him holding two tubes, one of which she offered to him. He felt heat wash across his face. He accepted with a mumbled "thanks" and popped the tag that released the drinking straw. Mango and strawberry juice flowed down his throat. He thumbed his cube to music and the soft trilling of flutes flowed out through his ear buds and down his nerves.

"Are you feeling OK? You don't look well." Emily stood six inches taller than Jamison, and her thin form looked light enough to blow away in this gravity. She wore a white stocking cap on her close-cropped head, yet somehow didn't look ridiculous. She peered at him solemnly, the only person at the station who would look in his eyes, and waited for his reply.

Yes, he felt better now. The flutes had shifted to the complex rhythm of conga drums, their rapid beat matching time with his heart. The buzz of the crowd faded, and he felt another beat, a counterpoint to the congas. His head jerked around as he sought the source of the new rhythm, but couldn't find it.

"Clay, what's wrong? Talk to me." Emily's voice snapped, all professionalism, suddenly more doctor than friend.

"I'm fine, really." He tried a big smile, then sucked on his juice straw to buy some time. He never knew what to say to other people. And this was Emily. She looked skeptical, though, so he added, "It's just…all the people." He waved a hand, managing not to knock anything, and thought he saw O'Brien smirking at him. "It hurts being in crowds."

"You know there are medications, therapies for that." Emily was all Dr. Bork now, but they'd had this conversation before. She knew him.

"Not for me. People like me." She knew that, too. She also knew, everyone knew, there were no people like him. Not anymore. Or not yet. His stomach twisted. His mother had sent him to an earnest woman who wore saris and a bindi, with a lot of letters after her name, to discuss, as she told him, his feelings about his place in the world. She was nothing like Emily. "Besides, even though I can't stand crowds I need other people." Jamison hoped his smile looked reassuring.

Emily's expression softened. She glanced around the room, where the other scientists bobbed and gestured in the slow motion pantomime required by the low gravity. "Let's go to my lab." She shrugged her shoulders. "I wouldn't mind someplace quieter myself."

"Um, OK. Sure."

He drew deeply on his juice tube before navigating his way out to the corridor, and succeeded in veering past everyone. He thumbed his cube controls and the flutes became the discordant bass and guitar of classic punk, one of his mother's favorites from her own childhood. The driving beat erased all other dissonance, and he felt safe again inside his skin.

Emily shared her tiny lab with two others, both of whom were probably at the party. Once they had clipped their boots to the chair anchors their knees almost touched. To hide his confusion Jamison made a show of finishing his drink and stowing the plastic tube in the recycler. He thumbed his cube and timpani twined around horns and strings, darting in and out softly in his head. He took a deep breath, swallowed, and faced Emily. "You wanted to talk to me?"

Her face flushed. He couldn't decide if she was angry. Or embarrassed? He couldn't imagine what someone so collected could be ashamed of.

"I wanted to ask you about your work."

"Oh." He slumped in his chair, as much as was possible in the low gravity. He'd never thought of her as a little green men fanatic. Or maybe O'Brien had put her up to it.

If she'd noticed his reaction she ignored it. She pursed her lips. "I wondered if—. Well. This may sound foolish, but…"

Jamison sat straighter and leaned forward. "Go on."

"My research on long term effects on humans in space, well, something's off. I'm not sure if it's physical or psychological." Jamison knew those studies well, after the barrage of tests he'd experienced since joining this research program. He hadn't seen or felt anything "off." Not anything anyone else would notice.

Emily continued, "Since we arrived I've been familiarizing myself with the notes left by the last team, and they're … odd." She shrugged. "None of this appeared in the official reports, and I can see why. The scientists claim they heard … music."

Jamison laughed, but he felt cold inside. He pulled his cube out of his pocket. "I hear music all the time."

"Not like that. Not electronically. Not coming from Earth at all."

He laughed, but inside he felt only confusion. Why was Emily making fun of him? "Little green men with orchestras. I see why you wanted to talk to me." He unhooked his anchors and stood up. "I'll let you know if I see any batons."

Emily slumped in on herself. Her voice came out in a whisper. "Clay, I hear the music, too."

Jamison fled. There was no other word for it. He careened off Emily's office mate, who was entering just as he rushed out the door, but met nobody else as he glided down the cold metal corridor. Was this some kind of sick joke? From Emily? Had O'Brien put her up to it? He thought she knew O'Brien well enough to steer clear of him. Or maybe everyone was in on it.

"OK, stop," he said aloud to the empty hallway. He refused to be that paranoid. And he couldn't really believe that Emily was that cruel. Besides, everyone knew about his music, but he never spoke about it or let others hear it. Not on purpose. The others had, before they died, but never him. So what did it mean? He needed to get to the scopes.

The rumble of the generators in the wall beside him brought Jamison back to the present. His cube played one of his attempts to recreate yet again what he'd heard as a small boy. Each time, each new mix of pulse and vibration, each new instrument and noise, he came closer to understanding. Emily's words ran through his mind. Would he have it right after all these years?

"Stop music."

Silence, and more silence, except for the rumble in the walls and the quiet chitter of equipment. Maybe Emily was that cruel.

"Play."

He practiced his glide on the way to the astrophysics module. He thumbed the cube to one his favorites, a mixture of classical punk mixed with Andean pan pipes, which came fairly close to what he'd heard in Pocatello years ago. He smiled. The radio telescopes he planned to use tonight were paired with optical telescopes. His project's measurements occurred over an array of equipment spread out across the Daedalus crater. This set of optical telescopes, with their affiliated computer, provided a general view of the stars. A view more like a boy would see, lying out on a dark night.

He made it to the observatory without mishap. His palms felt sweaty, and it took two tries for his fingerprint to work on the lock. He paused on the threshold before stepping through. He'd made his goodbyes with his mother years before, when illness took her. He missed her, but the joy at the thought of others like him muffled the ache of farewell. He would not miss O'Brien, or Clements, or the other scientists. He started a careful step, then paused. His jaw tightened. Or Emily. He stepped into the observatory.

When he stepped inside the dim room lit with red bulbs a voice echoed across the room. He could make out the forms of lab assistants but couldn't make out at first who had spoken.

"Clements, are you back? I don't need to hear any more of your whining." O'Brien's voice came again more clearly, angry and tense. Jamison saw the other man career off the ladder to one of the larger scopes before coming to an uncertain halt. He wasn't bouncing.

"You." There was venom in his voice. "Why are you here so early, Chief? Something wrong with your project?"

Jamison threw his hands up in the air in exasperation, sending himself into the start of a backwards roll that he stopped by grabbing on to another ladder. "Why are you here? You can't delay my testing."

The larger man laughed and turned away, as if he hadn't heard. Jamison wondered if he'd been drinking.

"I should have known you'd be early. Even Emily couldn't keep you from your ET's." Spit came out with O'Brien's words, floating in the light gravity.

Jamison felt heat flush through his body. "What did you do?

Did you sabotage my radios?" He took a step toward O'Brien, his fist clenched. The other man didn't move.

"Why would I hurt your toys?" O'Brien laughed again. "You're my meal ticket. No one would give me the time of day until I promised to make your microphone work." This time O'Brien's laugh had a touch of hysteria to it. "DJ to the stars, that's what you'll be. And I've turned your sound up to eleven."

Jamison knew O'Brien had to be drunk. Could he have damaged something accidentally, while trying to do whatever he'd been up to? Jamison felt O'Brien's presence burning through his veins, mixing with his own anger and confusion. He stumbled past the larger man, pushing aside lab techs until he reached his control station. He had to know, he had to hear for himself right away.

He felt other regulars moving toward him, coming close behind him, but he paid them no mind. The controls hadn't been tampered with. He slid his finger over the computer's security screen and his workspace came alive. He brushed his hand over the view controls of the strongest scope and revolved it towards Libra, then he turned toward the scope itself. At the same time he thumbed his cube…and the music didn't stop. The same, or almost the same, music flowed, this time into his mind directly, though now he heard the chittering sound entwined with the notes.

He heard voices behind him, voices of regulars. Clements and the other scientists from dinner. He wasn't listening. Not to them, anyway. The music tugged at his mind, almost making sense. Someone grabbed his arm.

"Jamison, tell us what's happening."

He stared blindly, mouth open, seeking words to reply with but finding none, the melodies blocking his way.

"What are you doing? What's going on?" The tugging continued, the voice insistent.

Jamison pulled away and glided to a display for an optical telescope. As he adjusted the screen he heard a low rumbling bass, so deep his back teeth ached.

The stars glowed, filling his eyes, as piccolos scurried above the throbbing bass. O'Brien spoke, but Jamison didn't understand his words and didn't reply. He opened the panel that controlled the radio transmitters. His fingers flew across keys, programmed with the music he'd spent his life composing. He now spoke only in melodies and counterpoint. More tones joined in, sounding less and less like the instruments of his life on Earth. "Welcome," Jamison said, in the language of music and light. "Who are you? Who am I?"

The bass lightened and quickened, reeds pranced, sounds of instruments he could never put a name to filled him with joy and a returning welcome. *You are part of us. You came from us.*

Hot tears ran down his cheeks. He had a list of questions SETI officials had drilled him in, some their own, others from the U.S. government and the U.N. He asked the only question that mattered. "When can I come home?"

The melody continued, but discordant notes, like a banjo out of tune or a dropped hand bell, melded into the symphony of his thoughts. He tried again. "When can I join you?"

This time the rattle of rice in a gourd, and the rude blat like someone blowing a raspberry. For a moment he thought it was O'Brien. He was sure he heard O'Brien shouting at him. There was a pause, stillness and quiet, then his mind and heart raced together, tumbling along other minds. This time, instead of thousands of ants crawling inside his veins, he felt velvet slide against his mind. He felt syrup covering his loneliness. He felt snowflakes, melting into tears. He heard a trill like a flute, a trumpet's triumph, the gentle buzzing of bees. He shared his joy. Was that love he received in return? The music rose to a crescendo, his heart rising with it—

207

Silence fell like the iron portcullis of a medieval castle, heavy and forbidding, shutting him away from his people. The display of stars darkened to black. Jamison jumped back from the console. He touched the screen, slid his fingers over command after command, yet his people had left him. For now, anyway, he told himself. He still heard sounds, the humming of computers, his own heavy breathing.

He turned abruptly, sending himself and his chair into a spin. O'Brien stood several yards away, typing casually at a screen. The technicians still sat at their stations. Jamison started laughing, a deep belly laugh, his voice echoing off the station walls. As his chair slowed his laugh died. Why had the conversation ended?

He wanted to speak with people again, feel the music of their being flow through him. He…missed them. His quick glance at the technicians told him they hadn't moved, or even reacted to his laugh. He stood and glided over to O'Brien. As he opened his mouth, the other man spoke.

"How may I help you, Jamison?"

Jamison stared. Was O'Brien making fun of him? He didn't care. He hadn't felt this light and happy since he was a little boy. "Did you hear it? Wasn't it wonderful?"

O'Brien's fingers kept up their dance across the console in front of him. "I don't know."

Jamison looked at what O'Brien was working on. "Is that the test you were doing for your collider's heat signature?"

"Yes."

Jamison scratched his head. "Did the test pass?"

Instead of exploding in anger or making a rude comment, O'Brien answered, "The collider project will proceed as planned."

"What were you testing for?"

"The heat bleed coefficient had been set too high. If I had not

208

reset it, your radio signal could potentially damage a receiver."

Jamison stood for a moment, but O'Brien stayed silent. He shrugged. Maybe his nemesis had decided to join his team. He didn't care. He didn't expect to be here much longer. He couldn't wait until he spoke to his people again. He laughed again as he glided out of the lab.

Not many regulars passed him in the corridor. He saw a woman wearing a pale scarf and thought of Emily. Emily! Maybe she had heard his people, too. If she really had heard the music before.

As he neared the intersection where the corridor split toward the dining hall he saw a knot of regulars gliding and bouncing. The special party must be over. Something seemed off, though, and as he mingled with them he saw that instead of pairs and groups each of the scientists walked alone. Clements passed him with the others from his dining group nearby, but with none of the spirited conversation from earlier.

"Hello," Jamison tried.

"Hello."

Clements kept moving, but sounded normal enough. Jamison glided next to him, trying not to jostle anyone.

"Did you resolve your argument...er, discussion? About the collider?"

Clements smiled. "Yes. We all resolved the problem. The coefficient is correct now."

Which was what O'Brien had said just now. So how had Clements known? Or if Clements and his group had solved the problem since dinner, how had O'Brien found out? He wished he could talk to Emily. He wondered where she was, and heard himself ask out loud, "Where's Emily?"

"Dr. Bork is in her laboratory," Clements answered.

Jamison stopped his glide. "What? How do you know?"

Clements didn't stop and didn't answer. The other scientists

209

glided past Jamison, still in the middle of the corridor, none of them bumping him and none of them speaking. Jamison shivered. The need to see Emily filled him like hunger, and he kicked off toward her lab. He used scientists as bumpers in a slow-motion game of bumper cars as he zigzagged through the eerily silent station, arriving in her doorway out of breath.

Emily sat at a console, her fingers slipping rapidly over the display. She still wore her silly white cap but she looked...different. Odd. Like O'Brien and Clements. He cleared his throat. She looked up at him.

"How may I help you, Jamison?"

He felt a stab in his heart. Jamison, not Clay. She must still be mad at him. He stood there, mouth open, mind blank. What did he want?

"I can't hear the music," he whispered.

"The music is inside us now." Emily smiled.

"You can hear it?" His voice was louder, rougher.

"All the people hear it." She tilted her head as if studying him. Probably wondering if he'd finally gone crazy. Though he wondered if she had, like the rest of the station.

"I don't understand. Where are my people? When do I get to leave?"

Emily shook her head. "You're not one of the people. You're the explainer. You taught us all to understand each other. The amplifier has been in the asteroid belt since before we caused you to be born, and now you've unified us all."

Jamison sat in the nearest chair, sinking slowly down. "We? Us? What, are you an alien now? Why aren't your eyes silver? And what did you do with Emily?"

The woman who used to be Emily laughed, but not like he had heard her laugh before. "I'm still here. I'm just not alone. None of us ever have to be alone again."

Jamison was trembling, heat washing down his face and filling his body. He clenched his fists and stood up, taking a slow step towards Emily. "Except me. Aren't you forgetting someone? Nobody ever has to be alone again except me." His voice had risen so that now he was screaming. "Why? Why are you shutting me out? Again?"

All of his dreams had vanished; all of his hopes had betrayed him. And standing here telling him of this monstrous betrayal was Emily. She smiled at him again, and said earnestly, "You have friends. We're all your friends."

No, he had no friends, not with Emily gone like this. O'Brien, Clements—they didn't matter. Now he was truly, finally, alone. He wobbled unsteadily out of the lab. He wandered blindly through the quiet station, the scientists and technicians staying out of his way. He didn't know where he was going until he found himself back in his own observatory.

O'Brien and the technicians had left, though their consoles stood active. Security must not matter when everyone was the same person, he thought bitterly.

"Time for lunch!"

Jamison jerked sideways, his heart pounding in his chest. His momentum sent him in an arc toward the equipment and he thudded into O'Brien's console. He didn't see anyone else in the room.

"Of course," he announced to the empty room. That was a reminder from his cube. Time for launch, for the launch of the collider project. All the scientists would be gathered around monitors to check the results when the collider started. What had O'Brien said about the heat exchange coefficient? He needed to set it lower so that when its excess heat was converted to energy and used to boost the contact signal sent by Jamison, it wouldn't destroy the equipment receiving the signal.

Jamison touched a spot on the console and a model of the solar system glowed around him where earlier he'd displayed the stars. The asteroid belt was closer than his project had originally planned for, so a high energy signal could do massive damage. Maybe destroy not just the receiver, but an entire relay station. Jamison saw where O'Brien had been working. He didn't like O'Brien, never had. But Clements could be OK, and some of the other scientists he'd worked with. And Emily.

He thought about his mother. He never knew his father, human or alien or some combined DNA. He probably never would. His father had abandoned him, left him alone, but he had still given him life. He'd never meet the aliens, either, even though he'd dreamed of doing so for as long as he could remember. His people. He sighed, then clenched his teeth. He knew who his real people were.

A few quick touches reverted O'Brien's recent changes. The collider would start soon, and when it did Jamison had some music to share.

Ragnarok and Roll
– Keith R.A. DeCandido

Author's Note: "Ragnarok and Roll" combines my fascination with Norse myth (which I freely admit was prompted by reading Thor comics as a kid), my love of rock and roll music (which has been in my bones pretty much since birth), my deep, abiding love for the island of Key West (the only part of Florida I can tolerate), and a character I actually created in the 1990s: Cassie Zukav, weirdness magnet. If all goes according to plan, this is not the last you'll see of Cassie or of 1812....

Ragnarok and Roll

It was Thursday night in Key West. Thursday, Friday, Saturday, and Sunday nights always meant the same thing for me: head to Mayor Fred's Saloon, order a pint of beer, and sit down to watch 1812 play.

So I was kinda surprised to walk in and see a different band on stage tuning up.

"What the *fuck?*"

Mira, the Goth waitress (not to be confused with Adina, the mousy student waitress, or Lainie, the beach bunny waitress), was walking past me as I entered the open-air saloon and asked that very loud question. She stopped in mid-delivery of two glasses of some kind of froofy pink concoction—yes, I'm female, but I don't do girly drinks—to say, "Hey, Cassie. Yeah, 1812's kinda takin' a break."

I frowned. "Hey, Mira. What does that mean, exactly?"

Mira tilted her raven-haired head to the side in a manner she probably thought was meaningful. "Well, they *still* can't find a drummer after—you know."

I nodded. Zeke Bremlinger, their drummer, was killed by a

nixie in the Gulf of Mexico last month. "This island's *full* of musicians, they can't find a drummer?"

"Not a permanent one. C'mon, Cassie, you *know* what drummers are like." Mira shuddered.

"I *told* you that Terry was a bad idea," I said with a grin. Terry was a drummer Mira had dated for all of two weeks before he flaked out on her, which was a week-and-a-half longer than I thought it would take him.

"Yeah, yeah." She rolled her eyes. "I'm surprised Bobbi didn't tell you."

"She didn't dive this week." I worked part-time as a divemaster at Seaclipse, a dive shop on Stock Island, and 1812's guitarist Bobbi Milewski was one of my regulars. "In fact, she cancelled Tuesday. Now I know why, I guess."

"Uh huh. The usual pint?"

I nodded. "When you get a chance."

She moved on to serve her customers. I looked around for an empty table, of which there were many. When 1812 was playing, I usually sat to the left—as far away from the pool tables as possible, as that would only get me in trouble—but near the front. That gave me a nice view, but allowed other people to get closer. Or I'd sit by the big ficus tree that Mayor Fred's had been built around; back in the 19th century, it was Key West's hanging tree.

This time, though, I thought maybe it'd be best to take a table near the back, by the big glass table where they sold Mayor Fred's merchandise: T-shirts (I was wearing one tonight, as it happened), shot glasses, postcards, mouse pads, keychains, and so on, all with Mayor Fred's logo. The merch table was conveniently located near the exit, the ideal place to be in case this new band sucked.

Which, let's face it, they probably would.

All right, it was only fair that 1812 needed a break. Having your drummer get killed by a mythical creature really took the

215

zing out of your motivation to play music four times a week. But dammit, they were *good*.

I made a mental note to give Bobbi a call tomorrow. Wasn't sure what more I could do—I already killed the damn nixie—but what're friends for, right?

Still, it was weird not seeing them on a Thursday night.

Upon achieving my hard-won Masters Degree in English Literature from UC-San Diego last spring, I'd decided to spend a few months driving across the bottom of the country in Rocinante, my battered old 1985 Ford F-150 pickup truck: Grand Canyon, Albuquerque, Austin, New Orleans, Biloxi, the Everglades, and finally Key West. I figured I'd stay for a week or so, spend my days scuba diving, my nights at the bars on Duval Street, and then head back home to start on my PhD.

After two nights of karaoke, mediocre cover bands, old farts with acoustic guitars, silly dance halls, and more covers of "Brown-Eyed Girl" than I ever expected to hear in a 48-hour time period in the places on Duval, I finally turned the corner onto Greene and found this open-air bar with a huge fish over the entrance, a big tree in the center, and a four-piece band on the stage, plowing through "Sunshine of Your Love."

Two were up front: On left-handed guitar, a short blonde white woman in a white T-shirt and blue sweat pants; on bass, a tall black man with dreadlocks, wearing sunglasses, an open button-down T-shirt, and drawstring pants. Behind them were another short blonde on the keyboards—she came up front to play a second guitar or mandolin every once in a while—and a short, round white guy with a shaved head, and the world's longest chin-beard behind the drumkit. That last was the late Zeke Bremingler.

Bobbi's the lead guitarist, and she was like a buzzsaw on Clapton's riff. They followed that with "Love Reign O'er Me," where the keyboardist—Jane Ann Naharodney, who insisted on the stage name "Jana Naha"—made the piano sound like a waterfall. But what won me over was their cover of Paul Simon's "You Can Call Me Al." Not only did Chet Smith nail the bass line, but Jana whipped out a tin whistle for that solo. Even Simon used a keyboard for that when he played it live.

Best of all, they didn't play "Brown-Eyed Girl" once. Or "Freebird," for that matter.

After my week-long trip entered its second month, I started talking to the band. By then I'd spent enough time at Seaclipse that they were thinking about hiring me, especially since I was a certified dive-master *and* I knew how to steer a boat. Luring not only Zeke, Bobbi, and Jana, but all six of Bobbi's dive-nut brothers to take their business to Seaclipse did the trick. I'd become good friends with Bobbi, Jana, and Zeke, and Chet tolerated my being in his presence. (He's a bass player, what do you want?)

Nine months later, it was a rare 1812 gig I didn't show up for. Sometimes there were odd circumstances—I was sick, they needed me to run a night dive at Seaclipse, having to get that dragon out of the garden of the B&B I was living in—but I'd tried very hard never to miss a gig.

This was the first one *they'd* missed.

I looked at the new band. They were setting up, plugging in, tuning, and so on. Well, most of them were. There was this one guy, not too tall, with flowing blond hair, a red-blond goatee, ice-blue eyes, and one of those physiques that men probably thought impressed women, but which bitter experience has told me usually meant the guy was compensating for anatomical deficiencies elsewhere. He was standing off to the side, trying to look important while not actually doing anything.

He just *had* to be the lead singer.

Mira came over with my beer. "So who are these guys?" I asked as I grabbed it and gulped down a quarter of it at once.

"They're called Jötunheim."

217

Running the back of my wrist across my mouth, I asked, "Seriously?"

Nodding, Mira said, "Yeah, with those two dots over the O."

"An umlaut? Geez." I shook my head and looked over at the lead singer, who was now chatting with a woman in a tank top and shorts who'd just come out of the rest room. "How Nordic. And short, blond, and sinewy over there looks like a Viking who wandered into the wrong century anyhow, so the name kinda fits."

"Actually, he's kinda cute."

I whirled and stared at Mira. That drummer, Terry, that she dated? She went out with him because he was very tall, extremely skinny, and had dark hair, which put him in company with every other guy Mira had dated in the nine months I'd been living in Key West. Jötunheim's lead singer was the exact opposite of her type.

She also had this goofy smile on her face. Mira had dark hair, pale skin, wore all-black even in the hot sun of Key West, had black nail and toe polish, and smoked like a chimney. I think I've seen her smile once, maybe.

So why the hell was she getting moony-eyed over *that* guy?

A signal from another table got her attention and she went off to help them, so I didn't get the chance to ask her about it. Reaching into the pocket of my shorts, I pulled out my smartphone and looked up Jötunheim. Unfortunately, all the references I could find online were either to Norse mythology, Marvel Comics, or World of Warcraft, so not much help there.

By the time my beer was down to almost nothing, the band was ready to start. Ihor, the bartender, grabbed the PA microphone and said, "Okay, everyone, let's have a big Mayor Fred's welcome for Jötunheim!"

The applause that followed was a mix of excited and reluctant. I went for a good old-fashioned golf-clap, myself—just enough to be polite.

"Good evening, Key West!" the singer said into the microphone up front. Next to him, the two guitarists—one acoustic, one electric—and the bass player were doing some last-minute tuning. I noticed a violin on a stand on the floor next to the acoustic guitarist, and I shuddered. A good fiddler was a noble thing, but a bad fiddler could absolutely and irrevocably destroy a band's entire sound forever.

"My name's Gunnar Rikardsen, and we are Jötunheim."

I shook my head and chuckled. With a name like that, he almost *had* to call the band Jötunheim, didn't he?

The electric guitar broke into the eleven-note riff from the Beatles' "Day Tripper." As openers went, it wasn't a bad choice. Everyone knew the song, and it bounced, so it might get a few feet onto the dance floor—which at Mayor Fred's was just the bit of floor between the stage and the bar.

Having said that, the rendition wasn't anything special. I mean, the notes matched what Lennon and McCartney did, but there wasn't any *oomph*. So imagine my surprise when the song ended and the applause practically shook the beer glasses off the tables, it was so raucous.

I'd only heard applause like that in Mayor Fred's once before, about two months back. That night, 1812 was particularly *on*. It was Saturday, the place was packed, including about a dozen college students there for somebody's birthday, and they'd just *killed* with everything they did. The birthday boy asked for a Bob Dylan song, and they decided to do "Like a Rolling Stone." Jana's keyboards pierced the crowd, filling the room with the five-note organ bit during the chorus, Bobbi did a buzzsaw of a guitar solo, and Chet, Jana, and Bobbi all sang "How does it feel" in three-part harmony with so much energy that I got goosebumps just listening to them. I still get them, thinking about it.

The Thursday night crowd at Mayor Fred's, which was about half the size, responded with the same enthusiasm to this mediocre version of "Day Tripper" that Saturday night crowd two months ago to the most transcendent version of "Like a Rolling Stone" I've ever heard in my life.

And it only got worse. Don't get me wrong, they were a perfectly adequate cover band, but that just made them like everybody else on the island. None of the musicians screwed up anything—which actually put them one up on some of the guys on Duval Street—and Gunnar had a nice little tenor that he didn't strain too much.

But the crowd just ate it the hell up. It was like they'd gotten into a time machine to see the Rolling Stones in 1971 or something.

There was only one other person who didn't seem impressed: an older guy with a shock of white hair, sitting up front near the speakers. He nursed an amber drink of some kind—bourbon? Scotch?—and seemed to be very much not enjoying himself. I wondered why he didn't just leave.

I wondered the same thing about myself. After the crowd went batshit for the most uninteresting version of "House of the Rising Sun" ever, I noticed the second guitarist picking up the violin, at which point I finally gave up. No way was I subjecting myself to that.

I finished off my second pint of beer, got up, and headed out. I didn't pay my tab before I left. Normally that wasn't an issue, especially on a Thursday, because I'd be back the next three nights. Now, though, I wasn't so sure.

Still, everyone who worked there knew where I lived and where I worked. Hell, Mira, Lainie, and Adina probably all had my debit card number memorized…

I walked out onto Greene Street, the evening breeze blowing through the rat's nest of blond curls that I laughingly refer to as my hair. It wasn't even midnight yet, so there were plenty of folks on the street, and I found my mood—already soured by what just happened in Mayor Fred's—worsened by having to landshark through throngs of drunken tourists, drunken college students, and drunken locals.

(The way you told them apart, in case you were wondering, was simple. The tourists crashed into you and then apologized; the students crashed into you and *didn't* apologize; and the locals were able to avoid crashing into you.)

Luckily, after I made the right onto Duval, it was only a couple of blocks to Eaton Street. Cover bands, drunken shouting, and wretched karaoke all competed for my ears' attention. I was so used to closing Mayor Fred's down at four in the morning that I forgot what a zoo Duval turned into between the hours of ten p.m. and two a.m.

Just as I was about to cross Caroline Street, walking past the Bull and Whistle, a shit-faced white guy walked up to me, beer dripping from his five-o'clock shadow—which was getting into prime time at this point—and asked, "Where'za strip clubs at?" Then he squinted. "You're fuckin' tall, lady."

"I'm also tall when I'm celibate," I said with a smirk. At 5'11", I got that a lot. Then I gave him directions to the Mel Fisher Maritime Museum, which closed over six hours ago.

"Nicely done," came a voice from behind me. I turned to see Lio, the six-seven, no-necked bouncer for the Bull. "Shoulda known you could handle his drunken ass on your own, but I was here for backup just in case."

"'Preciate that, Lio," I said with a smile. I'd never actually en-countered Lio anywhere but in the doorway to the Bull, but since that bar was a block from where I lived, and halfway between it and my primary night-time destination, we saw each other a lot. I was fairly certain I'd never told him my name, and I had no rec-ollection of how I learned his.

With a nod to Lio, I continued to Eaton, turned left, and walked the two hundred feet to a white house with a big blue porch, on top of which was a sign that read BOTTROFF HOUSE BED & BREAKFAST. For the first month, this was where I'd stayed. After that, with my cash reserves starting to run out, I offered to update the B&B's web site. The owner, Debbie Dellamonica, had web skills that were probably cutting-edge in 1996 when she created the site, and as far as I could tell, she hadn't updated it since. I brought it into the 21st century, and she let me stay there *gratis* as long as I maintained the web site and did whatever other work around the B&B needed doing.

I walked around the main house, wandered through the garden's palm trees, past bushes and our parrot Harry S—who was asleep, thank goodness—before arriving at one of the rear cottages. I trudged up the wooden stairs to my second-story place, using my key to open the sliding glass door.

"My goodness, are you ill?"

I sighed. Somehow, I just *knew* that the captain was gonna give me shit. "No, I'm not ill, I just decided to call it an early night."

"The only time in the past you have returned from your drunken perambulations before the witching hour was when you were suffering an illness."

I pulled off my cream-colored Mayor Fred's T-shirt, which I knew would get the old bastard's blood boiling.

Sure enough: "Must you do that?"

"It's my damn house, I can undress if I want to." I had on my one-piece bathing suit under the shirt and my shorts anyhow.

"In fact, it is *my* residence, bought and paid for by the fruits of my own labors, thank you very much."

"Cap, I'm really not in the mood for the usual banter tonight, so can we just skip to the part where I take my clothes off, you disappear in a huff, and I go to sleep?"

Now he sounded concerned. "You *are* ill."

"No, just cranky."

"Oh dear. It's not your moon time, is it?"

I stopped in mid-shorts-removal. "'Moon time'? Okay, now you're just making stuff up. They didn't really call it that in the nineteenth century, did they?"

"My wife did, on those rare occasions when she spoke of such things before me."

"Which was never?"

There was a brief, semi-awkward pause. The captain and I had those periodically.

Look, I don't know why no one else who stays at the Bottroff House can see or hear the ghost of Captain Jeremiah Bottroff, the wrecker captain who built this place in the 1840s, but I can. He's been my *de facto* roommate since I first started staying here, and he's also far from the weirdest thing that's happened to me. I didn't talk to Debbie about it—or anyone else, for that matter— but I'd kinda gotten used to being his Mrs. Muir over the past nine months.

There was a sudden breeze in the room, which meant he was gone and I could strip in peace. I'd long since stopped being self-conscious around the captain, but I didn't always want to fuck with his head, either. It wasn't his fault I was his first, and so far only, source of conversation the past 150 years.

Since it was still spring, I didn't need to turn on the AC. Keeping the windows open and the wooden ceiling fan over the bed going did the trick. So I just fell onto the bed without even bothering to pull the covers down. My head hit the pillow, and then I proceeded to stare at the ceiling fan for a very long time.

You ever try going to bed five hours earlier than usual? I know people who can do it, no problem. Me, I tend to settle into a rhythm, and it's a bitch to get out of it. In college, I got up every morning at the time of whatever my earliest class of the week was, even if I didn't have that class that day. Drove me nuts.

I tried everything, from trying to let the oscillations of the ceiling fan hypnotize me to getting up to check my e-mail to taking a

223

quick shower to tossing and turning. For all that, I didn't actually fall asleep until almost five.

Like clockwork, I woke up at 11, crawled out of bed, guzzled some of Debbie's amazing coffee—she always served Hawai'ian Kona and it was to die for—and hopped into Rocinante in plenty of time to drive down Route 1 to Seaclipse. As I inched along behind all the other cars on the only road that traversed the entirety of the Florida Keys, I wondered why that old man at Mayor Fred's stuck around so long to listen to Jötunheim when he obviously was as indifferent to them as I was. Was he related to someone in the band, maybe?

According to an e-mail this morning, I had four people for my one o'clock dive. I recognized three of the names: a couple who'd been diving every afternoon for the past week as part of their week-long vacation (I'd already warned them not to get sucked in the way I did), and Rany, a local who dove with me every Friday. The fourth was new, probably a tourist, named V.E. Bolverk.

Just before the bridge to Cow Key, I turned right and drove down to the coast, pulling into the large driveway that Seaclipse shared with the Waterfront. The latter was a restaurant that survived mainly because people were usually starving after a dive and would eat anything, no matter how wretched, a maxim they proved after every Seaclipse dive. I always swore I'd never eat at the Waterfront again after each time I did the Salmonella Shuffle there, but I kept going back anyhow. Bastards.

Anyhow, my couple was already there. So was the old man from the bar last night.

I nearly dropped my air tank.

This was my first good look at him—I only saw the right side of his head at Mayor Fred's—and I realized that he was missing his left eye. No eyepatch, no prosthetic, just an empty socket. Weirdly, it looked right on him. His white hair, which had been hanging loose at the bar, was now tied into a small ponytail, and he was already wearing the neoprene suit.

He and the couple were all looking at air tanks to rent. I had my own—why else do you think I drive around in a 25-year-old pickup? it's the best way to haul the tank around—but most people just rented when they dove. Especially travelers; you don't want to try and get a giant metal tube through airport security…

The female of the couple noticed me first. "Hey, Cassie!"

"Hey, Hannah—David. And you must be Mr. Bolverk. I'm Cassie Zukav, I'll be your dive-master."

Bolverk stepped forward and offered his hand. "A pleasure, Ms. Zukav. I'm sorry we didn't get to speak last evening at the saloon, but you departed before I had the opportunity to introduce myself."

I smiled. "That was going to be my line. Only, y'know, with fewer words. Why'd you stick around so long?"

"I am acquainted with the lead singer."

"Not even a relative, huh?" I chuckled. "Well, you're a better man than I am. We're just waiting on one more—"

From behind the desk, one of Seaclipse's owners, Cara Zimmerman, said, "Rany just called—he can't make it."

"Okay, then." Rany usually only made it to two-thirds of his appointed dives, anyhow. "Which one we got, Cara?"

"We've left *Harpo* for you."

"Great. Let's go, guys." Seaclipse had three dive boats, which Cara and her husband, Andy Wasserstein, had named *Groucho*, *Chico*, and *Harpo*. I usually preferred *Groucho*, but as a part-timer, I never got first pick. As we boarded the boat, I asked Bolverk, "Have you ever dived in the Gulf of Mexico before?" He had to be an experienced and certified diver, otherwise Cara and Andy wouldn't have signed him up for a dive.

"No, only in the northern Atlantic."

My eyes widened. "Really? Yowza." I cut my teeth in the Pacific, which was horribly frigid compared to what you got off the

Florida coast, but the northern Atlantic was like diving in ice water. "Well, this should be nice and warm for you."

Because Hannah and David had already done the close-by dives, I went out a little further to where I knew there were some nice fish and beautiful coral reefs—David had purchased an underwater digital camera, so I went to where he'd get some good shots.

Since there were only three customers, I had to go underwater also, since you didn't dive without a buddy. Obviously, the happy couple stayed together, so I got to dive with Bolverk.

I anchored *Harpo* and put up the red flag with the diagonal white stripe that signified that we were a diving boat. We all checked each other's equipment one last time, and then we all went under.

It's so beautiful underwater. There's really nothing on land that can compare to it. There are so many different shapes, sizes, and colors, and the water embraces you and takes you in.

Bolverk and I went down by a beautiful coral reef. This one had so far remained undamaged by pollution or carelessness. Picture a cauliflower made of porcelain, and you'll have an idea what an unspoiled reef looks like.

There were critters all over the place, too, and I made sure to snap a few pictures. I got an especially nice shot of a blue angelfish. A moment later, something caught my eye. I swam over to the other side of the reef.

Something was poking out from under the sand at the bottom. It looked like something that had been deeply buried, and then unearthed by the current. The two ends of it looks to still be pretty well buried.

You found all sorts of garbage down here, but this one looked different than the usual detritus that collected. It actually looked like the tail of a lizard—but the scales were a deep, emerald green that was sharper than any amphibian I'd ever seen. And between the scales, it almost looked like a tinge of gold...

Someone less scrupulous than I would have tried to unearth it, but there were several issues there. For one thing, it was just a small tube- or tail-like piece that was buried on either side, and there was no way to tell how deep it went. For another, I preferred to leave the ocean be. I saw myself as an observer, not a participant, in what was going on down there.

After a while, Bolverk and I swam back to the boat, making a safety stop partway up. When we clambered back into *Harpo*, I saw that Hannah and David were already in the boat, the sun reflecting off the drops of water on their face and hair and on their neoprene suits.

"*There* you are," Hannah said with a grin. "We were starting to get worried."

I chuckled. "Sorry, found something weird." I turned the digital camera's display on and scrolled over to the picture of the weird lizard-tail thingie. "That look familiar to any of you?" I showed it to Hannah, David, and Bolverk in turn.

"Nope."

"Don't look like nothin' I ever saw, no."

Bolverk frowned. "It looks like nothing seen on Earth."

"So what," David said with a laugh, "you're sayin' it's alien? That's rich."

"I said no such thing," Bolverk said gravely.

There was a brief awkward pause. I started *Harpo* up and steered her back to Seaclipse.

Neither Cara nor Andy recognized the tail either. I sighed and wondered if I should've bothered getting prints of the pictures I took. Prints of my digital photography graced the walls of the Bottroff House. But I preferred ones I could identify.

Bolverk signed up for more dives for the next several days, which I took as a compliment. It was a relief, too, since I had no idea how he'd liked the dive, and I'm usually pretty good at reading people.

As I was loading up Rocinante, my phone beeped with a text message from Bobbi: "Going to Fred's to see new band. Coming?"

Oddly, I hadn't decided what I was doing tonight. I couldn't recall a Friday night where I didn't know what I was doing since I came down here. I didn't really want to go see Jötunheim again. But if Bobbi was going to be there, maybe I could get a straight answer about what was going on with 1812.

Bolverk passed me by in the parking lot. "Will I see you this evening at the saloon?"

That clinched it. I needed to know more about this guy, especially since he was the only other person who seemed unaffected by whatever mind-altering substance Jötunheim put in their amplifiers.

"You bet," I said, even as I texted a similar sentiment back to Bobbi.

Bolverk nodded, and walked off through the parking lot and continued in the general direction of Route 1. I wondered if he was going to walk all the way to Key West.

I climbed into Rocinante and pulled out onto the road, but I didn't see Bolverk anywhere. Maybe he just parked somewhere else.

That night, Mayor Fred's was *packed*, way more than was normal, even on a Friday night. All the seats were taken, and people were jammed onto the dance floor. I procrastinated getting there, so the band was already on stage, and meandering through a lackluster version of Led Zeppelin's "Whole Lotta Love."

I found Bobbi and Jana both leaning against the merch table. Gratefully, I walked over to them.

Of Bolverk, I saw no sign. But the place was so crowded, he could've been almost anywhere in the bar, and I wouldn't have seen him.

They finished butchering Zeppelin and the room exploded in applause. Bobbi and Jana were among them, to my disgust.

"Hey, Cass," Bobbi said. "Aren't these guys *great?*"

"Fuckin' A," Jana added. "They fuckin' *rock*. Yeah!"

"Really?" I just stared at them. "They're *not* that hot. Certainly nothing on you guys. What the hell happened, anyhow?"

Bobbi and Jana exchanged glances. Then Jana said, "I need a cigarette."

The three of us went out onto Greene Street so Jana could suck on nicotine and we could talk in peace. Given that Jötunheim's next song was "Money for Nothing," which was a) one of my favorite songs, and b) eerily appropriate from my POV, I was just as happy to be farther away from it.

While Jana lit up, Bobbi said, "We just can't find a damn drummer, and hiring one's proving impossible. They either cost too much or they won't take the rehearsal time."

I couldn't help myself. "You guys rehearse?"

"Ha-fuckin'-ha, Zukav," Jana said. She had a thing for referring to people only by their last names. "We *gotta* get a drummer up to speed and in sync, and we can't do that with a new guy every damn weekend. Some of us have lives, y'know?"

"Since when?" I thought those words, but it was actually Bobbi who said it. "Anyhow," she continued to me, "we figured we should just take a break. Didn't realize they'd go and hire someone so awesome."

"Okay, seriously?" I shook my head. "What is the big deal about Jötunheim? I mean, they're okay, but you guys are six times the band they are."

"That's sweet, Zukav," Jana said through a cloud of exhaled cigarette smoke, "but you gotta say that 'cause you're our friend."

"No, really, I don't. If you guys sucked, I'd say so."

Bobbi regarded Jana with a smile. "She's got a point."

Jana shrugged and took another drag. "Still, these guys fuckin' rock. Pity they don't have keys."

"Yeah, I just hope we get the gig back when we finally do find a drummer. We're holding an audition in the garage Sunday afternoon." Bobbi looked at me. "Wanna come watch?"

My feeling on music has always been similar to what they say about sausages: love 'em, don't wanna see the behind-the-scenes stuff. Luckily, I had a good excuse. "Can't, I'm doing two dives on Sunday."

"Shit, Zukav, they got you doing the morning dive?" Jana was laughing at me.

"I can set the alarm."

"Yeah, and get Debbie to give you the coffee through an IV and you *might* manage to be awake before 11." Bobbi chuckled. "C'mon, let's go back inside."

"Nah," I said with a sigh. "It's just not the same in there without you guys. I'm gonna head back."

We exchanged good-nights, Jana finished her cigarette, and they went in while I headed home. Briefly, I contemplated trying another bar for the evening, but I found my enthusiasm oddly waning. I just wanted to go home and curl up in a ball.

I arrived just as Debbie was locking the front door for the night. "Hiya, Cass," she said. "We got a new one in six—big old guy with only one eye named—"

"Bolverk?" I asked in surprise. Room number six was the downstairs of the cottage next to mine.

With similar surprise, Debbie said, "Yeah. You know him?"

"Uh, he was on my dive today."

"Well, thanks for telling him about us. G'night."

I hadn't told him about the Bottroff House—which was a failing on my part, since I made a habit of talking the B&B up to Seaclipse customers. For that matter, I always talked up Seaclipse to the B&B guests.

But now I was starting to feel seriously stalked by this guy.

This time I didn't even try to go to sleep, just spent the night downloading my pictures from the dives, catching up on e-mail, web surfing, and trading insults with Captain Bottroff.

The rest of the weekend got progressively weirder. Bolverk kept signing up for my afternoon dives. I didn't make it back to where that weird tail was again, as the other divers made specific requests for other spots, and the customer was always right.

And Jötunheim kept playing to bigger and bigger crowds at Mayor Fred's. In fact, their biggest crowd was Sunday night, which was usually the second-deadest night of the week after Tuesday.

To make matters worse, the three surviving members of 1812 were there both nights, and they were all bopping to the music. Even Chet, who doesn't bop to *anything*.

I stuck around both nights, partly because I wanted to keep an eye on Bolverk—who was sitting there nursing what Adina told me was bourbon every night—and partly to see if maybe I was just missing something. Whatever it was, though, I couldn't find it.

Sunday night, between sets, I was standing in line for the women's room—something I'd never had to do on a Sunday night before—and Gunnar noticed me. Wasn't sure why—beyond the fact that, at 5'11" with a mess of blond curls, I tend to stand out—but he peeled off from these two brunettes who were hitting all over him to say, "I have been noticing you."

I stared down at him—he was half a head shorter than me. "Oh yeah?" I tried to put on my best Southern California "what-*ever*" voice.

"Yes. You are the only woman in this entire place who is not having a good time. Yet you keep coming back."

I smirked. "Maybe I'm a glutton for punishment."

"I am simply surprised." He showed perfect teeth when he smiled, and I swear to God, his eyes glinted. "Do you not find it odd that no one else in this establishment feels as you do?"

"Yeah, well, I can't stand *American Idol* or Steven Spielberg movies, either, so I guess I'm used to it." Thankfully, the line moved forward, and I was able to enter the inside of the women's room, the one place where Gunnar dared not follow. As the door closed behind me, I saw two more women glom onto him like moths dive-bombing a candle.

Okay, so the guy was the lead singer of a band that had been packing the house like no one had packed it before, but even taking that into account, ego much? He's got half of Key West falling at his feet, but he's gotta know why it's not half plus one?

I sat fuming during the second set, made worse by how much Bobbi, Jana, and Chet were enjoying themselves. First off, Chet enjoying himself was just *weird*. Though in some ways, it was worth hanging out listening to Jötunheim's drivel just to see this sight, if for no other reason than it was bound to provide black-mail material down the line.

But more importantly, these guys were totally eclipsing 1812. Every other band in the universe would be ripshit over what these guys were pulling off, but there they were, just bopping along.

After the final song—an appallingly uninspired version of "Join Together," about which the nicest thing I could say was that Gunnar played a decent harmonica—I left without even saying goodbye to anyone.

It was around three, but since it was Sunday night (Monday morning, whatever), the streets were pretty sparsely populated. Some of the bars closed early on Sundays, and the ones that were open weren't all that crowded.

So I was all alone at the corner of Duval and Caroline when the giant jumped me.

We're talking an *actual* giant here. He was at least eight feet tall, and that's *not* an exaggeration. He had a thick beard, a huge nose, and breath that came straight from Satan's ass. His arms were also the size of my entire torso, and one of them was grabbing right for me.

"Hey! Leave her alone!"

The voice came from my left, and was oddly familiar. Sure enough, it was the guy who'd asked me for directions to a strip club and commented on my height Thursday night. He was running up to the giant, screaming at him.

At least, he was running until the giant backhanded him across the face, sending blood flying out his nose and his entire body skidding across the street. A woman screamed.

I just kept staring at the giant. I'd seen some weird shit in my time, from the nixie that killed Zeke (and a bunch of others) to the dragon in the garden to Captain Bottroff—and that was just here on Key West. You don't even want to *know* about that thing I stumbled across in San Diego…

Now that I was over the initial shock, and since my drunken admirer had been kind enough to distract the giant at the cost of some serious pain, the least I could do was take advantage.

I kneed him in the groin.

Like any male, the giant screamed in agony at that, right in my face (since he bent over after I damaged the family jewels), at which point I realized that his breath didn't come from anywhere as nice as Satan's ass.

"Step away from the lady nice and slow, chuckles."

I turned to see Lio pointing a gun at the giant. The giant snarled at Lio.

Lio pulled the trigger.

I'd never heard a gun fired in my life up until that point. My parents were crunchy-granola Southern California types, and I honestly thought everyone in Key West—beyond, y'know, law enforcement—was too laid back to pack heat. For the record, it doesn't sound *anything* like a firecracker or a car backfiring or anything else I've ever heard. It's also incredibly fucking loud, especially when it's fired less than fifteen feet from you. If I didn't spend four nights a week listening to loud music, it might have

233

messed up my hearing, but mine came pre-damaged.

Another scream from the giant, and then he turned and ran around the corner.

Shaking my head, I chased him, but as soon as I turned onto Caroline, there was no sign of him.

Lio ran up right behind me, holding the gun with both hands. "How the hell'd a ten-foot dude disappear like that?" he asked.

"Dunno—but thanks, Lio."

"No problem."

I shook my head. "My name's Cas—"

"Cassie Zukav, I know. Debbie told me." He grinned. "Figured you'd let me know in your own time. C'mon, let's see if any'a these fools called 911 on their cell phones."

Two of them had, as it turned out. I went over to my admirer, who was sitting up on the pavement of Duval Street, his head leaning back while a brunette woman cared for him. "I can't believe you did that," she was saying.

"You okay?"

"Yeah." The woman was holding a tissue to his nose as he leaned his head back. As I got closer, I saw that his nose was still bleeding. He had a gummy, nasal voice, probably from all the blood and the wadded-up tissue. "I guess now we're even."

I frowned. "Huh?"

"I was *really* drunk Thursday night, and if you'd given me the right directions, I'd have wound up at an actual strip club instead of a closed museum, and Tanya here'd have killed me."

The brunette shot him a disgusted look. "You were going to a *strip club?*"

"I didn't, though! And it's 'cause'a this lady."

"So you got your nose broken for her? Jesus, Billy."

Leaving Billy and Tanya to their domestic bliss, I hung out until the cops and the ambulance arrived. Wasn't sure what to tell them, but—well, one of my closest friends was a federal agent, and I'd never hear the end of it from him if I didn't make a proper report.

That particular ordeal took a couple of hours, and I finally stumbled back to the Bottroff House at five. The captain actually sounded relieved when I showed up. "Thank God. I was beginning to grow concerned. First your uncharacteristic early returns, and now tardiness."

"I've been late before," I muttered as I took my T-shirt off.

The captain didn't even make a fuss, which told me a lot right there. "Tonight is far from a standard night."

I wasn't really in the mood for riddles. "What's that supposed to mean?"

"I mean that the occupant of the ground floor of the next cottage over attempted to gain ingress into this dwelling. However, I was able to drive him away."

It took me a moment to parse Bottroff's words. "Hang on, Bolverk was here?"

"Indeed."

"And he *saw* you?"

"Yes. Had he been a less belligerent sort, I might have welcomed another to share words with, but he seemed intent upon seeing you. He used a phrase I've heard you utter from time to time: 'low key'?"

I snorted as I climbed out of my bathing suit and crawled into bed. "Yeah, low key isn't exactly this guy's style. And he's the least of my problems tonight." As my head sunk into my pillow, I gave the captain the brief version of the night's events.

"That settles it, then. I will brook no argument, Miss Zukav—I will remain vigilant tonight, to guard against any further assaults upon you."

It was a testament to how incredibly tired I was, that it never occurred to me that the captain's notion was at all creepy until long after I woke up the next morning.

235

The next few days were shockingly normal. I did my afternoon and occasional evening dives at Seaclipse, I helped Debbie out around the B&B, I saw very little of Bolverk, and no giants leapt out at me on Duval Street. Apparently Bolverk did a couple of dives with Andy during the week. I tried not to be insulted.

I was almost starting to believe things were getting back to normal until I was greeted by a text from Bobbi when I woke up Thursday morning: "Jana quit 1812. Drinks after diving?"

I stared at my phone in disbelief. Bobbi and Jana had been best friends since kindergarten. 1812 was their baby. How could Jana quit?

I texted back a simple, "sure," then got ready to head to Seaclipse.

Bobbi wouldn't even talk about it during the dive. Afterward, we went straight to the Waterfront and sat at the long wooden bar. "Two beers, Jack," Bobbi said to the bartender as soon as her ass hit the stool.

Grinning, I added, "And I'll have two beers, too."

"Very funny," Jack said with a sour face, and he went and got us each just the one beer.

"I cannot *believe* her," Bobbi said after Jack handed her a full pint. "The whole week, all she's talked about is Jötunheim and how good they are, and how if they just had keyboards they'd be perfect. We're trying to audition drummers, and she's talking about this other band! So when we finally get someone, she quits on us."

That surprised me. "You got a drummer?"

"Yeah." She smiled. "Another girl, believe it or not. Poor Chet's gonna be the only guy now."

I rolled my eyes. "Yeah, he must *hate* that."

"Well, you never know with Chet." Bobbi sighed and gulped down more beer. "Anyway, it's not *just* that Jana quit. I mean, bands don't last forever, and teaching takes up a lot of her time,

236

and it was always kinda in the back of my head that the band could fall apart, y'know?" She sipped some more beer. "But to go another band? I mean, 1812 was *us*. It's like she's not even my best friend anymore!"

Frowning, I asked, "What other band?"

"Didn't I tell you?"

"Uh, no."

"Oh, sorry. Yeah, she quit to join up with Jötunheim."

I thoughtfully sipped some more beer before making my next statement. "How do you plan to kill her and how much help do you need from me to dispose of the body?"

"Don't tempt me." Bobbi shook her head. "What especially sucks is, I got us a gig at the Hog's Breath tomorrow night." That was a completely open-air bar on Duval, about half a block from Mayor Fred's. "Looks like now we're gonna have to do it as a trio."

"Well, the Hog's Breath has a tiny stage, anyhow. Jana would've had to use the Casio, and you know how much she hates that."

"Yeah." Bobbi finished off her beer. "You wanna meet the new drummer? She's meeting me and Chet at Fred's tonight."

I stared at Bobbi as if she'd grown another head. "Excuse me? Why're you going to Fred's?"

Bobbi shrugged. "Jana's first night on the keys. When we were eight, we were both already singing and playing music a lot, and we pinky-swore to each other that we'd never miss the other one performing. There've been a few we've missed because of other commitments—and I won't be able to see her tomorrow—but I've got no excuse tonight."

"How about, 'Sorry, but you just pissed all over our friendship, so I think I'll skip it'?"

"Tempting, but it *was* a pinky-swear."

"When you were eight," I said slowly. "Seriously, you're gonna torture yourself for this?"

Bobbi grinned. "Do not mock the sanctity of the pinky-swear." Then the grin fell. "Besides, there's two other things. One is: she'll make Jötunheim sound even more awesome. And also? I want to remind her that *I* still think our friendship means something."

That drew me up short. Holding up my pint, I said, "I'll drink to that."

We risked actually eating the food at the Waterfront, and then headed back to Key West. After I changed clothes, I wandered up to Greene Street. Lio nodded hello as I passed by the Bull, and I nodded back.

"You hear if they caught the guy?" I asked.

He shook his head. "Nah, I ain't heard shit about it."

"Figures."

When I got to Greene Street, there were already people spilling out on the sidewalk, as Mayor Fred's was packed to the gills. The show hadn't even *started* yet. I didn't even want to think about what Ihor, Mira, Lainie, and Adina were going through inside.

I saw Bobbi and Chet standing with a short redhead. Bobbi waved when she saw me coming toward them. "Hey, Cass! Can you believe this?"

"No. In fact, I'm pretty well convinced this is a mirage."

"Good thing the PA pipes the music out here, too." Bobbi looked over at the redhead. "Ginny Blake, this is Cassie Zukav, our biggest fan."

I winced. "Seriously? *That's* how you introduce me? Not 'my friend Cassie,' or 'my dive-master at Seaclipse Cassie,' but 'our biggest fan'?"

Chet stared at the crowds all around us. "This rate, you gonna be the only fan we got *left*."

Ginny held out her hand. "It's a pleasure to meet you, Cassie. I've heard a lot about you."

Returning the handshake, I said, "Well don't believe any of it, I'm actually pretty damned awesome."

"Good to know."

Ihor's voice came over the PA. "Ladies and gentlemen, put your hands together tonight and now *every single night* for Mayor Fred's new house band, Jötunheim!"

Everybody around us cheered wildly and clapped. My jaw fell. I leaned over to Bobbi. "*Every* night? What about Fiona and those two guys with the beards?"

Bobbi shrugged. "Guess they'll have to play somewhere else."

So the Monday and Wednesday acoustic acts got screwed along with 1812, not to mention losing the Tuesday open mic. I mean, all right, you can't argue with crowds like this, but it still wasn't fair.

The piano opening of "I'm Still Standing" came over the PA, and 1812 had covered this often enough for me to know that it was Jana's fingers tickling the ivories. Obviously they were taking advantage of their new band member right off.

Sure enough, the next three songs were all keyboard-heavy. Jana was a virtuoso, and Bobbi was right—she improved Jötunheim's sound tremendously. But she also showed up how mediocre the rest of the band was.

At least, to me. Everyone else was eating it up, with one exception: Ginny seemed unmoved by all of this, too.

I leaned over to her after she golf-clapped while everyone was having orgasms over a blah version of "Kashmir." "It's about time someone *else* was unmoved by these guys."

Ginny just smiled.

I added, "It's like someone cast a spell over the whole damn island."

She raised her eyebrows. "Maybe someone has."

Just after she said that, I felt something brush across my nose. Looking up, I saw white flakes start to fall from the sky.

Okay, I'm from Southern California, and I live on Key West. It took me few minutes to recognize snow. Ditto most of the folks around me, since snow is just about the last thing anyone expected to find in South Florida in springtime.

Within a few minutes, the snow was really starting to pour down. And it was getting *cold*.

"I gotta go," I said. Besides the fact that listening to Jötunheim suck while standing on a street being snowed on was pretty low on my list of ways I wanted to spend my Thursday night, I had a feeling that things were gonna be bad at the B&B.

After navigating the throngs of very confused people on Duval, I got to the Bottroff House. I arrived just in time for Debbie to beg me to drive to the storage unit down on Virginia Street, since I was the only person she knew who owned a vehicle that could handle snowy roads.

Two and a half hours later, and after using the heat in Rocinante for the first time since I left San Diego, I stumbled into the snow-covered garden, my feet like ice cubes from walking through snow on flip-flops. Just getting to the storage unit and back, all of a mile from the B&B, took ninety of those minutes. The rest of the time was spent distributing heaters, extra blankets, and other stuff I liberated from the unit and tossed into the back of Rocinante.

By the time I got to my cottage, the final space heater in hand for my own room, my bones were cold. I'd never been this chilled in my life.

Bolverk was sitting on the steps.

"Shouldn't you be in your room hiding from the weather?" I asked tiredly.

He rose to his feet. "I was waiting for you, Castor Lisbeth Zukav. We must speak."

I winced at his use of my full name. My twin brother was named Pollux. Yes, really. Talk to my parents. We went by

"Cassie" and "Paul" for a reason.

"Can't it wait till morning?" I asked plaintively. "I have a bed that desperately needs to have me sleeping in it." After all this running around, I doubted I'd have trouble sleeping this much before my bedtime.

"No, it cannot. Fimbulvetr is upon us, which means that Loki's plan to bring about Ragnarok has started to come to fruition."

I blinked. "Okay, basically *none* of that made any kind of sense."

"The man you know as Gunnar Rikardsen is, in fact, the trickster Loki. He is my blood-brother. I am Odin, the Allfather of the Aesir. And we do not have much time."

I remembered some of what I saw online when I was doing my search on Jötunheim's name. "Hang on—Loki, Odin—you're a Norse god?"

"Of course."

"Right, because that's the most natural thing in the world." I sighed. "Says the woman being snowed on in April while on her way to the room she shares with a ghost. All right, fine, let's get in out of the cold and you can tell me *all* about Loki and his evil plan."

Pulling my keys out, I walked past Odin up the stairs while he started to explain himself. "Fimbulvetr is the eternal winter, and is the first stage of Ragnarok. Soon Loki will be powerful enough to sunder Yggdrasil, the World Tree that binds the Nine Worlds together."

I unlocked and slid open the door, only to be greeted by Captain Bottroff. "You should heed what this—this person says, Miss Zukav."

At that, I *almost* dropped the space heater onto my foot. I *did* drop my keys onto the white-carpeted floor. "You're kidding, right? The guy whose favorite epithet is 'Mary, Mother of God' is telling me to listen to the pagan deity?"

"I still believe in the Lord God and His Son, our Savior, Jesus Christ, as I did in life. But the *after*life has taught me that there is more to this world than I could have imagined. I have learned that there are other gods, and they cannot be labelled 'false' as the vicars of my youth insisted. Therefore, yes, I do believe that you should listen to what this person has to say."

"Your friend's shade speaks truth," Odin said as he took a seat in my white wicker chair.

"Jesus fuck, it's cold." I plugged in the space heater and turned it on, standing as close to it as I could while rubbing my goose-bump-covered arms. "Fine, so Gunnar is really Loki. How'd he get to this point?"

Odin had a sonorous voice that was well suited to storytelling, and I found myself almost mesmerized by his story. "Loki tricked Hoder into killing Balder in an attempt to bring about Ragnarok—the end of all that is. But he failed, and he was punished. Loki was trapped in a cave with a serpent dripping poison onto his face forevermore. However, Loki's wife Sigyn remained loyal to him, and held a bowl to catch the poison before it struck him. Unfortunately, she had to periodically empty the bowl, and when she did so, the poison struck Loki's face, and his convulsions shook the very earth."

"Uhm—okay," I said, "why didn't she just have two bowls?"

That brought Odin up short. "I do not know. You would have to ask her that." He shook his head. "Regardless, Loki managed to free himself from his prison—how, I know not. But gods are only as powerful as their worshippers. When the peoples of the Scandinavian region believed in us, our power was at its zenith— but in time the Aesir were forgotten, given over for other gods. Today, we are little more than an academic curiosity, or fodder for popular fiction. Our end was prophesied to come about via Ragnarok, but instead we simply faded."

"Not with a bang but a whimper, huh?" I shook my head, the

242

space heater having managed to get my blood actually circulating again. "Okay, fine, so you all faded away."

"Save for a few of us. I still live, obviously, as does one of the frost giants, Geirrod, who is loyal to Loki. I believe you had an encounter with him."

"What, the lunatic outside the Bull? He's a frost giant?"

"Indeed."

"So why the hell did he want to kill *me?*"

Odin stared at me with his one eye. "Loki sent Geirrod to kill you because he sees you as a potential threat. As one of the Dísir, you are immune to his glamour—and one of the few who can stop him."

My eyes widened. "Excuse me? I'm one of the *what*, now?"

"The Dísir. The fate goddesses. The Norns are Dísir, and periodically a set of triplets is born on Midgard who are also Dísir. You are one of three, are you not?"

Now my heart was pounding against my ribcage. Yes, Mom had triplets, but Paul's and my never-named brother was stillborn.

I found myself with the need to sit down. The heater had only just started to warm up the room, but I no longer felt the cold— or, really, much of anything. I planted myself on the edge of the bed, since Odin was in my only chair.

"Yes," I said quietly. "I'm a triplet."

"Just so. Why do you think you are able to speak with the shade or survive an encounter with a frost giant?"

Before I could elaborate on the role that two other people played in my driving Geirrod off, Bottroff finally spoke up again. "If such is the reason behind our ability to communicate, Miss Zukav, then I, for one, am filled with gratitude."

I stared at the captain. In nine months, that was the nicest thing he'd said to me. Unable to entirely parse this, I forced myself to focus on the point at hand.

"Okay, hold it—the band's using magic?"

Odin nodded. "Loki is using a glamour, yes, to make his music more appealing. It is a minor glamour, not strong enough to affect me as the Allfather, nor you as a Dís. He was unable to revive worshipful interest in the Aesir—our time has passed. The Christians were little more than conquering fodder for Vikings in our heyday, but now you are everywhere."

I held up my hands. "Don't look at me, I'm Jewish." I sighed. "All right, so he formed a rock band. Figures—fan dedication's probably stronger than a church would be anyhow. So why here? Why Key West?"

"Because, as I said, the next step is to sunder Yggdrasil. And one of the roots of the World-Tree is –"

In an instant, I figured it out. "—the ficus in the middle of Mayor Fred's." I put my head in my hands. "Of course it is. So, fine, how do we stop him?"

"There is a counterspell that may be cast while Loki casts the spell to sunder the World-Tree. He will cast it tomorrow night—Fimbulvetr must last for at least a day before he may attempt it. You must cast this counterspell."

"Whoa, whoa, whoa!" I stood up. "You're the Allfather, the big badass of Norse myth. I'm just a tall chick with bad hair. Why aren't *you* casting the spell?"

"Loki is my blood-brother, and we swore never to harm each other. You, however, have made no such vow, and as a Dís, you can easily cast the spell."

"Oh, I can, can I?" This was getting insane. Insaner.

"Yes." He rose to his feet. "I must depart. I will return in the morning with the components you will need to cast the spell and instructions on how to cast it."

"But I've never cast a spell before!"

Odin slid the door open. "You are a Dís. You will be able to." With that, he left.

244

"Okay, then," I told the closed door, and turned to the captain. "You really believe this?"

"I believe that it is snowing heavily, a phenomenon I have never encountered in a century and a half. I believe that these musicians you have described are enchanting the good people of this island. I believe you were attacked by a vicious monster. I believe that the gentleman who just departed has a notion as to the reason for these occurrences and also the method by which they may be rectified."

"So you're saying I should see this through?"

"Yes. Yes, I am."

I collapsed on the bed. "Yeah, me too."

My dreams that night were filled with random images of Bobbi and Jana in a catfight, Gunnar giving Bolverk the finger while standing on Mayor Fred's stage, the Gulf of Mexico totally frozen over but Cara and Andy still trying to dive in it, Geirrod shooting Lio in the chest with a big shotgun, Ginny, Chet, and the rest of the crowd at Mayor Fred's giving Jötunheim a standing ovation, and a bunch more.

When I woke up, I frowned. Ginny *wasn't* into Jötunheim. How was she unaffected?

I put on the sneakers I hadn't worn since December, and hunted up the long pants I hadn't worn since I arrived on the island. The snow was still coming down and piling up in the garden. Seriously, this was the first time my legs hadn't been exposed to the open air in nine months.

"What a fucking nightmare," I muttered. "This is gonna cripple the island. We don't have salt, we don't have plows—hell, most of the people who live here don't own *socks*."

I trudged through the snow to the main house in order to get some of Debbie's killer coffee. Several guests were in the dining room, scared and subdued. Nobody knew what to do, and probably the whole island was shutting down. I had a text on my phone from Cara saying that Seaclipse was closed, to my lack of surprise. I doubted that any business was going to be open. Plus, how were deliveries supposed to get here on unpassable roads?

Then again, the world was going to end tonight, anyhow….

I trudged through the frozen tundra back to my cottage with an entire pot of coffee and then fired up my laptop to do a little online research before Odin came back. Sure enough, Norse mythology tracked frighteningly well with everything Odin said, including the whole eternal-winter thing.

When Odin arrived, he had the spell components: a bunch of really stinky herbs, a mortar and pestle, an electric mini-stove, and a familiar-looking lizard scale.

"You took that from the tail-thingie we found last week!"

"Indeed. It is from the Midgard Serpent, the creature that surrounds your world. That it has allowed itself to be seen is another omen of Ragnarok's imminence."

"Joy."

I spent the entire day in my room with Odin and Captain Bottroff going over how to cast the spell. Apparently, I had to get the mix of herbs *just* right, say the incantation *precisely* (in a language I totally didn't know or recognize), and time it exactly to when Loki cast his spell, which would be him singing a song with a set of lyrics in the same weird language as my spell.

But no pressure…

Debbie managed to provide enough food for me and Odin, as well as the other guests, though she wasn't sure what she was going to do Saturday, since there weren't going to be any deliveries.

That night, I drove to Mayor Fred's. Duval Street was eerily not crowded. A bunch of hearty souls were trudging through the snow drifts to the few bars that had decided to open up—which was maybe a quarter of them.

Rocinante was able to slowly plow its way through the snow,

and when we turned the corner onto Greene, I just parked right across the street. I couldn't park right in front, because it was packed with people. Even though snow was still coming down, *hundreds* of people were trying to cram into Mayor Fred's.

But this time, unlike last night, there was a clear path from one part of the entryway, past the ficus, to the stage. That meant I had a clear line of sight, although I'm pretty sure it was so *Loki* had that same line of sight...

Ginny Blake was in with the crowd outside, and when she saw me and Odin climb out of the truck, she walked right over.

I was about to ask her what she was doing here, but she wasn't paying any attention to me. She stared at my companion. "Hello, Odin."

"Greetings, Sigyn."

Son of a bitch. "*You're* Loki's wife? The one not bright enough to have two bowls?"

Ginny frowned. "Excuse me?"

"Never mind—no wonder you're immune to his glamour."

She smiled. "What wife can't see through her husband? In any event, after spending eternity protecting him from that serpent, he repaid my loyalty by abandoning me when the cave collapsed and he was freed. So I have followed him in the hopes of watching him fail." She turned to Odin. "I assume you are here to expedite that failure, Allfather?"

"Not I. I swore an oath not to harm my blood-brother, and I will not go back on it."

Ginny's eyes widened. "You mean there's a chance he'll *succeed*?"

I sighed. "Hope not. I'm casting the spell."

Staring at Odin, Ginny asked, "Are you out of your mind? She is a novice."

"She is a Dís. She can cast the spell." Odin's voice was absolutely flat.

"I don't care if she's one of the Norns, she's never done this before. The fate of all the Nine Worlds is at stake, and you're risking it on a promise you made to *him*?"

Odin stared down at her with his one eye. "Yes."

Ihor's voice sounded over the PA. "Welcome to snowpocalypse, ladies and gentlemen!"

"You don't know the half of it," I muttered.

"Tonight and every night, it's Jötunheim!"

The crowd cheered like crazy. This time I could see them— same short blond muscular guy up front, same other three, plus Jana on stage right behind her usual keyboard setup of a standup piano and two sets of electronic keyboards. They opened with an old Jethro Tull song called "Hunting Girl" that used to be an 1812 standard.

While they played the song, and I wondered why Jana was going around throwing her old band's music for these guys to play, I started putting together what I needed for the spell. As the song spiraled to a finish, Loki held up a hand. "All right, I need some quiet for this next one."

As he spoke, Jana started playing a soft, dirge-like melody very low on the keys, set to "organ" mode.

Slowly, the crowd started to quiet down, until there was total silence—something, I gotta say, I'd never heard in this part of Key West before, not even at four after the bars closed—save for Jana's organ playing.

Loki began to sing a song, in a language I didn't recognize.

Except I *did* recognize it. Odin had been giving me the words all day. I lit the mixture in the pestle, dropped the scale from the Midgard Serpent into the flames that licked up from it, and then started a chant of my own.

I had no idea what the words *meant*, but I'd been practicing them all day until Odin was ready to kill me (and I him, believe me), and damnit, I was gonna say them *right*.

Even as I said the words, I could feel—well, *something* pulling at my chest.

Loki saw me. Everyone else in the bar was mesmerized by the music; no one else even noticed me standing there with a flaming pestle in my hand. He finished what sounded like a verse of his chant, then looked at me with obvious annoyance. "I was wondering where Geirrod got off to. Couldn't even kill a Dís. Can't find good help these days, it seems."

I just kept chanting. Maybe he could afford to do his spell piecemeal, but I wasn't risking it. The pull on my chest got weaker as I went, which I hoped was a good sign.

"But there's nothing you can do, little Dís. Oh, if Allfather was doing what you're doing, I'd be doomed, but he won't harm me. His insistence on keeping his word is so charmingly old-fashioned, isn't it?"

He sang another verse. The pulling on my chest grew worse.

Sweat beaded on my brow, even though it was so fucking cold. I had come here wishing I had something thicker than a denim jacket, and now I was wishing I'd thought to throw it off before I started casting the spell.

The pull grew stronger, like someone had reached into my rib-cage and was trying to yank my heart out through it.

I kept chanting. I wasn't about to miss anything.

"Haven't you learned *anything*, Loki?"

That was Ginny, who my peripheral version told me was standing just behind me and to my left.

"Sigyn!" This time Loki cut off in mid-verse. The pull on my chest disappeared, and I kept the chant up, louder this time.

"Yes, Loki, I'm still alive. And you are about to fail to bring about Ragnarok *again*, just as you did last time. Oh, and you can rest assured that I will *not* be there to stay the poison from your brow again."

"I won't need it, *dear* wife of mine," Loki snapped angrily. He sang the next verse, and the pull grew even worse.

Thanks a lot, Ginny. If you were trying to distract him, that *totally* didn't work.

Suddenly, as a hand touched my shoulder, the pull stopped. The words, which were a bitch and a half to pronounce right even after a day's practice, were now coming easily, as if it was a language I'd spoken all my life.

And Loki stumbled on the stage.

"You're going against your word, old man?" Loki asked with a sneer.

Only then did I realize who was touching my shoulder.

"Yes," was all Odin said in response.

"We are blood-brothers! You swore an oath, Allfather!"

"And now I am breaking it. As you broke yours, many times. What good is my word, if existence ends because I held it?"

"What good is existence if your word while living in it means nothing?"

I got to the end of the chant. It was time to answer Loki's question, before taking the final step. "Words ain't no good if the music sucks."

I threw the pestle at the ficus. It sparked and shattered, yellow flame shooting out in all directions. The pull on my chest increased, and I fell to the floor.

Loki collapsed on the stage.

Wind whipped through Mayor Fred's, a cold, bitter wind that the body heat of hundreds of people couldn't warm. It blew out the flames caused by my shattered pestle. Then the entire world went white, as if we were all suddenly buried in a snowdrift.

I heard voices: Loki's, Odin's, Sigyn's. I had no idea what they were saying, but I heard them as I lay there on Mayor Fred's floor, unable to move. I struggled to get up, but whatever force had been pulling on my chest all this time was keeping me from moving. After several seconds of struggle, I closed my eyes, shivering from the bitter cold.

When I opened them, I was in my bed.

Captain Bottroff's ghost was standing over me. "At last, you awaken. Even one with your prodigious ability to slumber should not be in such a state for so many days."

I swallowed. "Days?" I sat up, realized I was still in the outfit I wore to Mayor Fred's on Friday night, minus the denim jacket, which was hanging on the back of the wicker chair.

"Yes. It is now Sunday. I will fetch the gentleman—he wanted to know when you awakened."

A breeze, and then the captain was gone. I sat up slowly, my stomach growling. Looking out the window, I saw that the sun was shining and there was no sign of snow. I could see the garden clearly, though some flowers seemed to be missing. I guess they got frosted to death or something.

First thing I did was get out of bed. That took longer than it should have, as pins and needles shot through my legs, and I had to stand at the side of the bed, hand braced on the mattress, for several seconds before I felt confident enough to actually walk.

My arms and legs felt like they were made of jello, as I shakily pulled my shirt over my head. Removing my bra proved an act of dexterity almost beyond my means, and I sat back down on the bed, not trusting myself to remove my pants while upright.

By the time Odin showed at the sliding door, I'd managed to get into a bathrobe. I cursed the fact that my bathroom only had a shower stall, since what I really needed was a long bath. For one thing, I wasn't sure I'd be able to stand in the shower for more than a minute or two without collapsing.

He slid the door open. "It is good to see you well."

"'Well' is a relative term, but I'm alive. I guess it worked?"

"Yes." Odin nodded. "I have accepted responsibility for Loki and Geirrod."

251

I frowned. "What does that mean, exactly?"

"No Midgard jail may hold either of them, and your enforcement officials cannot arrest someone who does not actually exist."

Nodding, I said, "Yeah, okay, good point."

"I must take my leave of you, Castor Lisbeth Zukav."

I winced again. "Will you stop that, please? It's 'Cassie.'"

For the first time since I met him, Odin smiled. "Very well, Cassie. I hope you continue to use your gifts as a Dís wisely."

"I didn't even know I had gifts."

Bottroff spoke up, then. "Yes, you did. And rest assured, sir, that I will endeavor to keep Miss Zukav on the proper path."

"You have *got* to be kidding me." I put my hands on my hips and stared at the captain. But I was smiling.

"Be well, Cassie." And with that, Odin departed.

My cell phone had been in my pants pocket, and had long since lost its charge. I plugged it in to find it had a dozen messages.

Half were from Bobbi. I called her back, and we filled each other in on what had been going on. Well, as much of it as I was willing to talk about in a phone call. Bobbi had become a dear friend in the past nine months, and if there was anyone I could talk to about being a Dís, it was her. But not now.

Eventually, we got around to talking about 1812. "Mayor Fred's actually asked us back. Without Gunnar, Jötunheim has just sucked. We're starting tonight."

"As a trio or a quartet?"

Bobbi hesitated for several seconds. "Dunno yet. Jana and I—" She sighed. "We got some stuff to work out."

I didn't know what to say. Jana's quitting wasn't entirely her fault, thanks to Loki's glamour. On the other hand, nobody *else* in 1812 quit and joined Jötunheim. That was something those two were gonna have to figure out.

We promised to have lunch the next day to catch up in more detail, and I promised to tell her everything. Then I called Sea-clipse, and worked out my schedule going forward. I told Andy that I wasn't up to working today, but I'd be okay tomorrow.

That night, after a not-nearly-long-enough shower during which I did *not* fall down and a huge meal provided by Debbie, I went to Mayor Fred's. Jana wasn't on the stage, but Chet, Bobbi, and Ginny were. I took a seat near the ficus tree. I suddenly felt protective of it. Adina got me a pint of beer, and Ihor came over the PA.

"Ladies and gentlemen, back after a brief absence, Mayor Fred's favorites, 1812!"

Bobbi walked up to her mic. "Good evening, Key West! This one's for our biggest fan."

Chet walked up to his mic. He wore sunglasses, like usual, so I couldn't tell where, exactly, he was looking. But I chose to believe he was staring right at me when he started singing their first song: "I Put a Spell on You."

Contributors

Sam Cutler has been at the center of some of the most exciting developments in the music industry and was the Tour Manager for The Rolling Stones and The Grateful Dead. He is the author of *You Can't Always Get What You Want* (ECW Press), an autobiography described as "an exhilarating, access-all-areas rock memoir from someone who has seen, and done, it all".

Patricia V. Davis is the author of the award-winning *Harlot's Sauce: A Memoir of Food, Family, Love, Loss and Greece*, and *The Diva Doctrine: 16 Universal Principles Every Woman Needs to Know*. She's the editor-in-chief of the non-partisan HS Radio e-magazine, where she posts editorials, conducts podcast interviews with intriguing people such as Neil deGrasse Tyson and James Redford, and hosts an "Expert in Failed Relationships" advice column there. Patricia holds a Master's Degree in Creative Writing and Education and was named one of Top 25 Mentors for Young Women and Girls 2010 and 2011, by the Hot Mommas Project.

Keith R.A. DeCandido is an author, editor, musician, podcaster, critic, anthologist, voice actor, karate student, library assistant, and probably a few other things that he can't remember due to the lack of sleep. He has written more than 40 novels, the most recent of which include the award-nominated *Star Trek: A Singular Destiny* and *Supernatural: Heart of the Dragon*, the genrebending police procedurals *Unicorn Precinct* and *Super City Police Department: The Case of the Claw*, the *Dungeons & Dragons* novel *Dark Sun: Under the Crimson Sun*, and *The Scattered Earth: Guilt in Innocence*. Other recent short fiction can be found in *Dragon's Lure, More Tales of Zorro, Star Trek: Seven Deadly Sins*, and *Liar Liar*, and he also scripted the *Farscape* comic book for BOOM! Studios in collaboration with series creator Rockne S. O'Bannon.

As a+ percussionist, he's been a member of the Don't Quit Your Day Job Players, and also backed up the Randy Bandits and Steve Rosenhaus, and currently provides the rhythm for the parody band, Boogie Knights (www.boogie-knights.org). Find out less about Keith at his mostly harmless web site (www.decandido.net), read his blog (kradical.livejournal.com), follow him on Facebook and/or Twitter under the username of KRADeC, or listen to his twice-monthly podcast *Dead Kitchen Radio* (deadkitchenradio.mevio.com).

Barbara Denz has been writing fantasy almost as long as she has been a singer, and that is a very long time indeed. Since she's a folk singer by choice (although classically trained), everything she sings is based in someone's fantasy. And she likes it that way.

Susanne Dunlap is the author of five historical novels, two for adults and three for young adults. A former professional pianist and music historian, musical themes are a recurrent counterpoint in most of her writing. She lives and writes in Brooklyn.

Kathi Kamen Goldmark is the author of *And My Shoes Keep Walking Back to You*, a novel; co-author of *Write That Book Al-*

ready!: the Tough Love You Need to Get Published Now, *The Great Rock & Roll Joke Book*, and *Mid-Life Confidential: the Rock Bottom Remainders Tour America with Three Chords and an Attitude*; and has contributed essays to at least half a dozen anthologies. With Sam Barry, she co-authors a monthly advice column in *BookPage* called "The Author Enablers."

Kathi is the founder and a member of the all-author rock band the Rock Bottom Remainders; host of a monthly music jam as leader of Los Train Wreck; president and janitor of "Don't Quit Your Day Job" Records; Author Liaison for high profile literary events; winner of the 2008 Women's National Book Association Award; and producer of the coast-to-coast radio show *West Coast Live*. She likes to think she is ready for anything.

Rain Graves is a Bram Stoker Award (2002) winning poet and writer currently living in San Francisco with one large black cat, and one small white cat. Publisher's Weekly has hailed her as "Bukowski meets Lovecraft," for her 2009 book, *Barfodder: Poetry Written In Dark Bars & Questionable Cafes* (Cemetery Dance). She has been published in the horror fiction and poetry genre since 1997, in various magazines, books, and webzines, and is a retired dance instructor, and former musician. Her latest book, *The Four Elements*, written with Linda Addison, Charlee Jacob, and Marge Simon will be out in Spring/Summer 2012 (Bad Moon Books).

Erika Jahneke is a fiction writer, occasional reporter, and blogger. She is proud that "Somebody" is her first anthologized work. Coming on the heels of her first national exposure in *Ellery Queen Mystery Magazine*, Erika is finally confident she did the right thing in sticking with creative writing over writing ad copy about toothpaste, and that it is much easier to be a soul fan to-day than in middle school during Simon Le Bon's heyday. She lives, writes, and fights the power in Phoenix, Arizona, where she is hard at work turning the adventures of paralyzed soul legend Darnell Watkins into a novel.

Roz Kaveney is a writer, reviewer, poet and activist living in London. She has written books on popular culture like *Reading The Vampire Slayer*, and was one of the Midnight Rose collective, co-editing *The Weerde* and *Villains!* shared world anthologies. She has one of those lives that sound like a list of cool stuff.

Brett Milano resolved at an early age to either become a famous writer or one of the Monkees. He wrote the books *Vinyl Junkies* (Griffin/St. Martin's, 2001) and *The Sound of Our Town: A History of Boston Rock & Roll* (Commowealth Editions, 2007). More recently he was main writer/researcher for "The Beatles: Rock Band" video game. As a music journalist he writes regularly for Sound & Vision magazine and various Boston outlets. His liner notes appear on albums by the Cars, the Smithereens, Todd Rundgren, the Tubes, the Continental Drifters, Robin Trower and Lee Michaels. As for the second ambition, he is still looking for the right size wool hat.

Charles Shaar Murray is an award-winning journalist and author of *Crosstown Traffic: Jimi Hendrix And Postwar Pop And Boogie Man: The Adventures Of John Lee Hooker In The American Twentieth Century*. He began his journalistic career in 1970 writing for the UK underground press, was press-ganged into the NME in 1972 and has been hanging onto the edges of the freelance precipice since 1980. He recently committed fiction for the first time, publishing his debut novel *The Hellhound Sample* in 2011.

Madeleine Robins has been, in no particular order, a nanny, actor and stage-combatant, administrator, baker, editor, book mender, typist-clerk for Thos. Cook's Houses of Parliament office, teacher, and through it all, writer. In that last capacity she is the author of eleven books including the Sarah Tolerance series: *Point of Honour*, *Petty Treason*, and *The Sleeping Partner* (Plus One Press). She is a fan of medical history, urban infrastructure, old movies, too many books, and her family. A New Yorker by birth, training, and inclination, she now lives in San Francisco with her family. She plays guitar badly, dulcimer unspeakably, has a decent voice and loves to sing.

Jeannette Sears is a rock lyricist who with her husband of 35 years, musician Pete Sears, has written many popular and critically acclaimed songs, including singles and title tracks on Gold and Platinum albums, and videos for MTV. She has recently written her first novel, entitled *A Light Rain of Grace*, about the life of a female rock star circa 1966 to the nineties.

Clea Simon spent the first half of the '80s as a rock critic for the Boston Herald, eventually contributing music journalism to everyone from Creem and Rolling Stone to American Prospect and Salon. Following a detour in straight journalism and three nonfiction books, she now writes mysteries, most of which involve music, cats, or both. Her eighth and ninth, *Grey Zone* (Severn House) and *Dogs Don't Lie* (Poisoned Pen), came out last spring.

A graduate of Harvard University, she lives in Somerville, MA, with her husband Jon Garelick, a jazz critic, and their cat Musetta. She can be reached via her website, www.cleasimon.com.

Karen Williams has worked for software companies in Silicon Valley for over twenty years. She is a second degree black belt in aikido, and lives mostly alone, with her two turtles Dymphna and G'Kwan.

258

Deborah Grabien can claim a long personal acquaintance with the fleshpots—and quiet little towns—of Europe. She has lived and worked and hung out, from London to Geneva to Paris to Florence, and a few stops in between.

After publishing four novels between 1989 and 1993, she took a decade away from writing, to really learn how to cook. That done, she picked up where she'd left off, with the five novels of her Haunted Ballads series being brought out by St. Martins Minotaur between 2003 and 2007. *Still Life With Devils*, a stand-alone thriller, was released by Drollerie Press in 2007. Dark's Tale, her first YA title, draws on her and her husband's experiences working with the San Francisco SPCA's feral cat program in Golden Gate Park. Her current series, the critically acclaimed *JP Kinkaid Chronicles*, are the books of her heart. Narrated by ageing rock superstar guitarist John "JP" Kinkaid, this character-driven mystery series not only takes the reader into the way rock and roll really works at the highest end, but illuminates what living with a chronic progressive illness is like. Like JP, Deborah herself has lived with multiple sclerosis for nearly a decade.

Deborah's been married to bassist Nicholas Grabien since 1983. They share a passion for rescuing cats, and are both active members of several local feral cat rescue organisations. Deborah has a grown daughter, Joanna, who lives in Los Angeles. These days, in between cat rescues and cookery, Deborah can generally be found listening to music, playing music on one of eleven guitars, hanging out with her musician friends, or writing about music, insofar as her multiple sclerosis will allow. See more at her website, www.deborahgrabien.com.

CPSIA information can be obtained at www.ICGtesting.com
Printed in the USA
LVOW121327060112

262726LV00001B/5/P